FOREVER MINE

FOREVER MINE
A Westin Pack Novel

By

Julie Trettel

Forever Mine
A Westin Pack Novel: Book Three

Cover Art by, Desiree Deorto Designs
Editing by, Sara Meadows of TripleA Publishing Services

Thanks and Acknowledgments

I swear the more books published, the harder these Thanks and Acknowledgments become, but first and foremost, I always have my husband James and our four awesome kids, Roman, Hope, Bethany, and Katy to thank. They sacrifice time and money and put up with me and my crazy writing obsessions. They are the greatest and so each and every book has to include a special shout-out to them, as well as my mom. She's always been supportive of me, even when she disagrees with my path in life. Writing has never been a disagreement though and she has been a great encourager and supporter every step of the way since before my first book ever published.

Beyond them it's tough to find new people to thank. I am grateful for a solid friend base in the writing community. You know who you are; I don't think I need to name each of you individually, but a special thanks to the overall 20BooksTo50K community. 20Books-Vegas, was an incredible experience this year and these men and women give information so freely it's insane and greatly valued. I'm not sure I could have gotten through self-publishing with them, but especially not my 3rd book in one year!

My ARC team, who I always acknowledge and don't think they ever see it, because I usually don't send advanced copies in the completed stage, which includes this section. Know each and every one of you is greatly appreciated and I take to heart every bit of feedback each of you gives. So many authors give away ARC's like candy on Halloween in hopes of receiving a small handful of reviews on opening day. My ARC team is small and mighty and I know I can count on each of them to leave that honest – sometimes brutally honest – review! Love you guys!

Liam

Chapter 1

I pinched the bridge of my nose and took a deep breath. Pushing back from my desk, I let the chair drift and looked around my office, reflecting over the last two years. Two years ago I was fresh out of college. I had majored in business, unsure of what aspect of the family company I wanted to someday work. All through high school and college, I had managed to stay as far away from the Westin Foundation as possible. So, what the hell was I doing here, a twenty-four-year-old CEO of a multi-billion dollar company?

The Westin Foundation was largely an investment firm. We had other holdings, and worked closely with a lot of charities, but for the most part that's what we did. Really it was just a front to legitimize the small town of San Marco, which housed potentially the largest pack of wolf shifters ever known. It was hard to know that for a fact, as packs were close units that didn't always share correct info due to old fears and rivalries, but Westin Pack was certainly large enough to be a top contender for the title. Even I didn't know exactly how many wolves made up Westin Pack—only the Alpha knew for sure—but we each carried a slightly unique pack scent that always let us know if someone was pack or not.

As a pup, I had grown up the second son and fourth child of the Alpha. My twin sister, Lily, was technically only three minutes older than me. She never let me forget it, either. Growing up in the royal family, so to speak, had its ups and downs. I wasn't ever one that required a lot of attention or enjoyed the spotlight. Good thing, too, with Lily always around.

Most of the spotlight revolved around my oldest brother, Kyle. Kyle was a great guy, and when the first battle of the war with the Bulgarians began, leaving my father critically injured, he had stepped up to become a great Alpha, too.

Before the war began, wolf shifters had lived in relative peace, governed by the Grand Council which was comprised of five men who gave up their own packs for the betterment of all wolf shifters. This had worked for hundreds of years and during this time of peace, my ancestors had started and grown what we knew today as Westin Pack, and also the Westin Foundation.

Wolves of Westin had much better lives than other packs because of the Foundation. All profits were split between the pack members providing us with a very comfortable lifestyle. Not all packs agreed with how Westin managed its pack, its money, or its wolves, but I'd learned through experience that it was mostly their jealousy talking.

My brother Kyle had ridden an emotional roller-coaster for a couple years after he'd found his one true mate, Kelsey. Wolves can only ever have one true mate. Wolves that didn't find their true mate at a young age often settled for a compatible mate, of which there could be hundreds or even thousands to choose from.

Kelsey was a lone wolf who moved into Westin territory without any proper protocol. I had been away at college for much of their early years, but even I had heard of the scandal and uproar it had caused. Kyle was CEO of Westin Foundation at the time, having taken the position over from our dad after he graduated college. He hired Kelsey and made it clear that no one was to touch her. It wasn't until years later that we found out the reason why was because he'd known she was his one true mate.

Then I saw how crazy the mating call had been for my buddy, Patrick, once he'd gotten a whiff of his one true mate, who turned out to be my other sister, Elise. I consider it a blessing that I was away during both those mating calls, especially since they had acted like idiots instead of embracing their one true mates sooner.

Later on we all learned that Kelsey knew she was a wolf, but she thought she was a werewolf like they depicted in scary movies. She didn't know anything about shifters. If Kyle hadn't been so stubborn, they'd have gotten together a whole lot sooner. Turned out there was a reason Kelsey didn't know who she was, though. Her backstory was pretty rough to discover. She's an Alpha she-wolf. For thousands of years, Alpha she-wolves had been thought too dangerous to live. Death sentences were placed on them at very young ages when their powers first surfaced. In Kelsey's case, that had been age four. She had been a triplet, and when her sisters were killed, their individual powers had transferred to Kelsey.

I didn't really understand how all that worked, but her parents had smuggled her out before she was killed and kept her hidden away until they were killed when she was twelve years old. They never told her what she was.

It had been difficult for her to find out everything, but also a relief to no longer be alone. Wolves by nature don't do well in solidarity, though sometimes it would be nice to have some alone time; having four siblings, even with all of us grown, means there never seems to be a dull moment or time alone.

Kelsey, we now knew, was from the Bulgarian Pack, and their Alpha broke all truces among the packs to get her back and finish what had been started when she was four years old. That didn't go over so well with the Westin Pack. Kyle and Kelsey had already mated by the time her past came to light. The first of several battles had left my dad near death—Mom, too, as they are fully bonded. Fully bonded mates share a strong connection that, once severed, destroys them both. If one mate dies, the other does, too.

My phone beeped with a reminder. My nephew, Zander, was turning one and the family was celebrating at Mom's Tuesday night family dinner. I still had to run out and pick up a gift for the little guy. I glanced at the time on my phone. One thirty. I had worked through lunch again, a bad habit I'd gotten into while trying to just keep things in order. There was always some sort of emergency or some fire to put out in the office. It was never-ending and often overwhelmed me.

If someone had told me a year ago that I'd be flying solo in the CEO position, I'd have laughed in their face. Kyle had been trying to transfer the position over to me before his baby was born, and Dad had recovered enough to try to step in to "help." I loved them, but they were both control freaks who weren't ready to let go of the reigns. Even after Kyle finally stepped back, consumed with his new Alpha duties, I still had Dad hovering around.

Dad's injuries in the first battle with the Bulgarians had been extensive. He had been in a severely weakened state and literally at death's door, so the pack power had automatically transferred to Kyle—who was next in line—without having to do the usual fight to the death match. So even though Kelsey had saved his life with her extra powers of healing, there was no way Dad could get the Alpha powers back

Dad would never fight Kyle for a position he would have eventually held anyway, so that left Dad plenty of time to groom me for the duties of a Westin Foundation CEO. It had been a very trying time for both of us, but after Zander was born, he and Mom were so consumed by love and grandparent duties that he had slowly eased up on me and channeled all that focus onto Z. Sorry, little man. Someday I was going to owe that kid big time for it.

I pushed the intercom button on my phone. “Chris, what's on my schedule for this afternoon?”

“Nothing, sir. You had asked last week to clear today for Zander's celebration.”

“Thanks,” I replied, grateful for the break.

Chris, or Christine Canine, was my administrative assistant. I hadn't wanted her to be at first, but she had turned out to be a damn good one. I couldn't function day to day without her . . . not that I'd ever admit that to her. Chris and Kyle had been close friends growing up, so I had known her forever. When they had turned eighteen and discovered they were not true mates, she had changed into someone I couldn't stand. Heck, most people couldn't!

When Kyle mated Kelsey, they had to face what we call the Challenges. It's a pre-determined period during which any wolf can challenge either mate for pack position. It's used often to advance one's place in the pack and as future Alpha, and with the Pack Mother role on the line Christine had jumped at the chance to battle Kelsey. She had lost, but while the challenges were usually a fight to the death, Kelsey had chosen to spare her at the last minute. The gesture had humbled Chris and although she could still be a bit high-strung, overall, we'd found an easy routine and worked well together.

Grabbing my keys off my desk, I headed for the door. “I'll be out the rest of the afternoon. Call my cell if there're any emergencies. I'm going to head down the mountain to see about a present for the little man.”

“Sure thing, boss. When I saw him last week at the park, he was mesmerized by a group of guys playing basketball. If he doesn't already have a hoop, consider that?”

Basketball? For a one-year-old? I shrugged. “Seems like a

weird gift for a toddler, but I'll look into it. Thanks for the suggestion."

The phone rang and I used it as my signal to leave. If there was one major fault with Christine Canine, it was that she loved to talk, and sometimes it was hard to escape her.

Driving down the mountain with the music blaring, I felt strangely relaxed. I had been so stressed as of late that I wasn't sure I remembered what it felt like. It was so nice of a change that I decided to stop at the Watering Hole to grab a drink before beginning my hunt for the perfect gift for my nephew. The Watering Hole was appropriately named, a restaurant and bar on the lake at the base of the mountain below San Marco. The views were gorgeous, and it was a popular eatery for tourists, too.

As I sat at the bar and ordered a root beer, a small child climbed up in the seat next to me. I looked down at him as he stared back at me. He couldn't have been more than seven or eight years old. The bartender noticed our new arrival and shook his head with a scowl.

"What's your son having?"

I started to protest, but the kid answered instead. "Chocolate milk, please."

"I know it's crowded this time of year, but kids really don't belong at my bar," the man said when he delivered the drink, though he did not force us to leave and for some reason I didn't bother to comment.

"I'm Liam," I told the kid.

He nodded with that serious expression he'd originally given me. "Oscar."

"Your folks here?"

He nodded again. "Mom, Mimi, and Papi. They're waiting for a table."

"Don't you think they'll wonder where you are?"

He shrugged and turned to scan the front waiting area. He waved at a man who didn't look much past forty, who waved back.

"That's Papi, its cool."

I was strangely impressed by the kid. I wasn't sure anything in this world bothered him. How I wished I could go back to those days when the weight of the world didn't feel like it was constantly pounding me into the ground.

I took a long sip of my drink. "You like basketball?" I asked the kid, remembering Chris's gift suggestion.

"Sure, who doesn't?"

"What's the usual age to start playing?"

He looked at me with an odd expression and smiled for the first time. "My mom bought me a basketball for my first birthday. Still have it. I've always played basketball."

I smiled. Maybe Chris wasn't so crazy after all. "Thank you," I told him. "My nephew's turning one today and I was trying to figure out what to get him for his first birthday."

"Oh, you can't go wrong with a basketball, and be sure to get the little kid hoop that adjusts down to his size. He'll love it!"

"They actually have something like that for a one-year-old?"

"Oh yeah. It adjusts. I grew out of mine last year and got my first real hoop for Christmas."

"You just might make me the coolest uncle ever then."

The kid scanned me from head to toe. I wasn't sure I had ever felt so exposed in all my life. Then he shrugged. "Maybe."

I laughed as I drained the last of my glass.

Offering him my hand, he took it and shook it. I left enough on the counter to cover us both. "It was nice to meet you, Oscar. Thanks for the advice."

"Sure, anytime," he said, and then tuned me out as the bartender turned on a basketball game on the big screen above the bar.

As I exited the bar, a sort of frenzied excitement hit me. It was so sudden and unexpected that it freaked me out. My skin felt like it was crawling and I had the sudden urge to change. Nothing like that had ever happened to me before. My wolf wasn't an Alpha, so I'd never had the struggles that Kyle did to control his wolf. I scanned the area in a panic, ready to run for my car. A commotion on the bench out front distracted me for a moment.

"Jane, honey, you're safe. I promise. We're not going to let anything happen to you."

"Annie, you don't understand. I can't explain it, but we cannot stop here. Please, just get them and let's go."

"It's not good for you to be so agitated. You were making such good progress."

I gawked awkwardly at the young woman pacing back and

forth. The hair on my arms stood up and I couldn't believe what my heart was telling me.

I saw her sniff loudly in the midst of her hysterics and her whole body froze. She turned slowly and golden-brown eyes locked with mine. My super charged body slowed and I think I forgot to breathe. Somewhere in the back of my mind I knew I was staring at my mate. My one true mate, but all I could think was, *this can't be real*. I was seeing a ghost. *Maddie*. An incoming group of people passed between us and just like that, she'd vanished before my eyes.

Maddie

Chapter 2

I had fallen asleep in the car. We were heading down to San Francisco. Jacob had a medical conference and I thought it would be fun for me and Oscar to explore the city. Out of fear I had chosen to homeschool him, but I often worried my son needed more than one-on-one time with his high school dropout mother every day. Sure, he was a great kid; I couldn't be prouder of him, but when the occasion presented itself, I tried to step out of my comfort zone and do what was best for him. He was so excited about the trip that even when my anxiety started to set in two days earlier, I just couldn't disappoint him.

Annie had given me a sedative of some sort for the ride, and for that I was grateful. It made things easier when traveling. I didn't do well in crowds. Not since the night it all happened.

I was sixteen years old. My best friend Jordan and I had gotten tickets to this concert for some big, popular boy band. They were great seats and we were so excited—so much so that I hadn't been able to concentrate on my chemistry test that day and though I tried to hide the resulting F from my dad, it had all snowballed on me and I'd been grounded.

Grounded? On the biggest day of my life? That was never going to fly. I snuck out and Jordan and I went anyway. The concert was really good, and some college boys near us had offered us some beer. I wasn't big on drinking, but they were college guys. I wasn't going to look like a baby and turn that down. Jordan had, and she'd gotten pissed when I hadn't. Just before intermission she had stormed out. I shrugged it off as no big deal and didn't go after her.

One of the guys started dancing really close to me and it

made me feel a little uneasy. He didn't know I was a wolf shifter and could have snapped his neck in two with one snap of my jaws. I remembered giggling just thinking it. Of course, I was only sixteen. My wolf hadn't emerged yet, but the signs were there that she would soon. Most shifters didn't change till sometime between eighteen and twenty-one. My mom always said I'd be an early shifter. I was very excited about it and couldn't wait for my wolf to show.

By intermission I'd had five beers and the room was spinning. I was upset with Jordan for not joining me, but I was having the time of my life. Six college guys and all their focus was on me. They told me they had a club box upstairs and invited me to join them. Hell, yes. I was ready to party!

The small room was so cool. My dad was our Pack Alpha, so I was used to luxuries that other shifters weren't, but this was just awesome. It was entirely soundproof. There was a private balcony of seats you could sit on for the concert, and if you opened the door you could hear the loud squeals and cheers as the band took the stage again. I opened the door and closed it three times, reveling in the noise to total quiet. The guys were fun and joined in with my excitement. One flicked on a button for speakers that suddenly had the concert music blaring inside the room. We danced and sang along. It was the best night of my life—and then it wasn't.

I don't remember any of their names. Only in my nightmares can I even remember the vaguest details of them. I was so drunk, and then the room started spinning out of control as we danced and my body went limp. Someone caught me before my head hit the floor. I couldn't move. It was like I was paralyzed.

"How much of that shit did you give her?" I remember one of them asking.

"Enough," someone else responded, laughing.

"I want her first."

I could move my eyes frantically, but for some reason I couldn't make a sound, and no matter how hard I fought with my own body, it wouldn't respond. I could hear them and see them, though. Stuck in that awful state of awareness I watched and listened as they each in turn beat and raped me to within an inch of my life, as they cheered each other on. A heightened state of awareness allowed me to feel every second of it, too. At some point I had blissfully blacked out, only to awaken two days later stuffed in a bag in a dumpster behind the coliseum.

A homeless man had found me and I was rushed to the hospital. I was too embarrassed to tell them my name. Annie Winthrop was my legally assigned, state-appointed guardian while they sorted it all out. I wouldn't talk to her or anyone. They listed me as Jane Doe and I kept the name Jane as the years went by. I was broken beyond repair and somehow, I knew that my wolf had died that day, too.

I was assigned to a girls' home, but continued to meet with Annie three times a week after they released me from the hospital. From the medical reports they had a pretty clear picture of what happened to me, but I never once told anyone, not even her.

The girls' home was hard. The others could be downright cruel, but by then I was so withdrawn and depressed that I just didn't care. There was no life left in me. They had destroyed me. Twice I was put on suicide watch, and for good reason.

Six weeks after being released from the hospital I had withdrawn to the point I wouldn't eat, and when they forced me, I'd just throw it up. Annie had fought for me. She begged me to live. She begged me to talk about it. I didn't want to do either. Then it was confirmed. I was pregnant.

Sixteen. Pregnant by a vicious gang rape. I couldn't go home. There was no way I could ever face my family again. The thought of a lifetime of grounding wasn't what scared me. I would be an embarrassment, a failure, the joke of the entire pack, and I could never do that to my parents, or my brother and sisters. My scandalous behavior would not destroy them as it had me.

Annie and her husband Jacob took me in after the pregnancy was confirmed. They were granted permanent guardianship of me and the baby until I turned eighteen. I didn't want a baby. I didn't want a constant reminder of what had happened to me. I would never even know who the actual father was. It was too much for one small girl to handle.

Annie sat me down one day and told me, "Jane, stop sitting around feeling sorry for yourself. I know whatever happened to you was horrific, but that child you are carrying cannot be blamed for it. You have to eat to be strong for him. You have to sleep so he'll rest, too. You have to get up and start living again, for him. God doesn't make mistakes with babies, but we humans can. You are going to be a mother for a reason child, now get up and start acting like it."

I hadn't spoken in days. My throat burned when I finally asked, "How do you know it's a boy?"

She had smiled back at me like she had all the secrets of the world. "I don't, but there's a fifty-fifty chance I'm right."

Six months later, making an appearance a little early at a whopping four pounds ten ounces, Oscar Jacob Winthrop was born. I had come back to life, for him. I had survived, for him. Seeing his tiny body stuck in the NICU those first few days had suddenly been the worst and hardest moments of my life as I watched my wee newborn son fight to survive. Not the rape. Not giving up everyone and everything I had ever known. Not a teenage pregnancy. Not even losing my wolf. That helpless feeling of watching my child struggle, knowing there was nothing I could do, that was the hardest thing I have ever been through.

I turned eighteen shortly after Oscar's first birthday and I prepared myself to leave the Winthrop's and set off on my own course in life, but they had other plans in store for us. They had opened their home, their lives, and their hearts to me and Oscar, and we would forever be grateful. They were our family.

Six years later, I still struggled with anxiety. Annie, who specialized in child psychology, attributed it to post-traumatic stress syndrome. She never pushed me to talk about what happened, but has been instrumental in helping me with coping mechanisms. For the most part now, I'm fine, but changes in life, even little ones like a trip to the big city, are difficult struggles that I push through for Oscar's sake.

He's a great kid. Super smart, serious, but also very much laid back, and calm. He soothes me in a way I can't fully articulate. I honestly do not believe I'd still be alive today if it weren't for him.

Waking up groggy, I knew I shouldn't have fallen asleep in the car. I mean, I was grateful for the sedatives Annie gave me, but when I did finally wake after the usual flood of memories that haunted me, Oscar wasn't there. I still relied on smells more than a normal human. It's sort of a wolf thing and even though my wolf had never surfaced and I no longer felt the connection to her that had been starting to form before the rape, there were certain attributes, like smell, that I had never been able to fully stop.

One sniff of the air around me and I knew we were far from

home, but not yet in the city. There were too many unfamiliar smells, and I knew before my eyes opened that Oscar was nowhere around. That set my anxiety on high alert and I started to go into a panic.

I jumped from the car and searching around frantically, I was surrounded by a much too familiar scent. Wolves. Where were we? I quickly checked around the area and I knew we must be in or near Westin Pack territory. I had grown up attending summer camp every year with Lily Westin and her siblings. We had been practically inseparable. I knew it was a long shot, but someone could recognize me. I had changed so much, but it wasn't a risk I was willing to take either. By now I knew my family would have celebrated my death, made their peace, and moved on. I wouldn't give them false hope that I was still alive, because the Madelyn Collier they knew wasn't. Jane Winthrop wasn't that same girl.

I spotted Annie sitting on a bench outside a restaurant we had stopped at. I didn't have to say a word; it was like she knew I was freaking out before I even reached her and she immediately began soothing me with confident, safe words. Sometimes Annie just seemed to have a way of knowing things she couldn't possibly know.

"Jane, honey, you're safe. I promise. We're not going to let anything happen to you."

"Annie, you don't understand. I can't explain it, but we cannot stop here. Please, just get them and let's go."

"It's not good for you to be so agitated. You were making such good progress."

Goosebumps stood up across my entire body and I quickly scanned the area, settling on a man. He was tall, muscular. I could tell even with the impressive suit he wore. He had sandy-brown hair and when I met his golden eyes I felt more exposed than ever. A ripple of calmness started to flow through me from my head down to my toes. It freaked me out resulting in a full-on panic setting in.

When a group exiting the restaurant broke my view, I turned and grabbed Annie and dragged her into the building. They were just calling Jacob's name for a table and he smiled as we approached, then instantly frowned.

"What's wrong?"

"We have to go. NOW. I can't explain it, just please. Where's Oscar?"

I could feel my heart beating fast in my chest and I was struggling to breathe evenly.

"Okay, okay," Annie said, rubbing my back in a soothing manner. "Jacob, get Oscar and meet us in the car. Jane, just breathe, sweetie. In and out. In and out." She kept talking calmly all the way to the car.

When Oscar saw me he just smiled sadly, climbed into the backseat next to me as Jacob started the car and pulled out, and wrapped his small arms around me. "It's okay, Mommy. Their chocolate milk wasn't even that good."

Liam

Chapter 3

Scanning the area, I couldn't find my mysterious woman. Maddie. Madelyn Collier had disappeared when we were teens. She and Lily had been close childhood friends, and while I had my own friends, I always hung out with my twin, too, especially when Maddie was around. Her father was Alpha of the Collier Pack in Wyoming. I had visited her family on numerous occasions. Their land was magnificent, even better than Westin with its wide-open fields to run in. They weren't the largest pack in numbers, but their massive property was quite impressive.

I remember the day we found out about Maddie's disappearance. I spent much of that weekcomforting Lily, distraught over the news of her friend. All anyone knew was that Maddie and a friend from the pack had snuck out to attend a concert in a city several hours away. She had been grounded and told not to go, but when Madelyn Collier set her mind to something, there was no changing it.

Her friend's account said that they arrived and were having a good time when they met some boys who offered them beer. Jordan, the friend, said Maddie accepted, but she did not. When Jordan went to use the restroom during the intermission of the concert, Maddie refused to go with her and when she returned, Madelyn was gone. Vanished. No sign of the boys either, but there wasn't a good enough description of any of them to track them down.

Madelyn had never been seen again. It was largely assumed that something awful happened and she was dead. The family even held a memorial for her to help the pack, but I knew her father was still looking for her, holding on to the hope that she would one day return home.

I hadn't thought of Madelyn Collier in years. Something about the frightened woman had triggered my memory of her. I had heard the woman with her clearly call her Jane, not Maddie, but I couldn't stop the feeling of unease that arose in me. Something was clearly wrong, and it hadn't gone entirely unnoticed that my wolf had recognized her, too. She had to be a shifter for that to happen.

Mate. The word kept playing over and over in my head. Impossible. Still, it freaked me out enough that I started walking the parking lot looking for her. I saw the boy I'd shared a drink with at the bar get into a car. He smiled sadly at me and gave a little wave. I watched as the car pulled away and only as it passed by, did I realize the woman I was looking for was sitting in the backseat with him.

I rushed into the restaurant and gave the hostess a description of the man that the boy had pointed out as Papi, who was waiting for a table. She looked it up for me, even while telling me she wasn't supposed to. Jacob Winthrop. The hostess was a chatty one and started telling me how odd it was, that the girl had come in freaking out and just as their table of four was called, they all left.

Jacob Winthrop.

It wasn't much, but it was something. My wolf was restless and my skin was itching as it did when I needed to shift. No way was that happening here. I took a deep breath to calm myself. It backfired. All I could smell was her lingering scent above all else. It was so strong I dared to believe that I could actually track her. Leaving the restaurant, I sat in my car and took out my phone. Pulling up a web browser, I typed in the name Jacob Winthrop.

The first site on the list was for a genetics conference in San Francisco, where guest speaker Dr. Jacob Winthrop would be speaking on some new gene found in humans. Blah blah blah, I didn't really care about the details. The picture on the website confirmed he was the man I was looking for. Nothing was going to stop me from going after her and getting to the bottom of who she was.

My phone rang in my hand. I glanced down and saw my twin's face on the screen. Sighing, I answered. "Hey, Lil."

"You still down in town?"

"Yeah, just about to head out, why?"

"Can you stop at the party store and pick up another bag of balloons?"

Balloons? Oh crap, Zander's birthday party! In the time since I'd first laid eyes on the woman, I had completely forgotten about my nephew's party.

"Um, yeah, sure."

"What's wrong?" Lily knew me better than anyone. I wouldn't be able to hide this from her, but I wasn't ready to share it either. She had this sixth sense when it came to me. I sometimes pretended I could feel and understand things about her too, but only because it made her happy to know I felt the connection. It was all a bunch of bunk, that twin bond and stuff, but she believed so much that I just played along.

"Nothing's wrong, Lil. I have one more stop anyway and then will head back. I'll get your balloons."

"Something's wrong. I can feel it."

It did sort of creep me out at times, like this when she actually got it right. Something was definitely very, very wrong.

"You're being ridiculous. I'll be home in about two hours. Plenty of time for the party."

"Okay, see you then. You're sure nothing's wrong?"

"Positive. Bye."

"Love you."

"Love you too," I said, rolling my eyes.

Before I put my phone away, I scrolled through emails, quickly finding the one I had just read yesterday inviting me to a fundraiser in San Francisco on Friday even ing Double-checking to confirm the convention Jacob Winthrop was speaking at would last through the weekend I quickly RSVP'd my acceptance and sent Christine a text to book me a room. I was leaving in the morning. I knew I wouldn't find any peace until I got to the bottom of the Maddie look-alike called Jane.

Stopping by the supercenter store, I picked up the balloons first. I knew Lily would never let me hear the end of it if I forgot them. Next, I wandered through the children's clothing section on my way to toys and sporting goods at the back of the store. I found I cute little suit complete with bow tie that I knew would drive Kyle nuts. Even as the former CEO of Westin Foundation, my brother hated dressing up. I didn't mind. I knew I looked good in a suit and tie, but I doubted Kyle had put one on since his last official day at the Westin Foundation. Our little man was going to look sharp.

I also grabbed a pair of baby Chucks to go with it. While I didn't mind the suits, I despised the normal footwear. Zander was going to be the coolest kid around in this outfit. I threw in a couple pairs of PJs he probably didn't need and headed for the good stuff.

Walking through the toy aisle, it was one electronic thing after another. I already knew Kelsey really didn't like him having those. A small part of me was tempted to get one just because of that, but I suspected Chase had it covered already. Stuffed animals were too girly for me. I looked at the small bikes, but he seemed too young even for those. That's when I remembered—basketball.

My thoughts immediately went back to the kid and the mysterious woman I could only imagine was his mom. A clone of Maddie that my wolf was so worked up over, but she couldn't be her. Maddie wasn't old enough to have a kid that age, but the resemblance was uncanny. I was already obsessed. It wasn't like me to behave in such a way.

Girls were a dime a dozen, and I knew I could have my pick, and I didn't want to settle down, anyway. My wolf had never responded to a female the way it did to this Jane chick, though. I didn't want to believe it was the girl herself, just the mystery behind her resemblance to an old friend who had disappeared without a trace. Still, I knew I had to see her again.

Oscar had been right; they actually did make a basketball hoop for toddlers. It said eighteen months and up on the box. Close enough for me. Plus, I was likely to have the biggest present of the day. I knew it shouldn't be a competition, but of course I wanted mine to be the best present of all. It came with a small soft basketball, but for good measure, I also got a smaller sized real basketball, too. I liked to play. Why not teach him? Oscar had lit up like a Christmas tree talking about basketball. Maybe it was an omen.

I grabbed several rolls of wrapping paper along with scissors and tape and headed out, I was suddenly thankful I'd taken the truck because otherwise, that beast-sized box would not have made it home. I was going straight there and didn't want the others to see what I'd gotten. Boy, were they going to be surprised.

It became a bit of a comedy act as I made a poor attempt to wrap the thing in the back of the truck in the middle of the parking lot. Two giggling girls took pity on me and came over to assist.

"Awe, it's so cute. Is this for your son?"

I knew she was fishing, but I answered honestly anyway. She was cute enough. Maybe she'd take my mind off Jane for a while. "No, ma'am, it's for my nephew. He turns one today."

"Awe, that's so sweet!" she gushed.

My wolf growled in my head and surged forward as she made an advance, placing her hand on my arm as she cooed. I bit back the growl, but the reaction stunned me stupid. What was going on? He clearly wasn't happy. It was strange. He never minded the ladies before, especially human ones. Feeling very off, I helped them with the last of the wrapping and thanked them before jumping into the truck and hitting the road.

"What the hell was that all about?" I asked aloud to myself, to my wolf, to the universe. I wasn't really sure which.

I cranked up the music and drove, feeling more at ease the closer I got to home. Still a little unsettled, I put on my best smile and headed inside. Carrying in the massively sized box that was easily five times bigger than the birthday boy himself, I yelled into the living room.

"Where are we putting presents?"

"What did you do?" Lily asked, frowning at me when she saw my gift.

I shrugged. "Wrapped it the best I could. It's not that bad."

"No, not that. What is it? It's huge. He's one. You do realize, right?"

I laughed and shrugged. "He'll love it. You'll see."

I passed her the balloons she had asked for, and Elise walked in and kissed my cheek. "I'm not even asking. I need you to hang streamers. Come on."

Grabbing me by the hand, she pulled me into the living room. Her mate, Patrick, was there, shaking his head and laughing.

"Recruited you too, yeah?"

"Looks like it. What else needs to be done?"

"I told you. I need you to hang the streamers. There. There. There and there," she said, pointing around the room to exactly where she wanted them. "It's Z's first birthday. It has to be perfect."

For two hours I worked mostly in silence next to Patrick. We rolled our eyes and laughed behind my sister's back, but neither of us dared cross her. You just didn't get in the way of Elise when she was on a mission. It was one of the reasons she made such a great VP of Human Resources at the Westin Foundation. She was super smart, quick-witted, and paid close attention to detail. Sometimes too close, I thought, as we moved the high chair for the fifth time, looking for exactly the perfect place for him to sit for pictures.

Patrick and I collapsed, bordering on exhaustion, onto the couch.

"Would you have mated her if you had known?" I asked him.

He grinned from ear to ear. "Absolutely," he assured me.

Elise had put Patrick through the ringer during their mating period. We had no clue for months that she was his mate, despite the full pack's attempt in helping him find her; despite the quick friendship he'd made with me and my siblings, he had no idea Elise was another sister of ours.

"Everyone in place," she exclaimed, rallying them all to the living room. Patrick and I didn't bother to move or get up. "He's here!"

As Kyle and Kelsey entered with little Zander between them, the entire family broke out into "Happy Birthday." The little guy squealed with excitement as he made his rounds of each person.

"Unkie Leem!" he chanted as he threw himself into my arms. Of course, I caught him and threw him up into the air as my mother and sisters scolded me and Zander yelled, "More. More. More."

Elise insisted on him opening presents first, before he got too tired to enjoy it. I waited patiently for him to get to mine last. His face lit up and he squealed at the sight of the basketball hoop and two basketballs, much like Oscar's had when he told me about it.

"Your gift just rocked that kid's world. What's wrong with you?" Lily whispered as she nudged my thoughts back to present. I had drifted back to thinking of Oscar and Jane and his Mimi and Papi. Who were they and why was I so consumed by them all?

"I'm fine. Knew he'd love it," I said, trying to add some usual cockiness to the statement, but not really feeling it.

"Tank you, Unkie Leem," Zander said, giving me a great big buddy hug only he specialized in.

"You're welcome, little buddy."

To my surprise, he wasn't just excited about the basketball stuff, but insisted on dressing just like "Unkie Leem" for his birthday dinner. I snickered watching my big bro squirm in annoyance, especially when Zander came strutting out in his new threads to the "oohs" and "aahs" of all the women present.

Family dinner proceeded with little incident. My phone buzzed in my pocket twice, but we all knew better than to check a phone at my mother's dinner table. Nothing was more sacred than her Tuesday night family dinners, except maybe today with the added bonus of it being Z-Man's birthday, too.

As soon as dinner was over and we had sung "Happy Birthday" again, watching Zander destroy the perfect little cake Elise had baked for him, that now covered the kid from head to toe, I checked my messages. Five texts from Christine.

CHRISTINE: Boss man, your hotel is booked from tomorrow until Sunday. Check email for reservation.

CHRISTINE: Rescheduled all but two meetings. Still working on it.

CHRISTINE: No-go on rescheduling Rogers, but agreed to teleconference instead of face-to-face.

CHRISTINE: Rest of schedule now cleared.

CHRISTINE: Thought you didn't want to attend this thing.

CHRISTINE: Oops, tell Z-Man happy birthday!

I knew there would be more questions about my sudden interest in a fundraiser I had refused to attend. I wasn't ready to explain it, and fortunately I wouldn't have to until I returned.

"You've been kind of lost in your head tonight. Are you sure everything's okay?" Lily asked as she plopped down on the couch next to me and rested her head on my shoulder.

"Lil, I'm fine. Just work stress. No big deal." I knew I had to tell her I was going out of town, and figured now was as good a time as any. "Hey, I'm heading out of town tomorrow for a few days. Work stuff. Just wanted you to know, 'cause I know you'll worry even when I tell you not to."

"Where and for how long?"

"San Francisco, and just 'til Sunday."

She nodded and yawned. It had been a long day for all of us. "Okay, please just call . . . like every few hours so I know you're okay."

I kissed the top of her head, knowing I would. Elise had been kidnapped a little over a year ago by the Bulgarian Pack. We were still at war with them. There had been a few skirmishes here and there, but nothing as serious as the kidnapping as far as we knew. Kelsey had lost contact with her aunt Raina, who was also Bulgarian and had promised Kelsey that she would be there for Zander's birth. She had never arrived and we all assumed she was just caught up in the war and forbidden to leave or contact anyone from Westin, but I knew it still bothered Kelsey that we didn't know for sure.

For the most part we hadn't had any major attacks or even contact with other packs in several months. Patrick was one of Kyle's Betas and he was in charge of security. All wolves had to train and adhere to a strict border patrol schedule. Patrick could be very laid back and fun, but not when it came to pack security. He was all business then, and we all felt a lot safer with him at the helm.

I knew I should inform him of my unscheduled trip, but I didn't have it in me to be interrogated over it. He wouldn't be happy about it, but he'd deal. It wasn't like we were confined to pack land or anything. I'd check in and let them know everything was okay. My thoughts and concerns revolved more around the Maddie look-alike than anything for myself.

Thinking of Madelyn Collier, I wondered again just what happened to her.

Maddie

Chapter 4

It had been awhile since I last had a full-on panic attack. Annie had to give me another sedative to get me out of the area and back on the road. They picked up drive-through at a fast food joint and we didn't stop again until we arrived at the hotel, well after nightfall.

I was too loopy from the drugs to be of much assistance. Oscar hugged me and tucked me in to bed, kissing me on the forehead and singing “Twinkle, Twinkle Little Star.” My heart nearly broke in two. That was my job, and no matter how bad off I had been in the past, I always made it a point of tucking my little man in. I understood why Annie gave me the sedative, but it’s just that I hated taking them and the way they made me feel. Helpless. Just like the night Oscar had been conceived.

I slept restlessly that night, despite the drugs. My dreams were haunted by old memories from my childhood. Golden-colored eyes followed me as I ran through the woods, as I jumped in the lake, wherever I went. There was excitement and comfort there, a familiarity I couldn't reconcile.

I woke up thinking of my childhood friend, Lily Westin. I hadn't thought of her for a long time. I tried hard not to think of anyone from my past, but no doubt being that close to her territory and smelling and seeing the wolf shifter at the restaurant had triggered it all. As the fog started to clear in my head, I realized that the male wolf whose golden eyes had captured me and froze me in place hadn't scared me. The fears that ensued after our eye contact was broken, were all my own. If I were to be honest for one brief moment, before I began to freak out, his smell had comforted me.

It was still dark all around and the soft snoring of the others told me I was the only one awake. I checked on Oscar and went to the bathroom, then buried my face in my pillow and just cried. It was a good cry, something I didn't allow myself to ever do.

Annie was constantly harping on me not to bottle things up so much. She said I needed to get it out, talk to someone, confront what happened to me, but that wasn't it. I needed to grieve the life I had lost and left behind. Understanding that was very different from allowing it to happen. I still missed my family. I missed my sisters and even my obnoxious brother, Thomas, who was God's gift to the pack after six girls.

I missed running in the wide-open fields, and hikes up the mountain. I was sad that Oscar would never know or understand that part of his heritage. For once, and only for that short time in the cover of darkness, I allowed myself to remember, and to feel the goodness of pack, refusing to have it darkened by the horrific things that had led me to leave it all behind.

As I cried myself back to sleep, it was with a smile on my face, staring into golden-colored eyes.

"Mommy! Mommy, wake up!" Oscar said, jumping on top of me.

I peeked up at him and when he looked away I leapt forward and grabbed him, tickling him as we collapsed back onto the bed. He squealed in delight, but I shushed him and whispered that he needed to be quiet.

"Are you feeling better, Mommy?" he whispered

I wasn't, but I lied. "Much better, Oscar," I said, looking around the room and finding the bed next to ours empty.

"Come on, sleepyhead, let's go get breakfast then. Mimi and Papi already headed down," he said.

"Well, come on then. What are we waiting for?"

I jumped up and looked around. I was still in day-old clothes, but didn't see my suitcase in sight and could tell Oscar was anxious to go. Sighing, I decided there were worse things than starting the day without a shower. At the door his small hand snaked into mine and squeezed. I glanced down at my son.

"Are you really okay, Mommy?"

I nodded. "Yes. Today is going to be a good day."

"Was it the woodsy smelling people?"

"Oscar," I started to scold him. "We don't speak of that, remember?"

He sighed sadly. "I know, Mommy, but I can't help what my nose tells me."

I smiled and gave him a squeeze. I didn't see how it was possible that he could have a wolf spirit, not when mine was dead and whichever of them fathered him was clearly human. Sometimes though, I did wonder. Oscar had shown a few minor traits common to wolf shifter pups. His heightened sense of smell was the most obvious. Without coming right out and telling him that normal humans didn't act like that, I tried to dissuade him as best I could.

We met up with Annie and Jacob in the dining area.

"There's my girl," Jacob said, rising and giving me a kiss on the cheek. "You are looking quite well this morning."

"Thank you. I'm feeling better. Sorry about yesterday." I knew I didn't need to apologize to them. They loved me and Oscar unconditionally and had dealt with worse from me than the attack the day before.

"Stop apologizing, Janie. I never much cared for the food there anyway." He winked at me and I knew it signaled the end of that conversation. They'd never mention it again.

Something about the place where I'd had the panic attack soothed and called to me as much as it freaked me out. Lily. It had to be Lily. I hadn't seen her, but there was a certain smell to those in a pack, and something familiar about her smell was all over that place. My heart longed for my friend, my family, my pack. In the eight years since I'd left, I had never felt it more profoundly.

Oscar filled the silence during the remainder of our breakfast. "The Golden Gate Bridge. Oh, and Alcatraz. Do you think we can actually tour the old prison? Can we go to the wharves? I can't wait to see the sea lions! And did you know that in Chinatown they make fortune cookies?"

Oscar for the most part was a pretty serious kid, but he loved history and research and he had been spending every waking hour for the last three weeks learning everything he could about San Francisco. He was a walking, talking encyclopedia now, and it was great to see him so happy and excited for a change. I knew I was going to have to push my demons aside and make this an awesome trip for him.

Annie was still watching me warily. I knew my panic attack had worried her. I hated knowing that, but I was determined to put on a good front for the day.

"I'm okay," I said, giving her a reassuring hug.

It had taken me several years to be able to do that comfortably, and I knew it meant a lot to Annie. I had never been an extremely touchy-feely kind of person, but after the rape, the thought of being touched or touching anyone was too hard. I struggled to connect and bond with Oscar when he was first born because of it. It was partly why he was so attached to Annie and Jacob. I felt guilty about a lot of things like that, but when people touched me even casually, like the brush of a hand or a hug, it triggered things I'd rather forget. Oscar was now the exception. It was kind of impossible to love a kid and not have them up in your personal space, but Annie knew my personal bubble boundaries and on rare occasions like a hug when it was breached, it had to be instigated by me, on my terms. I appreciated that they never pushed for more than I felt I could offer.

Her eyes were misted over when I finally pulled back.

"I need to shower and change," I said, pointing out my day-old clothes.

"Then we can head for the wharves?" an excited Oscar questioned.

"Yes," I said, ruffling his hair, "then we can head for the wharves."

I left them in the dining room to run back upstairs and shower and change. They had returned to the room by the time I was ready.

As we headed off on our adventure for the day, Oscar began again telling me how important it was that we go straight to this one particular charter down at the wharves to get the "real Alcatraz tour" that would let us on the island.

"Mommy, you don't understand. All the others only do boat rides around the island and don't let you on it."

When did my kid get to be so smart?

With Annie and Jacob, we all happily headed down to Fisherman's Wharf and to the only charter that Oscar approved. It broke my heart seeing the disappointment set in as we were told that all the tours were booked solid for the entire week we were there. He wouldn't get to set foot on Alcatraz Island, and we'd learned that we should have previously made reservations online. Now it was too late, since they were sold out, sometimes months in advance.

We headed over to Pier 45 to see the sea lions as a consolation and I promised we'd at least take one of the other Alcatraz cruises if he still wanted. He wasn't sure if he wanted that or not. Watching the sea lions battle for their place on the piers was entertaining and exciting enough to temporarily curb his disappoint.

Pier 45 was also home to the Musee Mecanique, home to a collection of classic coin-operated arcade games. That definitely lightened the blow some for Oscar. It hadn't hit his "things to do" list in his research, but was a small treasure of a place that I knew would entertain him for hours if I'd let him. He wandered some with Jacob while Annie and I stood outside enjoying the beautiful views. We walked up and down a few of the wharves, glancing around the various shops there.

"They won't come out of there on their own, you know," I told her with certainty.

"Oh, I know, but it gives us some good girl time. You want to talk about what happened?"

I knew it was coming. It always did. I should have known that's why she wanted time alone, away from Oscar. I shrugged. "I'm sorry, it just happens sometimes and I can't control it, Annie. It's just . . ."

"I know, Jane. It's hard to talk about things, but eventually you have to open up to someone, anyone. It's not healthy, and I'm worried about you. You were doing so well. I thought maybe the worst was behind us, but that panic attack was the worst you've had in years."

She brushed a stray piece of hair behind my ear. When I didn't flinch, she guided my chin up till I met her eyes. There was so much concern there and so many questions I didn't want to answer.

"Did you see him?"

I looked at her, genuinely confused. She was a psychologist, not exactly known for such direct questions. "Who?"

"Oscar's father?"

"What? No. Honestly, I wouldn't even know what he looked like anyway." I stopped myself mid-ramble. It was the closest I'd ever come to admitting the rape.

I knew she already knew about it, though. Without missing a beat or showing any sign of surprise, she asked, "Then what?"

"I smelled something familiar. You know, from my past, and it freaked me out."

Annie and Jacob were both too smart not to have recognized quirks like my heightened sense of smell over the years. I didn't even try to disguise it this time and I noticed her heart rate quicken just a little in interest. I would die before ever telling anyone my family secrets, but at times I just got the feeling they knew I was somehow different, special even.

We headed back to the museum in companionable silence. My answer seemed sufficient enough to stave off any further questions, for now.

When we entered the building I immediately saw Jacob, but I was also flooded by an all too familiar scent. I didn't see Oscar anywhere and panic began to spike in me.

"Hey, hey, hey, calm down," Jacob immediately started. "He's right over there. Hasn't left my sight for even a second, but he did make a quick friend, and it's good for the boy to have a male role model besides me, even if for only an hour."

I was furious. It was probably the only thing keeping me from a full panic attack. There was a wolf in the building, and he was alone. Wolves were pack animals. They rarely went anywhere truly alone and those that did were almost always trouble.

Could he smell me, too? Could he smell Oscar? I rounded the corner prepared to protect my son, only to be met by the golden eyes that had haunted me every second of the last two days.

It all suddenly clicked in my memory. Liam Westin.

"Liam," I whispered.

Liam

Chapter 5

When I arrived to check in at the hotel, there was the faintest smell of her lingering in the lobby. Somehow, I knew she was no longer there.

I checked in and went up to my room to drop my things. I had driven through the night and should have been exhausted, but I paced the floor of my room feeling more caged in than I had in years. My wolf was restless, despite having let him out for a run before making the trip. He had been agitated since we had first seen the girl.

I felt a brief tug towards the girl, but she was gone too quickly. My wolf was acting obsessed, like we'd just found our mate, but I knew that wasn't true. I mean, I'd know without a doubt, wouldn't I? I reasoned it was only the eerie resemblance to Madelyn that drew me to her.

I had made my way down to Fisherman's Wharf, figuring the open waters would be as much solitude as I'd find in this city, or at least give me enough of a false sense of open space to calm my wolf.

Wrong. There were people everywhere and that only heightened my agitation. I suddenly remembered an old video game museum, not like actual video games, but old pre-video game stuff, that I had visited on my last trip to the city. Maybe I could blow a few hours getting lost in a game.

Wrong again. Walking down the Pier and into the museum, I caught the faint smell that was uniquely hers, but stronger even was the kid's. I looked around, quickly spotting the older man he told me was his papi. Looking down, I could see the man holding the small hand of a kid just out of my sight.

I wandered around for only a moment before feeling a small

tug on the tail of my perfectly tailored suit jacket. I turned around, a little surprised to find the kid beaming up at me.

"It is you. What are you doing here?" he asked innocently.

"I'm so sorry," his papi exclaimed, reaching for the boy. "Oscar, you know better than to run off and talk to strangers," he started scolding.

"He's not a stranger. We met at that restaurant we stopped at. He bought me a chocolate milk."

I laughed. The kid definitely had a good memory. "It's fine," I assured the older man. "It's Oscar, right"

The kid excitedly nodded.

"Not every day you meet a kid at a bar, but boy was I glad for it. Gave me the best advice ever."

"You got it?" Oscar asked excitedly.

"Oh yeah. You gave me serious uncle points with your basketball and hoop suggestion. His mother texted me saying it was the first thing he ran for this morning, and all he's wanted to do today."

"See, I told ya." Then he turned to his papi to fill him in. "Remember my basketball hoop and basketball Mommy got me for my first birthday?"

The older man nodded and smiled affectionately.

"I told him to get the same for his nephew."

"Genius," I praised, surprised that I really meant it.

The man eyeballed me curiously for a minute, sizing me up, before extending his hand. "Jacob Winthrop."

"Liam Westin," I returned. There was a slight flicker of awareness in my name, but before I could consider anything, it was gone.

"Liam, will you come play this one with me?" Oscar asked.

"Mr. Westin," Jacob corrected.

"Liam's fine, really. Preferred even. Mr. Westin is my father," I joked. In actuality, since taking over as CEO of the Westin Foundation, I was "the" Mr. Westin of the family, but it didn't feel right to me coming from the kid.

"Well okay, then. You're sure he's not bothering you?"

"Nah, I love kids and I'm here for a few days early to enjoy the city. No plans or anything for today."

"Okay, if you're certain. I'll just be over there."

I gave him an encouraging smile and turned back to the kid, briefly wondering where the hell his mother was.

Aside from Zander, who was much smaller and didn't talk as much, I hadn't really spent much time around pups. Sure, there were always kids around San Marco, they just hadn't really affected me since the time I was one. If Oscar was any indication, they were pretty easy though. I just listened and kept feeding him coins while he prattled on.

He told me his mom was single and they lived with his grandparents who weren't his Mom's mom and dad. He was seven years old and in second grade, but was homeschooled, and he was obsessed with basketball.

I quickly realized the kid had no filter and began to question him being a shifter pup at all. Maybe I'd been completely wrong about the mom, too, and it was only her resemblance to Maddie that had me imagining it all, but then the kid hit me with something that had me second-guessing that theory too.

"I knew it was you the moment I smelled you." He shut his mouth quickly and turned wide, worried eyes towards me. "I wasn't supposed to say that. Mommy doesn't like me to talk about it."

I glanced at him, understanding what he was telling me. "How about I tell you a secret then, too?"

He nodded, still serious, but a little more relaxed.

"I can smell you, too."

"You can?"

I nodded. No idea why I had just told him that.

He leaned in and lowered his voice, very seriously asking, "Can you tell what I had for breakfast?"

The little pup was actually testing me. "Pancakes." I smiled. "But the dribble of syrup on your shirt would have made me guess that anyway." I wiped off the spot and he giggled.

Suddenly very serious, he leaned in and took a big whiff of me. "You only had coffee and your tummy's saying you're hungry," he whispered, a second before my stomach growled in protest. We both laughed. "I have good ears, too," he whispered. "Do you have good ears?"

I smiled. "Yeah, I do."

He got very excited about that. "You smell a little like me and Mommy."

It was only a statement. All wolf shifters had a hint of that woodsy, natural scent. It was the smell that alerted us most easily to others of our kind.

"Are you my father?"

I had just taken a sip from my water bottle and started to choke. It took me a moment of hacking and coughing to be able to talk again. "No, Oscar, I'm not your father," I told him, watching his big, brown, hopeful eyes turn sad. "How about another game?" I asked, not knowing what else to do.

"Okay," and just like that he transformed back to the sweet, chatty kid.

He won the game with only a little assistance from me. I gave him a high five then showed him how to do a secret victory first bump, when I smelled her. We both turned at the same time to meet furious, shocked brown eyes. It felt like I'd been kicked in the nads.

Mate.

The word played over and over again in my head. I was staring at Oscar's mom, Jane, the Madelyn Collier look-alike, my mate.

She was clearly just as shocked to see me. "Liam," I heard her whisper, making my heart flutter in a weird and unexpected way.

"You know my mom?" Oscar whispered, grounding me back to reality. His grandparents were standing just behind her, watching us closely.

I knew without a doubt I was staring at Madelyn Collier. Maddie was my one true mate. Knowing it didn't absolve the shock of it, but with all eyes on us, I chose the safest route.

"Jane, it's nice to see you."

Using the name I had overheard at the restaurant seemed to startle and confuse Madelyn, but she recovered quickly.

"Liam, what are you doing here?"

I didn't quite know what to say, so I grabbed Oscar and shoved him forward. "I'm playing games with the kid."

Oscar shot me a traitorous look.

"Oscar, how do you know this man?" she asked him.

"We met at that restaurant we stopped at the other day, and then ran into him here. Papi said I could play with him."

Smart kid. Throw the old man under the bus, but Maddie

wasn't taking the bait.

With hands on her hips, she turned back to me. I shivered at the clear display of mom eyes and my wolf cowered under the stare of our mate.

"Coincidence?" she questioned.

"Actually, yeah, it was." Though I didn't confess it was only because I was stalking her.

"Mommy?" Oscar interjected, taking the heat off me momentarily. "How do you know Liam?" His tone was accusatory and she sighed. Her shoulders started to sag.

"Liam and I grew up together. He has a twin sister, Lily." She smiled fondly as she said it. "We were best friends from about the time I was your age."

I caught a silent exchange between Jacob and the woman as Oscar's questions began flying from his mouth.

Maddie held up a hand and squeezed her eyes tightly, like she was counting to ten. "Oscar, why don't you go with Papi and Mimi, and let Liam and me talk for a bit?"

"But Mom, he's starving. He skipped breakfast. We should at least feed him first."

I suddenly felt like a stray dog that the kid was trying to ease in before asking to keep.

"I'm pretty hungry too, Janie. Why don't we grab some lunch? Let the shock of seeing an old friend sink in before talking," Jacob suggested.

"Fine," she said, like she knew she wasn't going to win that battle anyway.

"Would you like to join us for lunch, Liam?" The older woman with her asked.

I smiled brightly. "I'd love to."

"Oh good. By the way, I'm Annie, and it's so nice to meet an old friend of Jane's."

I smiled arrogantly at Maddie. "Jane and I go way back."

She glared when I emphasized the name Jane, and shoved me forward. Annie faltered a little and somehow I knew that this Jane didn't make personal contact much. I fought back a grin, taking it as a sign of her wolf recognizing me, too.

As we were heading down the stairs near the sea lions, Oscar grabbed my hand and pulled me aside, tugging me down to his level.

He cupped his hand near my ear and whispered. I think he may have spit a little in there, too. "Did you do something to make Mommy mad?"

"No."

"Did she do something?"

"No," I assured him.

"Okay, 'cause warning, that is not her happy face"

I tried not to laugh. "Thanks for the heads-up."

"Anytime."

I caught Maddie watching us, but couldn't tell what she was thinking. Oscar's small hand never left mine.

As we got back down to the pier, he stopped. Staring out across the water, he sighed. His whole body sagged, looking so much like his mother.

"Hey buddy, what's wrong?" Clearly the kid was upset by something.

Maddie came up behind us, rubbing his shoulders. "Oscar was excited to see Alcatraz. He researched everything about it, wrote a paper on it for school even. He found what tour would actually let us on the island, but they are booked solid all week."

"Oh," I said, wanting to make it all better. I took out my phone and started to dial a number. "What day and time were you hoping for?"

"Any!" Oscar told me with a pout and Maddie cast a concerned look my way. I knew I'd do whatever it took to get them on that island. Fortunately, I knew it wouldn't take much.

"All four of you?"

They all nodded, but Jacob added, "Well, Annie and I only have today and tomorrow for sight-seeing. I'm in town for a convention, but Oscar and Jane have all week."

I nodded and dialed Steph's number.

"Hey Lee, what do you want?"

I laughed. "Why do you think I want something, gorgeous?"

"Gorgeous? Oh, you want it bad. What is it?"

I tried to fake some innocence. "Can't I just call and check on an old friend?"

"Never. If you wanted to just check in, you'd have called Mark. If you need a favor, you always call me."

I laughed, knowing she was right. "Okay, you got me. I need

a tour group of five to the island."

"Private?"

"Of course."

"When?"

"Tomorrow. Anytime."

"Tomorrow? You ass, you're in the city and didn't call?"

"Maybe . . ." I gave her a sec. "So . . .we good?"

"It's a good thing you're so cute. One o'clock okay?"

I pulled the phone away. "One, tomorrow?" I asked as four shocked heads nodded my way. "Yup, one's great." I confirmed.

"You owe me," Steph said.

"My life," I responded. We always ended calls that way.

Hanging up the phone, I turned back to them, all staring awkwardly at me. I decided to address Oscar directly. "One o'clock tomorrow off Pier 37. I'll introduce you to my friend Steph, who will take you all out to the island."

He looked skeptical. "Is it legal?"

I laughed. "Yes."

"You're sure? Cause it's illegal to go without a special permit and there's only one charter that has it, otherwise we'd just take any boat over."

"I'm sure. Steph owns that company. She's a good friend and does private tours on occasion, or at least when I ask nicely."

"Wait, you've been there before?" he asked excitedly.

I laughed. "Yeah, a few times."

That started a never-ending stream of questions and information flowing from him as we headed across the street to a bakery for lunch.

Maddie placed her hand on my arm and moved closer to me. "Thank you," she mouthed, genuinely smiling.

My mouth went dry and my hands started to sweat. My wolf instantly calmed under her touch. We had just pleased our mate for the first time and the emotions that surged were overwhelming. I swallowed hard and nodded, unable to speak.

Clam chowder in a bread bowl was a personal favorite and popular request. I placed my order quickly and waited as the others did too, insisting on buying for everyone. I'm not sure Jacob entirely appreciated it, but he eventually conceded.

While we waited, Oscar dragged me around to look at the

crazy sourdough sculptures they had for sale, before finally settling on a bear. Maddie came over to protest, but I just looked at her and mouthed "Sorry" as the cashier handed me back my card. Oscar loved it. Sure it would probably never get eaten, but who cared. The kid was happy.

"Too late, Mommy," he gloated as I elbowed him gently in the back, and then gave him a serious look to be quiet.

She just shook her head and sighed. "Nothing good will come from you two meeting," she mumbled as she walked away.

Oscar helped me carry the food to a table they had secured outside. It was a beautiful summer day. Not too hot though, mild for San Francisco. The sun was shining and people were everywhere, some going about their daily routine, others clearly tourists.

"So what's next on the agenda, Oscar?" Annie asked.

"Cable car ride," he exclaimed excitedly.

Maddie looked at me and then back at them and before she could open her mouth to speak, Jacob intervened.

"That's what I've been most looking forward to doing with you. Would you mind if we ditched your mom and it was just you, me, and Mimi?"

Oscar looked at his mom and I noted the worry in his eyes. I instantly knew this seven-year-old felt responsible for his mother. Why? How did that happen? He was just a kid. I realized Maddie and I had a lot of catching up to do.

"Will you watch after my mom while we're gone, Liam?"

I was emotionally struck by the kid asking me. I could easily see his mom meant the world to him and his protective nature reminded me of Kyle as a kid. The boy was a natural Alpha.

I nodded seriously. "Yeah, I suppose I can put up with her for a few hours." He raised an eyebrow up at me in a comical way that made me laugh. "I'm kidding. Yes, I'll hang out with your mom. We have some catching up to do anyway. Won't let her out of my sight, I Promise." I grinned at Maddie over the top of his head, but the look in her eyes reminded me of a frightened wolf that had just been cornered, and I didn't like it. Neither did my wolf.

After lunch, we said goodbye to them and Maddie looked at me awkwardly as I offered her my arm. She seemed hesitant, but took it as I led her across the street. We walked along the wharves in an uncomfortable silence.

When we finally got through the worst of the crowds to the end of one of the piers with relative solitude, I turned to her. "Mad . . ."

"How did you know?" she interrupted.

"Know what?"

"To call me Jane. Why didn't you call me Maddie?" She struggled to say her own name and I wondered just how long it had been since anyone had called her that.

"I heard Annie call you that when you stopped at the restaurant. I might not have even noticed you at all, but you were having some sort of attack and she was talking loudly enough to draw my attention. I honestly didn't know it was you. I mean, you still look like you . . . well, sorta. More like a grown-up, more beautiful version of the girl I once knew." I couldn't stop myself from reaching out and caressing her cheek as I said it, but when she flinched away from me and then turned her back on me to walk to the water's edge, it felt like a punch in the gut.

I suddenly felt terrible for everything Patrick and my brother had gone through finding their mates. Neither one had an easy time with it in the beginning, but was this really how they felt through that whole time? Kyle had fought the mating call for two years. How had he survived if this was what he endured every day of that time?

Taking a deep breath, I walked to her, trying not to let my pain show, but I wasn't an Alpha like them. I wasn't as strong as they were and I was sure one look at me would show it all.

"So you are following me?" she accused with her back turned toward me.

"Not exactly. More like stalking," I said. That got a strong enough reaction that she turned quickly with wide, shocked eyes.

"Wh-what?"

I gave her the grin that typically got me out of anything and everything in life, the irresistible one, and I saw her melt a little. I was beyond relieved to find she wasn't totally immune to me.

"Look, I saw you, but for only a second. Then as you were driving away I saw the kid. Oscar and I had met at the bar inside the restaurant a few minutes before all that, so I recognized him. I went back in and asked the hostess about Jacob. I didn't know his name at the time, but Oscar had pointed him out to me and he was easy enough to describe. Jacob had left his name so I had a lead, at least. I

Googled him and found he was speaking at a convention here this weekend. I didn't know for sure you would be here, but I have a fundraiser here and a few meetings I needed to attend anyway, so I came down a few days early, hoping to run into you."

"Where are you staying?" she demanded.

"Okay, so I checked where the convention was and booked at the same hotel, which I would have anyway because my charity ball this weekend is also being held there. I was able to sweet talk the receptionist into confirming that Jacob at least was staying there. I wasn't certain, but had hoped you and Oscar were, too. I swear it was complete coincidence that I ran into him today. You just"—I took a deep breath, wondering how much I should tell her—"you just look so much like, well, you, that I couldn't stop thinking about you. I had only gotten a small whiff of your scent, not enough to confirm, just enough to set my wolf on edge. I had to see you and know for sure."

"Know what, Liam? That I'm alive? 'Cause I am, but please, do not run back to my dad and tell him you saw me. I can't go home. I can't. I have a life here, and it's a good one. They're my new pack now. My family will never understand and it's just all better if they believe I'm dead, because that's what happened, Liam. Madelyn Collier died eight years ago. She doesn't exist anymore and hasn't for a long time. You need to just go home and forget you ever saw me."

The pain that shot through my chest was almost crippling, and I stumbled back a little. She couldn't be serious. She was my mate!

"Maddie. Jane. I don't give a shit what you want to be called, but you know I can't do that. Please don't ask that of me. You're my mate. My one true mate."

Maddie

Chapter 6

I'm not sure anything had ever shocked me more than Liam's confession. His mate? He thought I was his mate? A small voice in the back of my head said, *You know he's your mate. You've known it since you first caught a whiff of him two days ago. Why do you think the panic attack hit so hard?*

"I can't be your mate," I whispered, not sure if I was actually speaking to him or myself. I wasn't at all prepared for the pain those words caused me physically, nor the sheer look of agony Liam was trying hard to reign in. I didn't know how to tell him. I didn't think he could possibly understand. I wasn't a wolf. I was different now. I could never be a proper mate for him.

He stared out across the water and his voice was hardened when he spoke again. "Like it or not, Maddie, you are my mate."

A tear slipped down my cheek. I made it a point never to cry in front of people; it had hurt my family too much during the years I had, but I cried openly now. Liam Westin was my one true mate. Eight years earlier I would have been ecstatic. I'd had the biggest crush on him for years as a little girl. I loved the Westin family as much as my own, and Lily and I would actually be sisters. It was like some sick twist of fate. The perfect fairy-tale I was meant to have and couldn't.

Liam's arms wrapped around me. I hadn't let anyone hold me like that since the morning of the day I ran away. I had been so upset about being grounded and Mom had wrapped her arms around me and just let me cry in her arms as I was doing now in Liam's. It should have felt wrong. Close contact terrified me, especially from a man, but it didn't. It was so perfectly right that I started to panic.

He must have felt the change in me because he started rubbing my back, "Hey, hey, what's happening here? Just breathe, Mad, just breathe. It's okay. It's going to be okay, but you have to talk to me. I need to understand and I need you to tell me how to help you."

"You can't help me, Liam. You can't fix this. This is who I am now."

"It's okay. It's okay. It's all going to be okay." He kept telling me that over and over, but it would never be okay. His soothing voice and the circles he was rubbing on my back finally started to calm me. I didn't know how he was doing it, but I started to breathe normally again. My panic subsided and so did the tears.

"Thanks," I said. I was mortified. This was Liam-freaking-Westin, and I just had a complete meltdown in his arms. I turned away from him to look back out across the water, but he stopped me.

"Don't do that. Don't turn away from me, Mad. If you choose to reject our mating call, that's going to be your decision and yours alone. I'll figure out a way to live with it and respect it, but at the very least, I think I deserve an explanation." He took in a deep, frustrated breath when I didn't respond right away. "Look, you of all people know how my family feels about 'one true mates'. I've waited my entire life to feel this, to find you, and so far, it really sucks."

I was so surprised by his confession that I snorted, trying to hold in a laugh.

"I mean really sucks! I'm dealing with a pair of humans, and a kid that might idolize me. I'm not kidding there—watch out for his request to wear suits." I laughed again, and he got even more dramatic. "You think I'm kidding, but I'm not. It's the latest fashion in the Liam Westin fan club, just ask Zander. It's coming. Oscar will be dressing like this soon. Just you wait and see. Oh, and I found my twin sister's obnoxious, bratty other half, and she's my mate? Yeah, what are the odds of that? I'd say I'm getting the raw end of the deal here." His voice softened and I realized he'd put me at ease and got me listening again. "So, talk to me. I need to know, 'cause spending the rest of my life without you and Oscar really isn't a viable option for me."

He included my son. It was more than I could have ever hoped for, but he didn't know me, and he didn't know what I'd been through. I had never told anyone and I wasn't sure I could start with him.

"I don't know how to explain it all to you, Liam."

"So, Twenty Questions then?"

It was an old game we all used to play at camp. I smiled, remembering the hours we'd spent just asking questions and talking. Life had been so simple back then. I had learned a long time ago not to focus on the what-ifs or wallow in what had happened, but right now, my dream man was within reach, and knowing what kind of wonderful life I had always imagined with him, it was really hard not to think about it.

"So that's a yes?" he asked when I didn't answer.

"Yes, but you've just wasted your first."

He feigned disbelief. "You little cheater. Fine. Was Oscar the reason you ran away from home?"

Wow, he was hitting the deep stuff right off the bat. "No, and yes."

"Come on, you can do better than that," he challenged.

"No way, I answered your question, and that was number two, so I get two to catch up."

"Fine."

"How's Lily?"

He smiled affectionately as we walked to a bench that had just been abandoned and sat down, facing the water.

"Lil's really good. She graduated a few years ago and went right to work at the Foundation. She loves it. Can't commit to a single job to save her life, so E reassigns her every year at least, sometimes sooner. Keeps them both happy. Mostly, she's still just Lily, full of life, true to herself, doesn't seem to care what anyone thinks or says about her, but we also know behind that is a heart bigger than that ocean out there."

I brushed another tear from my cheek. Instead of making it awkward he just said, "Next?"

I laughed, grateful he was keeping it mostly light. "Let's see, what about you? What do you do these days?"

He sighed. "I took over as CEO of Westin Foundation a little over a year ago. Kyle and Dad struggled to hand over the reins for a while, but I'm flying solo now."

"Wait, what? How did you become CEO? I always thought

Kyle would."

"Uh-uh, you already caught up. My turn. Plus, that was like a million questions."

"It was not."

"Was too."

I liked the easy banter between us. It made me more comfortable than I had been around anyone for a long time. "Fine, your turn."

"Explain your last answer."

"Not a question."

He glared at me trying to portray his frustration, but I just smiled back sweetly. "You always were too good at this stupid game," he grumbled, mostly under his breath. "Can you please explain your last answer?"

"No. My turn."

"What? Not fair!"

"I answered your question. My turn."

He crossed his arms over his chest and huffed.

I giggled. "Who's Zander?"

"What?"

"You said, 'Just ask Zander,' talking about your fan club and Oscar wanting to dress like you. So, who's Zander?"

He gave me a thousand-watt smile that made me swoon. "My nephew. Kyle's kid."

"Kyle has a kid?"

"Uh-uh, that would be two questions."

I smiled at him. "Okay, so ask yours already."

"How did you meet Annie and Jacob?"

He totally changed gears on me, and it threw me off a little.

"Annie was my appointed guardian until I turned eighteen. They took me in when I found out I was pregnant with Oscar and they just became family. I owe a lot to them both," I said honestly.

He seemed to consider that but didn't ask me to specify.

"Why are you CEO and not Kyle?"

He gave me a quizzical look, like, "How do you not know this already?" I could easily assume all wolf shifters were aware of the circumstances he was about to tell me. "Kyle was CEO until a little over a year ago. The Bulgarians started a war over his mate, Kelsey. Dad was seriously injured in the war and power transferred to Kyle before Kelsey saved him. He's fine now, but with the baby on the way then and taking over as Alpha years before planned, he had to step down as CEO, which forced me to step up. Like it or not."

It sounded a little resentful, but I didn't press. I knew it wasn't my turn. "Your turn," I said.

"You said Annie and Jacob took you in when you found out you were pregnant. Does that mean you were not pregnant when you left home?"

"No, I was not pregnant when I left home."

I could see my answer hit him hard as he tried to resolve what I wasn't telling him.

"I guess I thought from seeing Oscar that maybe that was why you left. You know, found out you were pregnant, got scared about how your dad would handle it and ran."

I shook my head no, sadly. "Um, has Lily found her mate yet?" I asked, trying to change the subject quickly.

"Nah. Kyle and Elise both have though, and now it looks like I'm up next." He grinned at me like he was happy about that, like truly happy, but he didn't know and I didn't know how to tell him.

"Look, Liam." I took a deep breath, trying to get my thoughts together. I had never said the words out loud and I guess a part of me hoped they weren't true. How did I tell my one true mate that my wolf spirit was dead? "I . . ."

I was cut off by a high-pitched squeal as a tall, sleek brunette threw herself into Liam's arms.

Liam

Chapter 7

One minute I felt like Maddie was about to finally open to me and the next I was being physically attacked.

"Lee-lee! Let me look at you." She pulled back and I couldn't help but grin as the outrageous Steph examined me closely. "You're looking pretty hot. I could kick your ass for coming into my territory without so much as a heads-up. Damn good thing you're so nice to look at." She hugged me close again and kissed my cheek.

A loud, aggressive growl sounded next to me. Steph froze in my arms and slowly backed up, glancing over my shoulder. I turned to meet horrified, embarrassed eyes. I quickly moved to Maddie's side. "Hey, it's okay," I reassured her.

"Uh, what just happened?" Steph asked. With hands on her hips, she demanded to know who had just growled at her. "And just who do we have here?"

I wrapped an arm possessively around Maddie and pulled her close to my side, but she was still tense from Steph's taunting.

"I'm so sorry, I don't know where that came from," Maddie started apologizing.

"Hey, it's okay. Trust me, it wasn't that long ago that E went through it, and Kelsey was way worse even. She growled at everyone."

She looked really upset and shook her head, "No, you don't understand, I can't—"

"Seriously, Lee, who is this?"

I knew Steph well enough to know it was only sheer curiosity, but I could see that Maddie's wolf was highly agitated and was seeing Steph as nothing but a threat to her mate. I was struggling to keep the grin off my face as I tried to console her.

"Dammit, Steph, back off and give her a minute."

"What the hell is this? The prodigal son returns without so much as a text or warning?" came a male voice from behind me that I'd recognize anywhere.

Maddie seemed to be relaxing just a little, still looking mortified about having growled at Steph. I took a step forward, careful to keep her safely behind me. I was aware that my wolf's instinct to protect her had just skyrocketed. I had never had many Alpha signs, but loyal, hardworking, and trustworthy were among my highest qualities. Trying to get a grip on these new and overwhelming emotions after finding and needing to protect my mate, I extended my hand and embraced Mark with my free one.

"You ugly mutt, what are you doing on my pier?" he asked affectionately.

"How the hell are you?"

"We're good. Man, it's good to see you. Never thought I'd miss that ugly face."

I grinned sheepishly, looking over my shoulder at Maddie. I motioned for her to come here and she hesitantly did, though I could see the caution clear in her eyes.

"Mark, Steph, this is—"

"Jane," she interrupted.

I nodded. "—Jane, my mate."

"Your mate?" Steph squealed and like a whirlwind, threw her arms around Maddie. I had learned enough in the last hour of talking with Maddie to know that this was not okay with her. Carefully orchestrating her removal, I sat down on the bench and pulled Maddie onto my lap. Her entire body relaxed and melted against mine.

"Steph, not everyone likes being mauled by you," I warned.

She just shrugged and took a seat between us where Mark had joined me on the bench. He immediately wrapped his arm around her and pulled her back against him.

"Sorry, Jane, she doesn't always get that normal people have boundaries," Mark said.

I laughed. "Mark and I were college roommates. Steph is his mate. They're sea lion shifters."

I'm not sure anything I could have said would have shocked her more. For the most part shifter groups rarely interacted with each other, but the Grand Council had been working with other shifters for years on a new integration program. A new college had opened, welcoming all shifters, and Mark and I had been in the first graduating class. I had quite the eclectic group of friends because of it.

"Seriously?" she asked.

"Seriously," I assured her. "Hence her lack of personal skills and boundaries." Mark laughed out loud, too, knowing it was true. "Did you watch the sea lions this morning and see how they all tried to lay on top of each other and wrestled for more space? Yeah, that's pretty much how it is with them all the time, too."

She stared at them with open curiosity. Mark just shrugged. "Hey, this guy carved out his space and practically peed all over it."

"I'm pretty sure he did, actually, from the smell of the place," Steph said.

We all laughed at the memory.

"Guess we all have our quirks," he admitted.

"So you live here, full-time?"

Steph looked out into the water with a dark, haunted look in her eyes. The sea lion population had started to dwindle and she and Mark had begun a repopulation program. I knew it was difficult for both of them, but especially for her. Our kind believes that God gave each of us a spirit animal to protect, and the duty to protect all the animals of our kind. By mating in animal form, we could reproduce animals. They were not born with a human spirit. The female had to stay in animal form throughout the pregnancy and most find it difficult to return to the human world afterwards, choosing to live out their lives as an animal alongside their young.

Mark and Steph were extraordinary in my mind. They had gone through the repopulation process at least four times that I knew of, but kept returning to human form to care for and watch after the animals. It was the ultimate sacrifice and it was easy to see how difficult it was on them.

He rubbed her back and kissed her temple. "We do. We're working on a repopulation program for the sea lions." He smiled sadly and I watched Maddie's reaction as she understood the full impact of what he was saying.

"They also run several charters, including the one taking us to Alcatraz tomorrow," I said in an attempt to lighten the mood. I saw an exchange of some sort pass between Maddie and Steph as Maddie quickly wiped a tear from her eye. Maybe it was a mother thing. I didn't fully understand it.

Steph morphed back into the carefree, playful girl I knew. "Ah, so that makes sense. You said five though, who else?"

"My son and his grandparents."

Her eyes widened in unrestrained curiosity. "You have a son?"

Maddie's chin jutted out in defiance, unnecessarily. I suspected with her young age, it was just a normal reaction to people questioning her motherhood.

"Yes, Oscar is seven, and his grandparents don't know about our kind."

I hadn't thought to warn them of that. I was proud of Maddie for thinking of it.

Steph nodded in understanding and I could see a million questions brewing just under the surface, but for once, she held back. It felt like there was some odd connection between the two women that Mark and I weren't privy to. I looked at him to confirm I wasn't the only one lost. He just shrugged and shook his head.

They had work to do, and excused themselves a little while later. Maddie and Steph actually hugged when they left, and Maddie didn't look like she was going to freak out.

Maddie turned and buried her head in my chest. "I can't believe I just did that!"

"What?"

"I growled at her, Liam. I growled!"

I laughed. "I told you, it's not that big a deal. Kelsey nearly snapped the heads off more than one unsuspecting she-wolf when she and Kyle were going through it. It's totally normal."

I didn't know what to say or do when she turned sad, watery eyes on me.

"You don't understand. You could never understand. I'm not like you. I'm not like her. I don't growl."

She was so distraught. "Talk to me," I begged her.

She walked away from me and looked out over the water, just crying for a minute before speaking again. It was the worst feeling of my life. I knew my mate was hurting, but I didn't know how to help her.

"The night I left—" she started, but was interrupted.

"Mommy! Oh my gosh, it was so cool!" Oscar hugged close to her side and looked up at her face. Angry, disappointed eyes glared back at me. "You said you would watch out for her. I trusted you!" he yelled, and I felt it all the way to my soul.

"Stop," Maddie told him. "Oscar baby, look at me. I'm fine. This isn't Liam's fault."

"Yes, it is. I thought maybe an old friend would help you. Make you happy, but he's only making you sadder. Mommy, you're crying. You never cry. Not in front of anyone else, at least."

She looked crushed at his confession. I knew without asking that she tried very hard to hide it from him, and I could tell by Oscar's reaction that it was not an uncommon occurrence.

"Come on, Mommy, let's go back to the hotel and I'll tell you all about it."

He was placating her, treating her like she was the child and he was the parent. She had been about to open up to me and now I wasn't sure I'd ever really know the truth. She looked embarrassed, mortified even, and I could easily see she was about to give in to the kid and do what he asked.

"Mm—" I almost slipped and said Maddie. "Jane, please don't."

She took a deep breath. Wiped her eyes and kissed the top of Oscar's head. "I'd love to hear all about it," she told him, completely ignoring me.

My wolf was frantic and I had to actually fight to maintain control when she turned sadly to me and said, "It was nice to see you, Liam. I'm glad we got the chance to catch up some."

I stood there and watched her leave. Jacob and Annie stared at me for a minute before turning to follow them. It was the lowest I had ever felt in my life. The thing was, I had never been mean to Maddie as a kid, but I had always shown her this cool indifference, because secretly I had always loved Madelyn Collier. I had been a good kid up until her disappearance. I rarely ever got into trouble and when I did I knew I could just schmooze my way out of it. I had the gift of charm, my mother said.

I had prayed and secretly hoped for much of my life that I would be blessed with Maddie as a mate, or at the very least, someone just like her. As far as I was concerned, the fates had smiled down on me today. The only girl, who had ever had my heart, even if she didn't know it, was the only one who would ever own it, but seeing the dejection in her as she walked away was breaking it.

When she had disappeared from my life the first time, I began heavily dating. I was known as a womanizer through college and I drank and partied too much. I was the fun, carefree guy everyone wanted to hang out with. Mark and Steph knew better, but the rest just saw me as they chose. I had straightened up and stopped drinking entirely after Dad's injury. I knew I would be called up to take over the family business, and I couldn't let him or Kyle down.

I haven't had a drink in twenty-one months, so why did I suddenly feel the urge to drown myself into oblivion?

I headed back to the hotel. It suddenly sucked that we were at the same hotel, because all I wanted to do was go to her. Instead, I headed for the bar.

"What are you having?"

I hadn't given up the bar life, I just ordered soda instead now. A part of me felt like I needed something a whole lot stronger, but then I thought of Maddie and I couldn't do it.

"Just a Coke."

As I was finishing my drink, Jacob Winthrop wandered into the bar. He sat down beside me. "Whiskey on the rocks, and another round for my friend. What are you having, son?"

"Coke," I said, causing me to smile for the first time since they'd arrived at the docks earlier.

He raised an eyebrow, but didn't ask.

"Janie assured us that you were not the cause of her being upset. I'm not sure Oscar fully believes it, but I do. There's been something different about her today with you around. So I want to ask, just how well do you know Janie?"

"I've known her since I was six years old. There's a lot of history there." He quirked his eyebrow at me again. I laughed. "Nothing like that. When we were kids she was my twin sister's best friend in the whole world. We spent every summer at camp together. We didn't grow up in the same—" I considered my words carefully, not knowing just how much of Maddie's life they truly knew. Certainly, as humans, they didn't know she'd come from a pack, or that she was a wolf shifter. How had she hidden from them for all these years? "Town," I settled on. "Our families are very close, though, so we got together as often as possible."

I could tell there was so much he wanted to know. They didn't even know her real name.

"How'd you know to call her Jane? We know it's not her real name, though I suppose using it for eight years now makes it as real as anything."

I guiltily confessed. "I heard your wife call her that, and figured if she was going by another name, then I should respect that."

"Don't suppose you'll tell us who she really is."

"No sir, not without her permission."

"Just as well. Shows me you can be trusted. Janie needs that in her life. She's had a rough run on things. Hasn't been easy on any of us, as I'm sure you picked up from Oscar."

"Sir, what happened to her? She was about to tell me about it when you guys showed up. That's what she was so upset about. Can you tell me what you know?"

His face softened and there was moisture evident in his eyes. "She was about to tell you?"

"Something, I don't know what, but yeah. She said, 'The day I left home,' and then Oscar grabbed her."

"Dammit, I'm awfully sorry. If I'd known, we would have stayed away longer. For eight years we've been trying to get that girl to talk about it. She just locks us out—locked everyone out but the boy, until you." He eyeballed me suspiciously. "Annie and I were watching, we saw."

"Saw what?"

"Oh, it's the little things, son. The way she reached out and touched you without hesitation. Close proximity. Personal space. That's all big issues with Janie, but you seemed to walk right past her boundary and she didn't even flinch."

"Will you tell me what you know?"

He nodded soberly. "Eight years ago, she was found in a dumpster. Two broken ribs, clothes torn and tattered. She wouldn't talk. A homeless man had found her and called 911 from a payphone. Annie was on call the night Jane was brought in. She's a psychologist and was working with child welfare services, so she was called in when they found Jane. She'd seen thousands of kids over the years, but something about our Janie just broke her heart."

He stopped and wiped a tear from his eye. "Janie spent three weeks in the hospital. They ran tests. We know she was raped, though she's never admitted to it."

Raped? Maddie was raped? Oscar was conceived from a rape? I was struggling to breathe, let alone keep my composure. I was grateful I hadn't caved to the desire for a real drink because I wasn't sure what I would have done. My wolf roared in my ears. *It was a long time ago. There's nothing we could have done*, I tried to rationalize with myself.

Jacob had given me time to let the news sink in. When I turned back to him, he nodded sadly. "That was about Annie's reaction, too. She was labeled a Jane Doe and sent to a girls' home. She still wouldn't talk and she wouldn't eat so she was practically skin and bones. When they forced her to eat, she'd just throw it all up afterwards. Annie was there every day checking on her for three months. That's when she started to suspect. She'd been given the 'morning after pill' in the hospital, but apparently it didn't work, because she was pregnant with Oscar."

I nodded, trying to reconcile his words to reality.

"Annie came home with her that night. The safety and one-on-one care slowly drew her out of her shell. She struggled to bond with the boy at first. That's part of the reason he's so close to me and his mimi. We couldn't love that kid more if he was our own flesh and blood."

"Thank you for telling me and for caring for them," I said hoarsely, my voice thick with emotions.

"Oh son, you don't have to thank me for that. That has been my greatest honor and privilege. You should know, Annie and I think of Jane as our daughter. We were never able to conceive ourselves. She and Oscar are our family."

"Tomorrow, I hope you all will still accept the trip to Alcatraz? I don't have to go if it's going to upset Oscar. Jane already met my friend Steph who runs the business. I really don't want him to miss out on that because he's pissed at me."

"No way are we missing that opportunity," he said with a smile, "and neither are you. We'll meet you at the docks around 12:30. Don't worry, I don't think Janie is upset with you, and Oscar will come around. He's very protective of his mother and doesn't like seeing her upset, that's all. If she was truly about to dive into her past and share with you, it's no wonder she was upset. Also tells me, you're exactly the one we need around her."

He winked at me as he stood and left the bar; and me with my thoughts on all he'd just told me.

Maddie

Chapter 8

All night I tossed and turned, worrying about whether Liam thought I was upset with him. I wasn't. I was worried about my son. Oscar had shown signs of a protective instinct towards me in the past, but never quite so aggressively as he had toward Liam.

When we returned to the hotel, I asked Annie and Jacob for a little time alone with him. I explained how seeing Liam had brought up some things from my past and that some of it made me sad, but that was not at all his fault. I tried to explain that it was important for me to talk to another grown-up and work through a few things. I also made sure to emphasize that he would always be the number one man in my life.

By the time Oscar was bathed and snuggled into bed, I thought we were at a better place, but the next morning we ran into Liam in line for breakfast. I hugged him and apologized for both my and Oscar's behavior the day before. He had tried to brush it off as no big deal, but I had seen his face as we left, and it had been a big deal.

The moment my arms wrapped around him, I felt a peace I'd never experienced before, but it was short lived as a small growl erupted from my son in warning for Liam to back off. I was so shocked I didn't know what to do.

Liam didn't hesitate as he knelt down to his level and talked softly to him. “Oscar, I know you don't like to see your mom upset, but you have to understand, I could never do anything to hurt her.”

Oscar looked so torn. He didn't understand what was happening to him emotionally. I had never told him about my heritage. Being half human, I had assumed it was impossible for him to have a spirit animal, but the way he was acting with Liam, I again questioned that theory.

"Mommy doesn't like to be touched," Oscar said. "She only likes it when I hug her, so stop touching her."

Liam put his hands up in surrender and I tried not to blush. "Okay, I can try to do that. Think you can stop growling at me long enough to enjoy our trip today?"

His eyes got huge with a mix of uncertainty and excitement. "You mean we're still going? But I thought that after yesterday you wouldn't want us to go with you."

"Not want you? Never. It was just a little misunderstanding. I didn't mean to make Mommy cry."

Oscar nodded like he accepted that as an apology. "It makes me really angry when people make Mommy cry."

"Lesson learned," Liam said good-naturedly, and my heart softened a little more for the only man I had ever cared about. "I can give you some pointers on how to control that growl, too," he whispered softly to Oscar, who nodded like that was a very good idea.

I needed to tell Liam that Oscar didn't know about our kind. I needed to tell him so much more than that, but I didn't know how or even where to begin. I had gotten up the nerve to start yesterday and it ended in disaster. I was hesitant to try it again.

Oscar got his food and went to sit at a table. I turned to Liam and whispered, "We need to talk."

He nodded towards a small veranda just off the breakfast area. I nodded before heading back to Oscar. I watched from across the room as Liam got his own breakfast and headed outside. When Annie and Jacob joined us, I excused myself and headed for Liam.

My breath hitched at the sight of him. He was perched on a concrete wall looking out away from the hotel. The morning sun was shining down on him and he looked more handsome and carefree than I ever remembered. Some part of me that had been dormant for a long time, or perhaps never even truly existed, began to awaken. Everything about him called to me.

"Hey!" he said, waving me over to join him, and I did.

"Hey." I didn't know how to begin but knew I had to be fast. "Look, we don't have much time before they come looking for me. You need to know that Oscar has been raised with humans. He doesn't know what you are."

I was careful not to say what I am or what he is, because I didn't believe in my heart either of us had spirit animals. I knew I couldn't shift, because I had never changed, not in all my twenty-four years.

I saw Liam struggle to accept that. His forehead crinkled in frustration. "But. . ."

I shook my head. "No buts, he's half human. He doesn't carry an animal spirit in him."

"You're sure? Because even in the little time I've known him, he has all the signs, Maddie, half human or not."

I shook my head no, wishing in part that what he was saying was true. "He's not."

"But how does he not know about you? I mean, I get you live among humans and must have gotten good about hiding it, but there's no way you can go all that long without shifting. I've been in this city right about twenty-four hours and my skin's already itching to change and run. How are you controlling it so well?"

My heart rate started to pick up and the palms of my hands began to sweat. Darkness started clouding my peripheral vision and I tried to take deep, calming breaths, but I could feel the start of another panic attack coming on. I needed to get away. I was withdrawing into myself quickly. I didn't want to have an attack in front of him. I didn't want him to know how weak I truly was. Thinking about it only made the feeling that more intense. I was losing myself to the fear and darkness once again.

"Hey, hey, hey. It's okay."

I heard him, though it sounded like he was a great distance away.

"Madelyn, I need you to breathe. In and out, just listen to my voice. In and out. You're okay. I'm here. Everything is going to be just fine. In and out. Just breathe for me, sweetheart."

The moment he pulled me into his arms, everything stilled. I gasped out a big breath and my entire body went limp, falling into him. I breathed in his scent and felt a sudden calm overcome me that made my whole body shudder.

"You're okay. I got you," I heard him whisper before his lips brushed across my forehead. It felt like an electric shock hit my body, causing me to jump from his arms. "Whoa, it's okay. Maddie, look at me."

I needed a minute to compose myself. I was no longer feeling pulled under by the anxiety. This was an entirely new sensation shooting through my body that I was equally unprepared for.

"I'm okay," I managed to whisper. "Just give me a minute."

I had never come out of an attack feeling quite so well. My body was warm and tingly all over, kind of nice. Normally I feel like a truck ran over me then backed up and did it again.

"How did you do that?" I asked him.

He shrugged. "One of my frat brothers in college served a few years in the Army and had some pretty deep battle scars. He'd get similar attacks from PTSD. We all learned to deal with them. Stay calm, keep talking, the faster you could pull him out the easier it was on him. I'd spend hours just sitting with him, waiting for the worst to pass. I promise I've seen way worse than this." He hesitated as he looked me over. "You okay now?"

"Um, yeah, I actually am. Thanks." I rubbed my thumb and index fingers together in circles. It was a coping habit of mine. He stared at my hands but didn't say anything or try to stop my fidgeting. "I, uh, I don't usually come through one so fast or so easily." My shoulders sagged and self-hatred flared within me. I was weak, that was all. Too weak to protect myself. Too weak to save my own wolf. Too weak . . .

"Hey, don't do that."

"Do what?"

"You know what." He stared at me so intensely I started to squirm. "My buddy—Andy, that was his name—he used to do that, too."

"What are you talking about?" I started to walk away. No way could he know what I was thinking or how I was feeling. No one could. "I said I'm fine, Liam."

"I know, but your eyes, they say otherwise. Andy"—he swallowed hard and he looked sad—"he used to do that, too. Beat himself up over the attacks, thinking he wasn't strong enough to fight his own demons, and that would snowball into every little incident that he had faced and maybe could have done something different to change the outcome, and truthfully, he couldn't. Sometimes bad shit just happens and you have to move on and learn to deal. Please, just don't tell me you're okay, when I can clearly see you're not, and it's okay."

Emotionally I was still better than usual, but I was a little overwhelmed that he seemed to get it, like really understand what I was going through. I couldn't dwell on it for too long before Annie and Jacob came out to find me with Oscar in tow.

Annie rushed to my side, shielding Oscar the second she saw me. "What happened?" she whispered while Jacob distracted my son.

"Nothing, I'm fine. Really, I'm fine, Annie," I added when she looked at me with more uncertainty. Was I? I took a moment to self-evaluate and was happy to see that yes, I really was fine. Liam, on the other hand, looked anything but fine.

As Annie signaled to Jacob in their unspoken way that I was okay, he excitedly announced that Oscar wanted to go see the sea lions again and spend the rest of the morning walking the wharves until time for the ride to Alcatraz. Liam sported an appropriate fake smile and joined us as we headed out for the day.

After arriving back at the wharves, Oscar led us straight for the pier with the most sea lions, and the biggest crowd. I didn't do well in crowds, but I was too distracted by Liam to really take much notice. It was like I could feel something was off with him, but I didn't know what, and I was compelled to find out.

Making sure Jacob and Annie had eyes on Oscar and seeing them all busily watching and cheering on a pair of battling sea lions, I pulled Liam to the side. "Hey, what's happening?"

"Huh?"

"What is wrong? I don't know how to explain it, I can just feel it. Something's really bothering you. Was it my panic attack?"

"No," he said, rubbing my shoulders, which seemed to relax him. "I'm fine. Just brought up memories of my own. Nothing to worry about it."

I realized, not for the first time, but perhaps more clearly, just how little I knew about Liam Westin. Not the Liam I grew up with and crushed on each summer, but Liam, the man standing before me.

Oscar abandoned the sea lions and came rushing over to us with Mimi and Papi following closely behind. He stopped before us and checked both of us out. I watched as Liam transformed, masking the pain I had clearly seen and felt from him.

"Liam, you want to play some more video games while we

wait?"

He smiled down at Oscar. "Sure, kid, come on."

They left with Jacob following, so of course Annie descended on me as soon as they were out of earshot.

"Janie, what happened back there at the hotel? You were so pale, and had a slightly glazed look. I thought for sure you were on the verge of another attack."

"Annie, I'm perfectly fine. Please don't worry. Nothing is going to stop me from enjoying this day with Oscar."

"And Liam," she added with a mischievous grin. "Oh, don't you even try to deny it. That man is good for you, Jane, and handsome, too. I have eyes. I see the sparks flying between the two of you." She sighed, looking a little conflicted. "Just be careful," she warned.

My cheeks felt hot and I'm pretty certain my mouth dropped open. "Annie! Don't you start now. Liam is an old friend, that's it." *And my mate,* I thought, but would never say aloud. She couldn't possibly comprehend what that even meant. Then again, neither could I!

Liam

Chapter 9

Hanging with Oscar was a safe and quick way to blow the morning hours. He was excited and talked non-stop, leaving me time to think without him noticing.

Maddie's anxiety attack had been on the cusp of being a bad one. I was starting to feel her emotions and knew that our bond was already beginning to take root. Jacob had given me enough information that I knew it was inevitable I'd have to face an attack with her, but I wasn't prepared for it to happen so quickly. I was lucky I didn't go into a full-blown panic attack myself. The only thing that had grounded me was, knowing my mate needed me.

Andy had needed me once too, but I had an important exam to take and was late for study group. I ignored all the signs, knowing he was about to have a major PSTD attack, and I left. He hanged himself that night. My friend had killed himself because I had more important things to do. That was the burden I carried. That was the awful truth I had to learn to live with.

I was drunk for two weeks straight after Andy's death. All my fraternity brothers carried guilt over his death, but none more than me. He had asked me to stay that night. I hadn't and that was a regret I would carry to my own grave. It took a trip to the emergency room to have my stomach pumped from alcohol poisoning to pull me out of the stupor, which was a huge contributing factor to me no longer drinking.

I had known exactly how to walk with Maddie through an attack, but there was something else that had happened between us that morning. I had seen my brother and sister and their mates constantly touching each other. I had harassed them all over it on more than one occasion, but I think I was beginning to understand it now. Every time I touched Maddie, a sort of warmth and peace washed over me. I suspected it was the same for her and that it was actually my wolf calming hers on some unseen level that caused her attack to end so abruptly.

Wolves cherished closeness and connections. I had heard about it. I knew it existed, but that in no way prepared me for the reality of it. I knew if it wasn't for the kid, I wouldn't leave her side, and I wouldn't be able to keep my hands to myself. The warmth that only she provided me was more addictive than anything I had ever experienced in my life, and I hadn't exactly been the poster boy for clean living in my fraternity days.

When we finally left the museum, I was surprised to see the sun already high in the sky. Glancing at my watch, I saw it was nearly noon.

"How about we grab a quick bite to eat before heading to the boat?"

The others agreed as Oscar announced he was starving. We walked to a nearby area with outdoor vendors. They had everything from tacos to lobster. The food was good and despite the tension the day before, everyone was relaxed and amicable.

As we finished our meals and headed back to the wharves and down to Pier 37, I hung back behind the others. It didn't take long for Maddie to slow down so she was walking next to me. Oscar was holding both Jacob's and Annie's hands, talking up a storm. When I reached for Maddie's hand, she didn't flinch away. I smiled down at her, feeling like the luckiest man alive.

We hadn't talked about what the future would hold for us, but with Maddie and Oscar by my side, I knew I could face anything. I felt stronger just being with them and protective in a way I'd never felt before. My mate. I smiled and shook my head. Lily was going to freak out when I told her.

Steph and Mark were already waiting for us at the dock when we arrived. Steph bit her lip, trying to hide her grin as she watched us approach. I knew they were happy for me, being true mates themselves. Steph squealed and waved. Before I could stop her she'd passed the others and launched herself onto Maddie. I was relieved and a little surprised that Maddie seemed okay this time.

"I'm so excited to spend time with you guys today," Steph started. "Now, who is it that wanted to see the island so badly that this fool called in a favor for it?"

"Me!" Oscar said, raising his hand and jumping up and down.

Steph turned to check him out. I took the moment to apologize to Maddie.

"Sorry," I mouthed.

She shrugged and leaned in to whisper, "I was ready for her this time."

I chuckled.

Oscar was already onboard and chatting it up with Steph and Mark as Steph made the introductions all around and passed out life jackets. We set sail as Steph gave us a quick list of rules. First, she gave the official tour at sea, circling the island and giving a history of the place. Of course, Oscar already knew every detail she shared, and he even told a few stories they hadn't heard before.

Annie had pulled Maddie over to sit with her, close enough to hear Steph's stories. I wandered more to the back of the boat to give them space as a family. It wasn't long before Jacob joined me.

"Annie's ecstatic at the progress Jane's making with you in such a short time. Don't let her fool you, that woman's got eyes in the back of her head. Always watching."

"Is that a warning?" I asked with humor.

"Jane looks happy when she's with you. That's all any father really wants, right? And make no mistake, in my heart, that girl is every bit my daughter."

"So you've warned," I said fondly.

"Your friends seem nice, but you're not from around here. How'd you meet?" he asked, referring to Mark and Steph.

"Mark and I were college roommates." I laughed thinking back on it. "Steph too for much of it, least it felt that way."

"It's nice to have friends like that. You can learn a lot about a man by the company he keeps. I'd say you're doing pretty well for yourself."

I blew out a hard breath and ran my fingers through my now windblown hair. "Some days, Jacob. I won't pretend it's always easy. I'm twenty-four-years-old and the CEO of a major corporation. Sometimes I wonder how the hell this happened. I mean, don't get me wrong, I'm grateful for the opportunities, and I always knew I'd go into the family business, but this was supposed to be my older brother's job, not mine. Life doesn't always quite work out the way we thought it would, does it?"

"No son, it doesn't, but that doesn't make it bad."

"No sir, I'm not complaining. Truth be told, I'm proud of the work I've done so far and have solid plans for the company's future."

"And what about your future?"

"What about it?"

"Being CEO, especially at such a young age, can't really afford you much free time."

I shrugged. "It's not as bad as it sounds."

"How about family?"

"My family is the most important thing in my life. There's nothing I wouldn't do for them."

"I meant your family. You want a wife? Kids someday?"

I grinned, thinking of Maddie and Oscar. As far as I was concerned, I had already found my family and I couldn't wait to take them home. I was already working out the plans in my head to build us a home and I hoped to fill it with even more kids.

Jacob noticed the direction my eyes had taken, focused on Maddie, and he nodded and grinned. I didn't think he'd disapprove one bit. Before he got a chance to confirm that, Oscar came over, excited to announce it was our turn to dock. We were about to go ashore.

I had been on Alcatraz a few times before when visiting Steph and Mark. It was a neat place. I liked the history of it and the movie *The Rock* was awesome, but never had I quite experienced the place until I watched it through Oscar's face. I was mesmerized by his excitement and captivated by his interest. It was literally better than seeing it for the first time.

"Hey look, Liam. That's the tower where Nicolas Ca—"

"What?" I interrupted the boy. Turning to Maddie, I quirked an eyebrow. "You let him watch that movie?"

She just shrugged and smiled innocently. "It wasn't that bad and he was so infatuated with this place I had to give him something."

"He's eight," I insisted.

"Technically, I'm only seven."

"Not helping," Maddie half scolded with a laugh. "Seriously Liam, it was fine. He loved it."

Oscar nodded enthusiastically and I suddenly realized just how difficult it was going to be to ever say no to the kid.

Alcatraz was a huge hit with him. Steph did a great job talking through the stories and engaging him. The others all seemed engrossed in the tour, too, but I just stood back and watched them all. Two humans were certainly an oddity to have for family, at least in our world, but I was grateful for all they had done for Maddie, and for Oscar. I knew we'd have to find some way to keep in touch and be a part of the family. Oscar and Maddie would need that as they transitioned to life in San Marco.

As the tour ended and we headed back to the boat, I was struck by just how beautiful my mate was. Madelyn had always been pretty. Even as little kids I had recognized that, but she had grown into a strong, quiet, sophistication that I loved.

I loved her, I thought. I paused a moment to let it fully sink it. I had never even had a serious relationship before, but somehow, I knew it was true. This wasn't just some stirred up mating hormones. I loved Madelyn Collier, Jane Winthrop, whatever she wished to be called. I loved her.

I was quiet, just watching them all on the way back to shore, content and happy with the life we had ahead of us.

Maddie

Chapter 10

Liam had been quiet much of the afternoon, but he looked happy. Oscar had been ecstatic and the entire trip was a huge hit with everyone. I knew I owed him big time for making my son's dream come true.

Earlier I had pulled Annie aside and asked her if she and Jacob could watch Oscar for the night so I could go out with Liam. I needed to thank him, but mostly we needed to talk. I had tried to explain some things yesterday; I told him I couldn't be his mate, but today felt different. Felt. That was really the biggest concern. I could feel him. I didn't think it should have started so quickly, but I somehow knew that even without a wolf of my own, our bond was forming and it had to stop.

I knew it was going to hurt like hell, but I'd been through worse. Hadn't I?

“Are you okay?” I asked him, seeing him jump a little like I had startled him. “You've just been really quiet this afternoon.”

He smiled up at me, the kind of smile that set my body on fire and made me sigh happily at the same time. *No, no, no,* I thought. It had to stop. He affected me too much and I cared too much for him to let it continue.

“I'm fine, just enjoying the views,” he said.

I gave him a puzzled look. “You've been staring at me, Liam, not the views.”

“Exactly,” he said, like that was the answer to everything, but then he laughed.

“Annie and Jacob are taking Oscar for the rest of the day. Are you busy tonight? I really think we need to talk, without little ears around, and Jacob's convention starts tomorrow. Single moms don't exactly get breaks often," I said apologetically, though I didn't know why. It was my life and he needed to understand that, too. I had a responsibility to my son above all else.

I felt a surge of happiness coming from him before he spoke. "Yeah, sure. I'm free anytime you need me to be."

He was so sincere and open in ways I wasn't sure I had the courage or strength to be. Knowing how difficult tonight was going be, I felt nothing but sadness. I knew by the confused look on his face that he was able to feel my emotions, too.

When the boat docked Oscar requested ice cream. Steph and Mark decided to join us. As we were walking to a nearby place, Steph came up beside me and linked her arm through mine. The others were just ahead of us.

"I'm really happy you and Liam found each other."

I cringed. "Don't be," I whispered.

Steph stopped and turned to stare me in the eyes. I had never felt quite so vulnerable in that way, like she could see all the way to my soul.

"You're certain? I mean I'll admit I was little skeptical when I heard you had a kid, but Oscar's great and Liam's going to be a wonderful dad."

"I know," I said softly.

"And you're sure this is what you want?"

"No," I said shaking my head, "but it's what I have to do."

She brushed a tear away and hugged me close. Panic flared inside for only a moment. I took a deep breath and was surprised to find I was okay.

"Do me a favor, and make it fast. He's a really great guy, and I don't want to see him hurt any more than needs be."

I nodded and started to cry. Oscar must have sensed it, as he turned to stare. I saw the disappointment in his eyes and quickly wiped my tears away.

"Mommy, what's wrong?"

I put on my biggest fake smile and lied to my child. "Nothing's wrong, baby. Mommy's just really happy for everything Steph and Mark did today and I was just thanking her. Papi has your ice cream so go and enjoy it."

Steph and I shared a look and I suddenly had a flashback to

my sisters. It was a similar look we'd give each other when we shared a secret. I took a deep, cleansing breath.

"It's going to be okay," I said aloud to no one in particular, or maybe just to reassure myself.

I watched Oscar finish his ice cream before I pulled him aside and stepped away from the others. I needed to give him a heads-up that I wouldn't be going back to the hotel with them, but that Mimi had promised he could go swimming after dinner, if he didn't give her too hard a time.

He was so used to always having me around that on the extremely rare occasion I left him, even with his grandparents, he pitched a fit. He would sometimes refuse to eat, or cry and throw a tantrum. Of course, it was much worse when he was little; now it was more of pouting and being stubborn.

To my surprise, he took the news better than I expected. He was still elated from the trip to Alcatraz and he didn't even bother asking me where I was going or anything. Sometimes in moments like this, under the scrutiny of his inquisition, it could feel more like I was the child and he was the parent, but he just smiled, hugged me, and told me to have a good time.

A short while later we all said goodbye as Annie and Jacob left with Oscar, and Steph and Mark said their goodbyes also . . . and then there were two. Just me and Liam. Suddenly I had no clue where to even begin.

"So, I have you for the entire evening?"

I nodded, feeling shy all of a sudden.

He grinned from ear to ear. "Perfect, come on," he said, taking my hand.

"Where are we going?" I asked.

"Come take a ride with me."

"Where?"

"You'll see," he said, reaching for my hand.

We walked back to the road and caught a cab to the hotel. Instead of going inside he escorted me to the parking garage where a sleek black SUV waited. He held the door and helped me up into it before walking around and climbing into the driver's seat, and then we were off.

We were both quiet as we drove along. I stared out into the bay and admired the beautiful Golden Gate Bridge as it got closer and closer.

"Are we going across?" I finally asked, excitedly. I had never been to the other side where the hills rolled high above in plush green landscapes. It was so opposite of the hustle and bustle in San Francisco.

"We are. There's a special place I want to show you. It may be a little weird, but probably my favorite place in the whole Bay Area."

For some reason I found just crossing that bridge and being on it, looking up as we crossed, to be magical. I was sorry it was over much too soon. Liam turned right almost immediately and pulled into a scenic lookout spot just on the other side of the bridge. We stopped and got out of the car. It was so surreal, looking back across the water at San Francisco, such a strikingly different view.

Liam took out his phone and immediately began snapping pictures. "Turn around and smile," he told me.

I froze. I didn't take pictures, ever. They were nothing more than validation that I, Maddie Collier, existed, and I couldn't let that get back to my family. It wasn't fair to them.

"What's wrong?"

"I, uh . . ." I didn't know how to explain it to him. "I don't like having my picture taken." I lamely tried to play it off.

"Don't be ridiculous," Liam said. Before I knew it he was standing behind me and holding the phone away from us, snapping selfies of the two of us. He started making faces and acting silly until I couldn't help but smile. "See, that wasn't so bad," he said triumphantly, kissing my cheek and sending tingles throughout my body. "Come on, we're not there yet."

"Wait, we're not?"

"Nope," he said as we got back in the car and headed out away from the Golden Gate Bridge. He took a left a little ways up and began a slow climb up the mountain. There were lookout stops all along the way, but he didn't stop until we'd reached the top and he parked the car.

"It's beautiful," I whispered.

"Yes, it is, but we're still not there yet, come on."

I laughed, getting out of the car. He came around, took my hand, and led me to an opening in the mountain. "Are we supposed to be here?" I asked as he led me into a dark and somewhat spooky-looking tunnel. Halfway through, the smell of urine was strongly mixed with the fragrance I knew to be spray paint. A small opening to our right appeared.

"You do not want to go in there," he warned, and I realized the smells were coming from inside. We moved past it quickly, coming out on the other side.

Everything was so green. A thick forest covered the hillside, and a cove with a small town surrounding it was seen far below. It was beautiful. I inhaled deeply, taking in the woodsy smells. The woods called to me like nothing else ever had before. It smelled a little like home.

My entire body sagged and I started to cry. Strong arms wrapped around me.

"I'm so sorry—I didn't know it would upset you."

"It's beautiful. It's just"—I sniffed—"it's just that it smells a lot like home."

He just held me and let me cry. Anyone else and I'd have been mortified, but not with Liam. When my sobs slowed to mere whimpers he hugged me tighter and finally spoke.

"Better?" he asked sweetly.

I chanced a look at him and wished I hadn't. I needed to just close my eyes and tell him everything and then leave and take Oscar and go home. My mouth was dry and my palms started to sweat. The darkness started to sneak into my peripheral vision.

"Hey, stay with me now. Just breathe in the fresh air," he told me in a soothing tone.

"I can't, it hurts too much."

"What? Why does it hurt, Maddie? I need you to talk to me."

I opened my eyes and looked straight into his. "Because it smells like home. The memories are too much. I'm not strong enough to face them. I can't. I don't want to remember."

"What don't you want to remember?"

"Them," I whispered. "I don't want to remember Mom and Dad, and my sisters, and Thomas. That's not my life anymore, and it hurts too much to remember them."

"Sweetheart, they are going to know you're alive. We're going to have to face the challenges and while many packs are not welcome into Westin territory right now, Collier isn't one of them. They're going to find out you're still alive."

My spine straightened and my body stiffened. "They won't," I said in a voice I barely recognized as my own, "because we aren't going through the challenges. I can't accept you as my mate."

I vividly felt his confusion and hurt. It was almost crippling.

"You don't mean that."

"Liam." I sighed. The last thing I wanted to do was hurt him. "There are things you don't know or understand about me. Just trust that I know what's best for both of us?"

"Do you? Do you really? Because this is not what's best for me, Madelyn." His voice was full of pain and despair and I could feel his resolve strengthening. He wasn't going to let me go without a fight.

I was grateful there was not a single other person around to witness.

"You're going to have to accept my decision, because it is final. And I would really appreciate it if you wouldn't share my whereabouts or even that I'm still alive with anyone. I need you to forget you ever saw me."

He snorted in retort. "That will never happen, and you know it. You only get one true mate, Maddie."

"My name is Jane. Jane Winthrop. I can't be the girl you remembered. She's dead, Liam."

"No, you're not, Maddie. You're right here. I'm right here."

I didn't know what was happening until it was too late. His mouth descended on mine with a wild desperation. Every part of me screamed to respond in kind and I tried not to, but it was so hard. I should have been panicked. I should have been quivering in fear at such dominance over me, but I wasn't panicked and I wasn't afraid—but I was enjoying it far too much.

I pulled back, breathless, trying to fortify the wall I'd attempted to erect between us.

"Please, just tell me why."

That was it, I couldn't take it anymore. I sat down hard on the ground just off the path and lay back into the grass. "I don't know how to make you understand without telling you things I've never told anyone."

"I'm your mate, Mad, there're no secrets between us."

I looked back into his hopeful eyes. It hurt me to see the hope there, knowing we could never be.

"Start from the beginning. Eight years ago, you went to a concert with a friend. She lost you in the crowd and no one ever saw or heard a thing about you since. What happened at that concert?"

I knew fear radiated from me. Joining me on the ground, he lay next to me and wrapped his arms around me, pulling me to him. He lay on his back while I found myself using his chest as a pillow. He stroked my back softly, begging me to answer. The positive of this position was that I didn't have to look at him.

I closed my eyes and began. "Jordan didn't lose me in the crowd that night. We'd met some college guys who were hitting on us—us, just two sophomores in high school and six hot college guys. They were drinking, and offered us some. Jordan wouldn't take any, but I did. She got upset with me for drinking, and left. The guys said they had a suite we could hang in, so we did. It didn't take long for things to change once they had me alone in the room."

I stopped talking. I couldn't tell him what they'd done to me. I didn't want to admit to him of all people how they'd ruined me, and how I'd likely never have another child because of it.

"Go on," he said, and I felt a surge of power crawl over me. I shivered at the sensation. It was Alpha power, but I didn't think Liam was an Alpha, so I wasn't sure how he was doing it, yet it was like I was compelled to respond.

"They hurt me. Please don't ask me to go into details. I have to relive enough of it every time I close my eyes. I don't want to talk about it. Just know that they did really bad things, Liam. I was drugged, unable to move or fight back, but coherent enough to remember it all, until I finally blacked out. According to reports it was several days later before I awoke, beaten and bruised, with several broken bones. I told them I didn't remember anything, but I did. I still do, every second of it all." I paused and let that sink in. His body was drawn tight and his heartbeat erratic. He was furious for what I'd been through. I knew it without asking or even seeing his face. "I found out a few months later I was pregnant with Oscar. I'll never even know which one of them fathered him."

He took a deep breath, and through gritted teeth said, "Go on."

Tears fell from my eyes and I shook my head.

"Maddie, go on, I need to hear it all."

"Why? 'Cause being gang-raped by six men isn't enough? I've

never confessed that to anyone and all you have to say is "go on?"

"Go on," he said again, as he released more Alpha power over me.

"They killed her. Is that want you want to hear? I can't be your mate because I don't have a wolf, Liam. She died, eight years ago, and so did Madelyn Collier." I had never said it aloud before and it nearly broke me. I sobbed loudly before the hysterics set in. I lay there crying once again in his arms until no more tears would come.

He didn't talk, not one single word. He just held me, and despite all the horrors I'd faced and shared, in that moment I felt loved and cherished.

Liam

Chapter 11

Nothing she could have said would have shocked me anymore. What was she talking about? My wolf responded to her. She responded to me. On some level, I felt her wolf. Didn't I? I was starting to second-guess everything.

"What do you mean you have no wolf? That's not possible." I could see how upset she was, but I had to know, so I pressed her to answer.

"There were signs she was going to emerge early. I could feel her, then it-it all happened, and when I woke up I was alone. All alone, Liam. She was gone. I don't know how else to explain it. I'm twenty-four years old and I've never shifted. I don't have a wolf."

"Maddie, I don't think it works that way." My head was spinning.

"Then how would you explain it?"

I could feel the frustration rolling off of her, mixed with anger and hurt. She sat, then stood and began to pace back and forth. I tried to hide my grin. Most shifters only did that when their wolves were agitated.

"You're a wolf shifter. My wolf would not have claimed you otherwise."

"Technically you haven't claimed me, Liam, and you aren't going to either. Oscar and I have a life. It's a good one, and I can't just give that up and go back to the life I left behind."

I jumped up; needing her comfort as much as I needed to comfort her. "It's not the life you left behind. It's not. A life with me wouldn't be the same. I can protect you and Oscar. I can give you anything you want."

"Then give me this. Let me go."

My heart was breaking and I was ready to beg her to change her mind, but I could feel her resolve. I'd found my one true mate, and she didn't want me.

"I guess that's it then. We should probably go."

"I didn't want to hurt you, Liam."

"Yeah, well, it's a little too late for that, isn't it?" I didn't mean for the sarcasm to cover my words, but I didn't take it back either.

Tension was high between us as I led her up and over the hill to the very top. The magical views of the Pacific Ocean, and the little coves, were wasted on us. I didn't stop at the place I had intended on taking her. I just glanced at the small rooftop of the old fort where you could stand and see San Francisco and the Pacific Ocean, seeing it now from an entirely different perspective than the one I had loved. Instead, we headed to the right and followed the path back around to the car.

When the sight of the Golden Gate Bridge and San Francisco beyond came into view, she stopped and her breath hitched.

"It's beautiful, isn't it?" I asked, breaking the silence between us.

She reached for me without thinking and touched my arm. I wished she hadn't; it gave me false hope and even consciously telling myself it meant nothing, it didn't change the way it made me feel.

"So beautiful. Everything looks perfect from up here."

I nodded. I had always thought the same.

We finished the walk down to the car in silence, but with less tension between us. I wasn't angry. I wanted to be, but I couldn't. I was just very upset. I needed time away from Madelyn to process everything she had said to me.

My phone buzzed a new text arrival as we got in the car.

LILY: 8 years today. Where are you? I need you.

Eight years today? I wondered what she was talking about.

LIAM: Busy, what's 8 years today?

LILY: I know you're busy. I just miss you. Always a tough day.

LILY: 8 years since MC disappeared. I still miss her.

I looked at the calendar. Sure enough, it had been eight years to the day since Madelyn Collier had disappeared from the earth. My twin still mourned her loss every year. In the past I had always done something special to help take Lil's mind of it all.

"Shit," I said to myself, feeling guiltier than ever. Not only had I forgotten the anniversary of Maddie's disappearance and didn't even check on my sister, but I had the real woman sitting next to me and something told me that she didn't want even her childhood friend to know she was alive and well.

"What's wrong?" she asked.

"It's, uh, nothing. Don't worry about it." I didn't want to burden her with guilt. It was kind of ironic, despite her ripping my heart out and dancing on it, I still couldn't bring myself to cause her anymore pain. I laughed to myself, shaking my head as I drove. The entire situation was beyond screwed up and I desperately needed a stiff drink.

"Liam, I can tell you're worried about something; what is it?"

"Don't, just don't, Maddie. You've made your position clear and I'm trying really hard to respect it. Acting like you care isn't helping."

"Well, I do care, Liam. If my situation was different in any way, we'd be having a much different conversation. You know that, right? I really need to know you understand. This isn't easy on me either, but I have to do what's best for me and Oscar."

"And clearly that's not me, or doesn't leave any room at all for me in your lives. I heard you, loud and clear."

She was getting more aggravated than upset. *Good*, I thought.

We made it back to the hotel without another word. I thought we'd say goodbye there and that would be the end of things, but to my surprise, Maddie followed me to the elevator. I briefly heard the receptionist call my name as the doors on the elevator closed. Being confined with Maddie in the car had been difficult because her scent had been everywhere, but stuck in the elevator with her was far worse. Not only was I consumed by her scent, but there were other male smells throughout which only heightened my awareness and fueled that stupid need to protect her.

As the doors opened she spoke. "Liam, I don't want us to part angry."

"I'm not angry, Mad. I'm hurt and in shock, but I don't think I could ever truly be angry with you."

"It's still early, and Oscar's going to worry if I come home too early."

She was fidgeting with the seam of her shirt and wouldn't look me in the eye.

"You can hang out in my room until enough time has passed." The second the words were out of my mouth, I wanted to kick my own ass. I didn't want more time with her like this. I wanted to curl up and lick my wounds.

She followed me down the hall to my room. I opened the door and held it for her to walk through. It was followed by the loudest screech I'd ever heard. My wolf leaped for control, which never happened with me, not since I first changed at the age of seventeen and learned to control him.

My only thought was that my mate was in trouble. I quickly shielded her, pinned against the wall as the door shut behind us and I carefully examined the room. Sitting on the small couch was a very pale, very shocked Lily.

"Dammit, Lil, what are you doing here?" I asked, trying to get my body to relax without much success.

Maddie was trying to push me out of the way and scramble for the door, but it was too late.

"Maddie?" Lily asked, tears already streaming down her face. "Is that really you? Liam, tell me I'm not seeing ghosts or something."

I sighed. "Lil, this is my friend." I hesitated. "Jane. And I'm pretty sure you just scared the life out of us both."

She tried to approach as I continued to shield Maddie.

"It's uncanny really. Look at her, Liam, and today of all days. Wow," she said, shaking her head. "I'm sorry, you just remind me of someone." She sighed. "Sorry, I can't help but stare. Tell me she doesn't look just like MC, Liam."

I followed my sister's gaze to my mate. Despite herself, Maddie smiled, and then tears started to spring to her eyes at the use of her old nickname that I'm pretty sure only Lily and my siblings ever called her.

Suddenly my vision started to darken around the edges and my palms began to sweat. As my heart started racing it dawned on me that I was fine, because it wasn't coming from me. I was feeding off my mate.

"Shit!" I yelled, picking Maddie up and moving to the couch where I cradled her on my lap. "Just breathe, sweetheart. Deep breaths, in and out. Listen to my voice." She clung to me, hiding her face in my shoulder, but my touch was calming her and slowly bringing her back before her panic attack could fully set in. Knowing she was going to be okay, I just held her close to me. "Lily, back off and give her a minute."

"What's wrong with her?" Lily asked after heeding my request.

I hugged her close. She was the most precious thing in my life and I already knew, I could never let her go. "She's just been through some shit. Sometimes, she has a hard time dealing and you freaked her out by screaming like a banshee."

"Sorry," she said to me, then addressed Maddie. "I'm really sorry. You really do look a lot like an old friend of mine." She sat down on the couch next to me. Lily always did have issues with personal boundaries. "I just really miss her. She disappeared eight years ago today. It's always been a hard anniversary for me, so I decided to drive up to see Liam. He always cheers me up on this day and I missed him." She elbowed me hard. "You could have warned me you were sneaking off to meet a girl."

"You could have, I dunno, actually asked first," I said.

"Why would I have any reason to suspect you'd have a girl up here? You haven't even dated since coming home from college. You're all work, work, work these days, so when you said you were coming up for 'work,' why would I think anything else?"

"Maybe it's just none of your business, Lil, and you don't need to know all of my personal business."

She snorted. "Yeah right, like that's gonna happen. Dream on. No offense, lady, but I can already tell you're calming down, so you have about three more minutes before the interrogation begins. This is my twin brother"—she overemphasized *twin*—"and it is my duty to make sure no one is going to hurt him. I take my twin duties very seriously, and just so you know, no one is ever going to be good enough for him, so the odds are already stacked against you. Jane, was it?"

Maddie giggled and sat up to face Lily. Her eyes were still filled with tears, but they looked like happy tears this time. She lunged off me and threw her arms around my sister, shocking us both.

"I love you, Lily Ann Westin," she whispered. "Eight years, and you even remember the day?"

"MC? Is it really you?"

She nodded her head yes. I couldn't let myself even think of what this meant. I sat and watched as the girls embraced and cried. I knew Lily would have a ton of questions and wanted to give them space to catch up, but I couldn't bring myself to leave Maddie's side. When they let go of each other, she sat back on my lap looking happier.

"I can't believe you even remembered."

"Not remember? Are you insane? Liam has to distract me every year on this day. We spent months hanging posters and looking for you after you left. Where have you been? Why didn't you come home?"

Sadness filled her. I could feel it. "It's okay," I reassured her, rubbing her back.

"I'm sorry, Lil, I really can't talk about it now. It's too hard, and today has been even harder." She looked at me and gave a small smile.

I returned a hesitant smile. Instead of sharing her story with Lily, she instead bombarded my sister with her own questions.

"What are you doing these days? Are you living in San Marco? How have you been? I want to hear everything."

Lily looked at me with a million questions in her eyes before answering each and every one.

"Okay, I've answered all your questions," Lily finally said. It was getting late and my stomach was rumbling. My leg had gone to sleep from Maddie sitting on it for so long, and I needed to stretch.

"If you two are going to yap all night long, I'm going to order pizza. I'm starving."

"Oh no," Maddie said, jumping up. "What time is it?"

"It's nine o'clock," I told her, seeing panic flash across her face.

"I have to go."

"No," Lily cried. "Please don't go. We have so much to talk about and I'm afraid I'll never see you again once you leave."

My heart hurt for both the girls, but I was afraid of the same thing. Maddie had leaned on me for comfort and support once again.

Could she really just walk out of my life forever? I wasn't sure I could just let her and Oscar go without a fight. They were both worth fighting for.

"Call them," I told her with more authority than I normally would.

She nodded without questioning me.

"Call who?" Lily mouthed while Maddie went to call Annie and check on Oscar.

When she returned, she looked relieved. She smiled and nodded. "Fast asleep."

"It was a big day, I figured he would be."

"Who? What are we talking about here?" Lily asked.

Maddie looked at me questioningly and I nodded reassuringly.

"Lily," she started. "I have a son. His name is Oscar. He's with his grandparents in our hotel room. I had promised him I'd be home in time to tuck him in, but he's already fast asleep."

I could see the guilt of missing bedtime written on her face. Without thinking I got up and walked to her, pulling her to my chest.

"Um, y'all want to clue me in what's happening here? 'Cause if I didn't know any better I'd swear you were . . ." I saw recognition flash across her face. I looked away from my sister and down at my mate in my arms as she stared up with a death look. I wasn't going to win either situation, so I let go of Maddie and backed away slowly. The girls could hash it out. "Liam Michael Westin, you better tell me right now. What is going on?"

"Mad, what do you like on your pizza?" I asked.

"Um, pepperoni and mushrooms," she said.

"At least no pineapple," I joked. Pepperoni, mushroom, and pineapple were my sister Elise's favorite toppings. It grossed us all out, but then we found out her mate, Patrick, loved it, too. Gross! I could tolerate just pepperoni and mushrooms, as long as there was no pineapple.

I was grateful to have gotten a suite where the bedroom had a door of its own. I walked in there and shut the door behind me. Madelyn could figure out what she wanted to tell Lily without me. It wasn't like I had anything to hide, except I really didn't want my sister to know I'd found my one true mate, especially if Maddie really did walk away from me.

I ordered the pizza and cautiously headed back to them.

"Do you have a picture of your son?" Lily asked.

"Yeah, it's . . . dead," she said with a frown, looking at her cell phone. "I guess I used up the last of it calling Annie."

I took the phone from her, bracing for the tingle I always got touching her, and plugged it into my charger on the desk in the room. Then I took out my phone and scrolled through my pics to find one of Oscar grinning happily as we landed on Alcatraz. I wondered how it could possibly still be the same day.

"So, he's with his grandparents?" Lily asked. "I know you don't mean your parents, 'cause I just talked to Shelby last week and they were planning the annual vigil they hold for you each year. They don't know you're still alive, but they still hold on to the hope you are." A sad look passed between them, but I was thankful Lily didn't press her about telling them. I could already feel the panic starting to rise in Maddie. "So"—she changed the subject—"it's not your parents, so are these his father's parents? Are you still with him?"

My twin had no filter. Most of the time whatever she thought would immediately spew out her mouth. It was something I equally loved and hated about her. My jaw set as that uncomfortable protectiveness flared in me. I shook my head no behind my mate so only my sister could see. Her eyes shone with both amusement and curiosity.

"No, we aren't together," Maddie said with disdain in her voice.

I could see Lily about to burst with more questions so I thrust my phone at her. "This is Oscar, Maddie's son." I told her.

Lily's eyes were huge. "Oh my gosh. How old is he?"

"Sorry, I don't know if you remember or not," I told Maddie, "but Lily has no filter. If she thinks it, she says it. Actually, I think half the time she says it before she thinks it."

"It's okay," Maddie reassured me. "I haven't forgotten. I've always admired her for being able to speak her mind like that."

"Hello? I'm right here," Lily said obnoxiously.

Maddie laughed, looking more relaxed than I suspected. "Oscar is seven, Lily. No, I didn't run away because I was pregnant and no, I'm not going to talk about it or try to explain it. I had my reasons and that's going to have to be enough."

"Okay," Lily said. I think my jaw may have dropped open in shock. Lily never caved when she thought she was on to a story, and she had to know this was a big one.

"Thank you," Maddie said in relief.

"Not getting off the hook that quickly, girlie."

Maddie

Chapter 12

Somehow finding Liam hadn't been nearly as shocking as seeing Lily. He had tried to give me an out. He introduced me as his friend Jane, but hearing how Lily still missed me, *ME*, so much that she even remembered the exact day I had disappeared, I just had to tell her it was really me. That day Maddie Collier had died, or so I'd thought. Being with them again, made me question everything—I felt like me around them. Not Jane Winthrop, the beaten and broken skeleton of a human, but me, Madelyn Collier.

"Okay," Lily started again, and I knew the questions were coming. "First, Oscar's really a cute kid. He looks really happy in that picture. I gather since it was on my brother's phone that he's met him?"

"I'm standing right here," Liam reminded her.

"Shush, and go away then. We're having girl talk. When was that picture taken?"

I smiled, fondly remembering the first part of our day, when everything felt just right. "Earlier today. All Oscar wanted to do on this trip was visit Alcatraz, but when we first arrived, we found out that the only tour to go on the island was booked solid. Liam was able to get us a private tour through a friend."

"Steph and Mark?" Lily asked, and Liam and I answered yes at the same time. "Haven't seen them in ages. How are they?"

Liam looked a little sad. "They're doing well enough, but it's always going to be hard on them. They seemed happy today, though."

My eyes misted over and I wiped them quickly.

Lily didn't mention the repopulation project and what they

were going through, but I could tell she knew all about it and exactly what her brother was talking about.

"So on to the next question then. If you're on vacation then you don't live here, I take it?"

"No, I don't. Annie and Jacob took me in a long time ago. They're the only family Oscar's ever known. They've been so good to us. You don't have to worry about me, Lily."

"Your reaction to seeing me after more than eight years was an anxiety attack. Yeah, I think I need to worry. But you asked me not to press you for details, so I won't. So, why don't you live in a pack? If they're the only family he's ever known, clearly you didn't take up in a new pack."

"No, I didn't. Annie and Jacob are human. We live in the human world." I decided straightforward, simple answers would be the best. I knew Lily well enough to know it wouldn't stop her curiosity, but hoped it would appease her enough for now.

"Do they know about you? I mean, that you're a wolf shifter and all? How do you hide that from them?"

"They don't know, and it's been easier than you'd think." I almost laughed in light of the situation. They didn't know about me because there was nothing to know, but I wasn't about to tell her that.

"Does Liam know why you left and stayed gone?"

I took a deep breath and met Liam's gaze. "Yes."

"Does anyone else know? Like this Annie and Jacob?"

"No. No one," I whispered.

Lily gave an evil grin I remembered all too well. It was the one she used when playing games that basically signified "checkmate." "So Liam's your one true mate then, huh?"

"Lily," Liam growled in warning.

My cheeks flushed and I didn't know what to say.

"Oh yeah, my twin, you got it bad," she continued to tease.

"Lily," I started to plead, but then shut my mouth, 'cause honestly what was I supposed to say?

"Are you happy about it?"

I know my face gave away my sadness. Was I happy it was him? Yes. But he knew the situation, and I couldn't back down from my stance to not accept him. I could never be a proper mate for him. He deserved so much better than me.

"It's, um, it's complicated," I told her.

She frowned at me, then rolled her eyes. "Been through this a time or two already. Seriously, what is wrong with you people? First Kyle, and then Elise, now you two? When will you all learn that you can't hide from your fated mate? If you really are each other's "one true mate", just accept it and be happy. It always leads to great happiness, so stop being stupid and just go with the flow."

"Like you're going to do when you finally find your true mate?" Liam laughed. "I can't wait till that happens and we all get to remind you just how simple it really is."

"I can't believe Kyle and Elise have taken mates. That's awesome," I said in a lame attempt to change the subject. "What are their mates like?"

"Oh, you're going to love them!" Lily said excitedly, like it was inevitable I'd be meeting them, but I didn't want to tell her I was rejecting her brother and going home to suffer in silence for the remainder of my life, so I encouraged her to keep talking. "Kelsey is the best, and she is one badass Pack Mother. Did he tell you Kyle took over as Westin Alpha?"

"Yes, he did," I confirmed.

"Okay, good. So, yeah. Kelsey grew up in the human world, too. Doesn't seem to have hurt her any. She's really cool. But she didn't even know she was a shifter. It's a long story. She and Kyle worked side by side for two years while fighting the mating call. Then Elise's mate, Patrick, he actually came from Ireland to challenge Kyle for Kelsey. That lasted right up to the moment he got a whiff of my sister. It was pretty funny. Everyone was so shocked when he reneged on the challenge then stayed to hunt her down. Her dumb ass hid for as long as possible, but in the end it all worked out. So again, why are you even bothering to fight this?"

"I told you," I said, unable to keep the sadness from my voice, "it's complicated."

I was so grateful when there was a knock at the door and the pizza delivery man arrived. Liam answered and paid for it. Sitting down to eat, he made Lily promise to cease with the questions, so it broke some of the tension in the room. I wanted to know what Liam was thinking. I couldn't read the expressions on his face as Lily grilled me. I knew I didn't have a right to know, but it didn't stop me from wondering.

We talked about lighter things after that and the time melted away. I stifled a yawn.

"Sweetheart, it's after midnight. Lil, I think that's enough for today. Tell you what, why don't I take Oscar out tomorrow and give you two some time alone?"

I was floored by his generosity. I had seen the hurt and pain I had already caused him, yet he would do that for me? Why? I couldn't help wondering. I looked to Lily to see what she thought.

"He's great with kids; Oscar will be fine."

I laughed. "I have no doubts on that. Would you want to hang out with me tomorrow?"

"Duh, of course I do. I'm scared if I let you walk out that door I'll never seen you again, though. Can't you just sleep here?"

"No, she can't." Liam intervened. "Oscar will freak out and worry if she's not back before he wakes."

Dammit, every time I thought I had a handle on him, he did or said something that made my heart melt again. I didn't know how to fully harden it with him around. I needed space and distance, but didn't think I was actually going to get it, no matter what I said to him, until this trip was over. *Just don't fall in love in with him*, I scolded myself, even knowing it was already too late for that.

"I promise, I'll see you tomorrow," I said, hugging Lily good night. It dawned on me how different and natural personal contact was with them. It didn't make me panic or even feel uncomfortable. It felt right, and that was wrong. I already knew it was going to hurt like hell when we said goodbye forever at the end of the week. I had tried earlier to do just that with Liam, but now with Lily in the mix, life just got all the more complicated.

"Hey, Lil?" I needed her to understand and promise me something. "Swear you won't tell anyone you saw me?"

She hesitated, then nodded. "I promise."

Liam insisted on walking me back to my room. When I tried to protest in the hallway that it wasn't necessary, he told me that Elise had been kidnapped in a hotel the previous year and with everything I'd already gone through, his wolf was feeling particularly protective and asked me to just humor him. I did, but was thankful he didn't draw out some awkward good night, or try to kiss me at the door.

"Just come by or call in the morning. My number's in your

phone," he said as he turned to leave, motioning me to close the door first.

I wondered when he had put his number in my phone, then remembered he had taken it to plug in after it had died. Then I figured he must have done it sometime while it charged and I talked with Lily.

I quickly went to the bathroom, changing into pajamas, washing up, and brushing my teeth before sneaking into bed next to my son. Oscar's little body seemed to relax, even in sleep, and he snuggled up against me. I held him close and kissed the top of his head, inhaling the sweet scent of his shampoo.

I wanted to reflect on the events of the day that felt more like a second lifetime, or in my case, I guess, a third. I smiled at the thought. As I closed my eyes and drifted into sleep, I dreamed of a third lifetime, with Liam.

All too soon it was morning, and a wiggling little boy woke me up. "Mommy, you're here! I'm sorry I fell asleep before you could say good night. I was really tired."

"It is fine, my sweet boy. Did you have a good time with Mimi and Papi?"

"Yes, it was great! I got to swim in the pool till bedtime."

"Wow, that sounds like great fun," I said.

"Did you have a good time with Liam?"

I tried not to think about the fort and all that had been said between us. Oscar was far too intuitive for a kid his age. Instead, I told him about happy things. "I did, and guess what? His sister Lily showed up and surprised us."

"Your best friend when you were my age?"

"Yes, that's the one. Now where're Mimi and Papi?

"They went down for breakfast and then were going to the conference. They said to tell you it runs 'til seven tonight, and they'd call later to see if we had eaten yet or not. So, it's just me and you today, Mommy!"

I felt guilty for the next words out of my mouth. "Actually, I was thinking. How would you like to spend part of the day with Liam so I can catch up with Lily?"

"Really?" he asked skeptically. "You don't ever let me go anywhere with anyone except Mimi and Papi."

It was true. I was fiercely protective of him. I may not have been the best mom and done everything right, and he may have had to deal with my issues more than I'd wish on any kid of his age, but I loved him with everything I had in me.

"I know, Mommy loves you so much that I hate sharing you with anyone, but if you'd like to hang out with Liam today, I would really love to catch up with my friend."

"Can I meet her?"

"Absolutely. She can't wait to meet you."

"Could we get breakfast first? I'm starving. Maybe they'd want to join us?" he suggested.

"I dunno, bud. We were up pretty late last night, so maybe we should let them sleep."

"But Mom, you're up. Maybe they will be, too. Can we check at least?"

"Okay, okay." How could I possibly say no to his sweet, hopeful face?

I dialed Liam's number and he picked up after the first ring. "Hello." His voice was deep and sexy with a hint of sleep to it. My body responded to it almost painfully in places I wasn't sure functioned properly.

"Um, good morning," I said in a breathy voice I barely recognized. "I'm sorry I woke you. Oscar demanded we see if you guys were up and interested in breakfast with us downstairs."

"Lil's probably dead to the world, but give me ten minutes and I'll head down."

"Is that Maddie?" I heard Lily ask as what sounded like a struggle ensued. "Give me the phone," a muffled Lily said.

"No, go away, you freak," Liam retorted. "Get out of my bed . . . Lil, I'm not kidding, go away."

There was a crackling of the phone and then Lily was suddenly there. "Good morning, Maddie."

"Good morning, Lily. I was just asking Liam if you two wanted to join us for breakfast."

"Of course we do. Downstairs?"

"Yes."

"Great, I'll be right down, but my brother just jumped in the shower. He could be awhile."

I laughed as I said goodbye and hung up. Lily was already waiting on us when Oscar and I got downstairs.

"Hello," he said, checking her over. Then he leaned in and sniffed her.

"Oscar," I scolded.

"Oh please, at least he didn't sniff my butt." She laughed at her own joke. I had forgotten to warn her that Oscar didn't know about our kind.

"You smell a lot like Liam," Oscar announced.

"Oscar, we discussed this," I warned him.

"But Mom, Liam smells good, too. He even told me, and she's his sister." He said it like it was the most natural thing in the world, and for a shifter it was, but he didn't know people like that existed. I had never taught him about the wolves, and I certainly had never encouraged the few signs he'd shown, but maybe it was being around other wolves that was calling to that part of him, because he had never before been so vocal and obvious about it.

"I'm sorry, Mommy."

"It's okay, kid," Lily said. "I know what you meant. I'm Lily."

"Hi, Lily, I'm Oscar."

"Well, look at you, a perfect little gentleman. You're a pretty lucky boy to have this lady as your mama," she told him, putting an arm around my waist and laying her head on my shoulder.

Oscar gave her a confused look. "Mommy doesn't like to be touched by people, ’cept me and Liam. Please back off."

Lily looked confused, but did as he asked just as Liam came up behind Oscar and picked him up under his arms. "Don't worry Lil, yesterday he gave me the same warning, only sounds like I've been upgraded in the last twenty-four hours."

"Liam!" my son squealed, turning in his arms and hugging him by the neck.

"We missed you last night," Liam said, tickling Oscar and making him laugh. "Hope it sucked, ’cause we don't want to make a habit of it. Mommy's nicer when you're around," he whispered to him, and I shot him an incredulous look that made Oscar laugh harder.

"Mommy says I get to hang out with you today."

"You okay with that? ’Cause otherwise we have to sit around and listen to these two yap all day long. It's not going to be any fun at all."

"Could we go swimming in the pool? That was lots of fun last night."

"I'm sure that could be arranged."

"Do you have a car?"

"I do. Why? Kid's starting to worry me," he said to me with a wink as the two of them headed off to fix their breakfast.

"He's really good with him, MC," Lily observed.

"I know," I said sadly.

"Why so sad then? I mean seriously. I know he's, well, he's Liam, but he's not the same annoying brother we grew up with. He's actually pretty cool. He has a great job that's he's really good at. And he clearly loves you and Oscar."

I snorted. "Lily, it's only been three days since I ran into him. You can't fall in love in three days."

"Girl, you are blind then, and clearly you have some missing memories, 'cause that boy has been in love with you his whole life."

I laughed, and it felt good. "What are you talking about?"

"Don't give me that, like you never knew. Why do you think he hung around us so much at camp all those years? I promise it wasn't because of me."

I was laughing as we filled our plates and joined the guys at the table.

"It's good to see you laugh. What's so funny?" Liam asked.

I blushed, not wanting to tell him how outrageous his sister was being.

"I like it when Mommy laughs," Oscar confessed and I suddenly felt guilty knowing how little he'd seen it in his lifetime. "What's so funny, Mommy?" No way was I sharing that with him either.

"She had no clue you spent half your life crushing on her, Liam," Lily said, to my horror.

He just laughed and took a bite of food, smiling but not denying it. I wanted so badly to ask him if it was true, but I couldn't. It didn't stop Oscar from asking though.

"Did you like Mommy when you were my age?"

"Very much," he said, and he winked at me. My heart fluttered erratically as Oscar giggled.

I couldn't seem to stop looking at Liam throughout breakfast, and the worst part was, he knew it too. Much too soon he and Oscar said goodbye and left for some adventure, and I had the entire day with my oldest and dearest friend. I knew it was going to be equal parts wonderful and hellish.

Sure enough, the second they were gone, Lily descended on me. "Okay, we need a place to talk. I know an old fort on the other side of the Golden Gate we could go to."

I looked at her with sheer horror. "Any place but there!" I said much too quickly.

"Ah, so that's the place you chose to shred my brother's heart then." It was just a statement, no judgment, but it made me feel so guilty. "Relax, I just want to catch up and talk. Have a little fun with an old friend. I promise not to grill you too much on all that or him."

I sighed in relief. "Okay, so what do you want to do then?"

"First up, shopping! I'm giving you a makeover."

"What? I don't need a makeover, Lily."

"Girl, you are twenty-four years old, and you dress like….a mom."

I laughed. "I am a mom, so that's not a bad thing."

"But you're still young too, just humor me, I promise, nothing too flashy, I can do conservative. Elise makes me conform every day for work."

I looked over at Lily, wearing six inch heels with her tight skinny jeans and crop top, sporting pink highlights streaking her blonde hair, and I could not even imagine what her idea of conservative was.

"Okay," I said hesitantly, unsure what I'd just gotten myself into.

She drove us to a shopping area I never would have found myself and we spent hours going from store to store. To my surprise, the girl had wonderful taste in clothes. She did convince me skinny jeans were the way to go. I had never even tried on something so tight, but I had to admit, they were really comfortable and I was in love quickly. Even though we were nearing the end of summer, in California it was going to remain hot for quite a while longer, so we also looked at summer clothing, too.

In the end I had a whole new wardrobe with several shirts and a few pairs of shorts that were arguably far too short for me, showing off way too much leg, but Lily was quite convincing that they were too perfect to turn down. I did say no to every pair of shoes she attempted to get me to buy. Sorry, but her cute heels were just not practical for me trying to keep up with a seven-year-old, but we did agree on a pair of cute flats that I fell in love with and a new pair of Chucks.

She also convinced me to try on some lingerie. I had never even looked at such things. My plain white cotton panties and sports bras had always been practical and sufficient. I had never had a girlfriend to discuss such things with and it was definitely a new, educational experience shopping with Lily. The new bras fit great and didn't make me look so flat-chested. I loved them. I felt taller and more confident in them. Who knew something so simple could affect me so much? I didn't want to admit it, but the lacy sets I had picked out also made me feel pretty and a little sexy. It was like opening up a whole new side of life, one I didn't like to think much about.

As we headed back to the hotel, I was exhausted, but I also couldn't remember the last time I'd had so much fun. I should have known Lily wasn't through with me. When she said makeover, she meant it. As if the clothes weren't enough, as I let us into my room and dropped off the bags, she informed me she had booked us at the spa.

I usually went to a local chain haircut place where Oscar and I could both get cuts for twenty-five dollars or less when they had sales. I almost had a heart attack at the prices when I asked. I worked part-time at a local pizza place in the evenings, so I could be home with Oscar. Annie and Jacob afforded most of our life and I was grateful to them for it, but also felt like some things I needed to provide myself and insisted on working, even if only a few hours while they were home to watch him.

The cost of just a haircut equaled a good night of tips. I couldn't afford Lily's taste. I had already exceeded my budget and caved to let her buy me a few things in the excitement of shopping. I couldn't let her pay for this too.

"Lily Ann, I can't do this." For one whole summer, she had insisted on being called Lily Ann instead of just plain, boring Lily, or so she had said at the time. Likewise, I had decided I didn't want to be a Collier anymore. Being the youngest of six girls, all of whom had done great things and excelled in nearly everything, left me little room to do anything but screw up, so I asked to be called MC instead. It made me smile when she called me that now.

"MC, stop it. This is my treat, don't take that from me."

"It's too much, I can't."

"We'll talk about that later, but trust me when I say I really, really want to do this, together. Please. My roots are already showing and I'm in desperate need of a touch-up. Please." She pouted in that same way I had never been able to say no to her. "Pretty please—it's totally my treat."

"Fine." I caved again much too quickly and she squealed and hugged me.

For the next three hours I was washed, scrubbed, and polished to a shine, then snipped and morphed into this beautiful woman I barely recognized. I pulled on the ends of my new haircut, admiring it all. She even splurged and literally got us makeovers. I wasn't much on wearing makeup. I didn't see the point, except on special occasions, but I figured this was a special occasion. We were there so long that they even served us a late lunch. It was a bit of a Cinderella kind of moment and I felt like I was living in a dream.

Finally done, she stopped me at the front as we were leaving.

"These," she said, pointing to pair of designer sunglasses. "These will look amazing on you. You have to have them."

I shrugged them off; they were over-the-top too much. The entire day had been, if I were honest. Of course, she bought them anyway and she was right, they looked awesome on me.

"I don't think I can handle much more pampering for one day. Thank you. I've never done anything this crazy."

Lily laughed. "Girl, there was nothing crazy about today. You totally forget who you're dealing with."

I fondly recalled several outrageous, crazy things she'd gotten me into as kids. She was right, this was probably mild for her, but it was absolute insanity for me.

She insisted we head back to Liam's hotel. I didn't mind, but his smell was everywhere in the room which made my growing hormones do crazy things to me on the inside. After everything I had been through, I didn't expect to ever even want to have sex again, though I knew the possibility of it would likely happen eventually. I tried not to make any personal or emotional connections with people to encourage it. I hadn't known if I would ever be ready for a relationship and then Liam walked into my life, and despite the barriers I was trying to keep between us, when I smelled his delicious woodsy scent, it set my body on fire and I knew without a doubt that everything would be different with him. I knew I didn't need to be afraid that he'd ever hurt me. His touch was always gentle, even when I upset him, or entirely pissed him off.

"Earth to Maddie." Lily interrupted my train of thought. "Where'd you go?"

"Just thinking. It was nothing."

"So, we're relaxed, we look hot and we are ready to take on the world. It's girl chat time. I have a few more questions for you."

I groaned. "I told you, I can't talk about it."

"But you talked about it with Liam."

"That's different," I insisted.

"'Cause he's your mate."

"Exactly," I said without thinking.

"OH EM GEEE!!!!! I mean, I guessed and teased you guys a little about it last night, but I wasn't actually sure. I mean neither of you would deny it, but you wouldn't confirm it either. This is so incredibly awesome. I can't imagine any other woman for him."

I thought we had already established we were true mates. I tried to think back over the talks the night before and couldn't remember one way or another.

"Lily," I said sadly. "Please don't get too excited. I've already rejected him. We aren't going to mate."

I'm not sure anything I could have possibly said would have shocked her as much. "You rejected him? When? 'Cause all cuddled up, hiding behind him yesterday when he was trying to convince me you weren't you, was not rejection. And the googly eyes you two were making at the breakfast table just this morning was not rejection."

"We were not. He knows it's not going to happen. We were coming back last night to finish talking and say our goodbyes when you blindsided us both."

"Thank God for that then. You two clearly need me for some intervention."

"Please don't. It's hard enough as it is."

"That's the thing, you stubborn fool—it's not supposed to be hard at all. Plus, you can't truly be that blind? That boy is already in love with you. Like head-over-heels, crazy-in-love with you."

"Listen to you, all knowing one. How did you become such the expert on mating? And love? It's only been three days, Lil. There is no way Liam's in love with me. It's best to just cut ties now before anything does start to grow."

She stared at me, making me uncomfortable. "Bullshit," she finally said. "Liam's been in love with you since we were kids. You reappear in his life like some ghost from the past, and then he realizes you're his one true mate. He's already a goner. You're going to destroy him. Do what you have to do, but I'm not in the business of sugarcoating things. Sure, he tried to hide his little crush on you when we were kids, but he wasn't fooling me. Plus, after you disappeared, you weren't there to see how bad off he was. We even went to Collier to help in the search. Liam was . . . I don't know how to put it. He was devastated. He had a good friend in college that killed himself, and Liam took that really hard, but still not as bad as when you left."

"His friend killed himself?" I asked, struggling to accept the rest of what she was saying.

"Yeah, he was ex-military, suffered from PTSD. He had a big anxiety attack and hanged himself. Liam blamed himself for a long time because he wasn't there to help him."

I felt terrible. Liam had mentioned the guy to me after one of my attacks, but he didn't tell me he'd died. No wonder he was so patient with my anxiety. The guilt must have eaten him alive, because I knew that was just the kind of man Liam Westin was.

"I have PTSD, Lil. Don't you see? He doesn't need me in his life. Nothing good could come of it for him."

"Wait, PTSD? From what?"

I shook my head. "I can't talk about it."

"You damn well better start talking. That's not the kind of stuff you just keep bottled up. What happened to you? You used to be so full of life, MC. I see glimpses of it here and there, but mostly you seem hollow inside, fragile, not things I'd ever think of remembering you."

I started to cry. "I know. I can't help it. It's why I can't go home, and if I went back to Westin with Liam, then my family would find out and I'd have to face them. Don't you see, I can't do that to them? It's better if they believe I'm dead."

"But they don't believe that. They all still hold on to the hope that you're coming home someday. Thomas is about the only one that seems to have given up on you. He goes out of town every year on the anniversary of your disappearance, refusing to have anything to do with it. But he's a complete asshole, so that's not saying much. You're definitely better off without him in your life."

"Thomas?"

"Oh yeah, he changed so much after you left that you'd be ashamed. I haven't seen him in years now, but I've kept up through your sisters. He's nothing but trouble."

"All because I left?"

"Oh no. You aren't putting that on yourself. He was always a self-righteous jerk—he's just grown into an even bigger one now. That's not your fault."

"I miss them, Lily. I don't let myself think about them often, but I miss them all so much. Seeing you and Liam has been wonderful and awful at the same time. No offense."

"None taken."

"It's just that I can't be that person anymore. Madelyn Collier died eight years ago. I'm Jane Winthrop now. No one in my life knows me by Maddie, including Oscar, so please try to remember to call me Jane instead, in front of him."

"Changing your name definitely hasn't helped anyone in the search for finding you. Whatever happened to you, MC, Jane, whatever you want to be called, I can tell it wasn't your fault. You scream victim here. Have you ever talked about it with anyone? A therapist? A friend? The people you live with?"

I shook my head no. "I told Liam yesterday, not every gory detail, but more than I'd ever confessed to anyone. That was the first time I'd ever talked about it."

"I'm a great listener you know, and I have absolutely no right to judge anyone. I know how that feels, so if you need a friend to just listen, I'm here. You're never going to fully move past it without talking to someone."

I nodded as the tears fell freely. "You sound like Annie. She's been trying for years to get me to talk about it, but it hurts so much to even think about it."

"Well, if you told Liam yesterday, it's still open and raw, so start talking."

I did. Once I started talking, everything poured out of me. I didn't hold anything back and I told Lily every sordid detail of what I had been through. She cried and hugged me and we talked through it together. I had never felt closer to anyone in my life right that moment with Lily Westin, and the emotional baggage I'd been carrying around for eight years, lifted off of me from sharing my pain with her and was a huge relief.

For the first time in a long time, I felt like I could breathe again.

Liam

Chapter 13

If I were being honest, by the time Oscar and I walked back into the hotel lobby, I was exhausted. Who knew keeping up with a kid could wear out a person like that? I'd never seen so much energy in one little person before, and now he wanted to go swimming, because I promised.

Maddie had left me their room key in case I needed anything for Oscar, like his swimsuit, so we headed upstairs and I let him into his room, wanting to just drop on the bed and take a nap. I let him change, then I did the same, as I had brought my suit with me, carrying it in my backpack all day. We went sightseeing and had spent quite some time just driving up and down the hills of San Francisco. I had let him use my phone to take pictures, but he couldn't get the shot he wanted. After about five passes in the car, I stopped and parked, and then we walked around until he was satisfied with his shots.

I figured I must be getting soft from working in the office too much, because my calves were cramping and I was beat. Maybe that was the kid's objective. Kill me off so I'd stay away from his mother. Wasn't it just yesterday he was growling warnings at me?

Oscar had already informed me that we had to wear shirts and shoes while walking through the hotel, and also that towels were provided there. I wasn't sure if they were actual hotel rules or Mimi and Papi rules, but I obeyed just the same.

We headed downstairs as I let Oscar lead the way to the pool. That's when it hit me.

"Hey, kid, can you even swim?"

He laughed. "Yes, can you?"

I'd never seen such a young person with such witty

comebacks. Without answering I kicked off my shoes and tossed my shirt aside before cannonballing into the pool.

"Cool! Did you see the size of that splash!" he squealed with delight, quickly following me in, with a less-than-stellar cannonball attempt.

We spent a little time working on his form till he had perfected it. I watched as he doggie paddled across to the wall to jump each time.

"So no one taught you to swim?" I had never seen a pup who didn't naturally doggie paddle, so I assumed.

"What do you mean? I'm a good swimmer."

"You definitely are," I agreed. "But have you ever seen swimmers in the Olympics or on TV?"

"Mommy doesn't let me watch very much TV, but we did a study on the Olympics last year and watched some events online."

"Okay, so you know what I'm talking about? Freestyle, backstroke, breast, fly, that sorta thing."

"I can't do that," he confessed.

"Of course you can. Come here." I lay him on his back. This was always the hardest stroke for a wolf shifter to conquer as it made our wolves feel vulnerable, but he only wiggled a little before settling in. He was a quick one. Before long I had him backstroking like a pro all over the pool. We celebrated with synchronized cannonballs before I had to cry mercy and take a break. I sat up on the side of the pool, watching him swim around as my mind drifted off to his mother and wondering what she and Lily were up to.

"Mommy!" Oscar yelled, echoing throughout the indoor pool area. "Whoa, you look beautiful."

I hadn't heard them come in, but my jaw hit the floor when I looked up and saw Maddie from across the pool. She looked different. I mean, she was always pretty, beautiful even, but right now, she was a complete bombshell. My heart started racing as I checked her out slowly from head to toe. The tight jeans, the tank top that fit just snugly enough to highlight her breasts, gave me pause to stop. I had to close my mouth to keep from literally drooling. She'd gotten her hair cut and she was wearing makeup.

She was checking me out too, not as obviously as I was gawking at her, but even from across the room I could smell her arousal and I was having a very hard time hiding mine.

"Ew, what's that smell?" Oscar announced, breaking us out of our mutual lust-induced trance. If I'd had any doubts about her wanting me physically after everything she'd been through, they'd just been laid to rest.

"Hey, champ, why don't we get out of here and let your mom and Liam talk for a minute? You can tell me all about your day."

"Mommy, is that okay? I'm really hungry. Can Lily take me up to the room to get changed so we can go eat?"

"Um, yeah, sure." Maddie said it like she was coming out of a fog. I tried to keep the smirk off my face. She handed Lily the card, and Lily left with Oscar in tow.

"Why does it stink so bad in there?" I heard him ask as the door shut behind him.

I laughed and jumped up, heading for my gorgeous mate.

"We may just scar that poor kid for life at this rate," I joked.

She looked a little uncomfortable, like she wasn't sure what to say or do. I didn't hesitate or give her a chance to argue, just walked up and took her in my arms, stifling the small gasp that escaped her as I crushed my lips to hers. It took very little prodding to get her to open up to me as I set about learning every inch of her mouth. It didn't take her long to begin her own exploration. I was thankful the windows were already fogged from the heated pool, 'cause I was pretty certain we would have fogged them up just from that kiss alone.

"Hi," she said breathlessly when I finally pulled back, unsure how long I could control things and keep them PG-rated.

"Hi." I smiled down at her, resting my forehead against hers and breathing in her scent. "You look amazing."

She blushed under my compliment. "Um, did, uh, did Oscar behave himself today?" she asked, struggling to find the words and attempting to change the subject.

"He did. He's a great kid, but I have to admit, I don't know how you do it. Do all seven-year-olds have that much energy all the time? I'm not going to lie, he wore me out."

She laughed and the discomfort she'd seemed to feel after our kiss disappeared. "I know he's a bit over-the-top sometimes. I hope he didn't drive you too crazy?"

"Nah, we had a good time. I may have to sleep for a week straight to recuperate, but it was all good. What did you and Lily do all day? Or rather, let me guess, shopping and spa time."

"Yeah, she got a little carried away."

"Elise is the only one who can come close to keeping up with her. Kelsey begs Kyle to warn her when Lily's in the shopping mood so she can hide." Maddie laughed, but I was being entirely serious.

"She definitely talked me into things I would never buy for myself."

I didn't hide my interest as I checked out her butt in the jeans. "She did good," I complimented.

"Liam, you can't say stuff like that." She scolded me like she would Oscar.

"Did you have a good time with my sister?" I asked sincerely.

"I really did. I've never really had a girlfriend to go shopping with and talk to like that. Not as an adult, at least, and it was really nice."

I heard a hint of sadness in her voice. "Did she pester you with questions all day?"

"She's Lily. You know she did."

Getting her to open up was like pulling teeth, but I waited patiently and kept it to simple questions. "Did you really talk to her?"

The eyes looking up at me were a little haunted, but not as much as they'd been. She nodded slowly. "I-I told her everything. It wasn't easy, but I think it helped some. I've"—she looked away from me and I thought she was going to shut me out, but she seemed to end her internal battle and looked back at me when she started talking again—"I've always been worried that if people from my past knew what had happened to me, that it would change the way they see me—that no one would ever be able to love or accept me if they knew. It's why I've never talked about it, no matter how many times Annie's badgered me about it."

"Hey, you know now that's not true, right?" I asked, wanting desperately to tell her I knew and I loved her, that she was deserving of love, but yesterday she had told me we would never be mates and today she had kissed me back. I didn't want to screw up the progress I felt like we were making, largely thanks to Lily's intervention, though I wouldn't admit that to her.

"She-she really hasn't treated me any differently. We cried

together a lot and I told her stuff I hadn't even been able to tell you. It felt good to share it with someone."

Her admittance was like a dagger to my heart. On the one hand I was grateful she could open up to my sister, but on the other, I desperately wished it were me she chose to confide in.

"Hey," she said, seeming to feel my disappointment. "It wasn't like that. I didn't tell her more than you, just different, and we talked about you a lot, too."

I perked up at that, unsure if that was good or not. "Uh, should I be thanking Lily or killing her in her sleep?"

Maddie laughed. "Verdict's still out on that one."

I could tell she was teasing me and it felt incredible, like we had reached a new level, and I was filled with hope once again. I wasn't going to push her. I had the rest of the week to convince her to come home with me.

"Hungry?" I asked and when she nodded yes, I took her hand and started to lead the way back to her room, stopping at the door and running back to grab my shirt and pull it on and slip on my shoes. "Sorry, Oscar's rules," I said apologetically, sensing her disappointment when I put my shirt back on. She nudged me in the ribs good-naturedly.

I swung by my room to change while she went to check on Oscar and Lily, then we all met in the lobby to go out to dinner. Maddie seemed relaxed; she smiled and laughed more. I was grateful for Lily's presence, knowing it contributed to it. It gave me hope that maybe Maddie would come around, and my life would not end up the living nightmare I had glimpsed the day before. I decided that I would not rush her or even discuss the future for the duration of our time in San Francisco. I'd simply enjoy every second she'd allow and pray that by the end of the weekend, she wouldn't be able to live without me either.

The four of us had a nice early dinner. I was surprised to realize it was already Friday. I had a teleconference starting at seven that I couldn't get out of, so after dinner I reluctantly dropped Oscar and the girls off at the wharfs. Lily swore they'd be careful, but they wanted to see the sunset.

I made a quick call asking Mark and Steph to keep an eye on them for me as I headed back to my hotel room for a meeting I wasn't looking forward to. Adam Rogers was a huge pain in my ass.

I wouldn't lose any sleep if we lost the account, but I had a duty to try to keep him happy. To my surprise, it went far smoother than I expected and ended just as the girls returned.

"Where's Oscar?" I asked, and was surprised by the quick panic that set in as my newfound protective instincts flared for the kid.

"We ran into Jacob and Annie in the lobby and he claimed he was starving again and asked to go with them for 'night dinner,'" Maddie informed me. "Is your meeting over already?"

I nodded, taking a deep breath, trying to calm my overreaction.

Once again Lily and Maddie stayed up late talking before saying their final goodbyes. Lily was heading home early in the morning and I knew it could be awhile before they saw each other again, so I kept to myself in the bedroom, giving them space.

I was pleased when there was a light knock on the door and Maddie came in, shutting the door behind her. I was honestly not expecting to see her and didn't want to push my luck by being too forceful, so I had already showered and was in nothing but my boxers. I pulled the covers over me so as not to embarrass her, but heard her quick intake of breath when she saw my bare chest. I couldn't help but grin in satisfaction.

"I, uh, I'm heading back to my room," she said softly, still openly staring at my chest. "I just wanted to say good night."

Screw her comfort. It was the first time my mate had actually sought me out, and I was out of the bed and crossing the room to her before I could stop myself. In one fluid motion, I swept her up in my arms and kissed her breathless. Leaning my forehead against her and grinning like I fool, I whispered, "Good night."

"Oh, okay then," she stammered in a fog. "I'll see you tomorrow."

She left quietly and I headed back to bed, falling fast asleep with a smile on my face.

The week had gone by faster than I expected. Lily headed home the next morning, but I had to stay for the charity event I had used as my cover to track Maddie down. I tried to convince Lily to stay and watch Oscar so Maddie could attend with me, but she said she couldn't without raising further suspicions, and Maddie was still adamant no one could know she was alive.

Only two days were left to convince Madelyn that she and Oscar were better off with me in their lives. I would do anything to keep them, even if it meant quitting my job and leaving my family behind to be with them. Whatever it took, I was ready to make that sacrifice. But I knew it would freak her out to hear that, so I kept it cool and enjoyed a relatively quiet day with her and Oscar, while subconsciously dreading the moment I had to finally say goodbye to prepare for the charity ball.

I dressed in my tux, alone in my room, hating the silence. Madelyn had truly come out of her shell with Lily's presence. The girls combined with Oscar's abundant chatter meant very little quiet, and even without Lily today, that hadn't stopped the momentum. The stillness in the empty room was depressing. I couldn't take it long. While normally I would show up deliberately late to such an event, I decided to head down early.

The charity ball was to raise money for the local sea lions. Of course I was happy to contribute on behalf of Steph and Mark. The host of the evening was Stephen Daniels, and Westin Foundation managed several of his charities. The man was extremely wealthy and giving, though I had heard he was quite ruthless in the boardroom, not someone you wanted to get on the wrong side of. Still, as far as Westin Foundation dealings went, he had proven quite generous. I had never met him in person, only talked to him over the phone. I was surprised to find I was looking forward to meeting him.

The ball was being held in the same hotel I was staying in, so a short elevator ride down to the first floor and I was there. People were already beginning to arrive in their formal best. The women wore gowns of every color with sparkles and shine that shimmered when they walked. The men were all in black tuxes similar to the penguin suit I wore. It was without a doubt the fanciest party I had ever attended. I immediately felt out of place and the various smells of perfume and cologne bothered my sensitive nose.

I looked around the room for any hope of fresh air to clear the smells some. I did not enjoy human events, which is why I had originally told Chris to regretfully decline this invitation. I didn't regret coming, though. It had allowed me to find my mate, my Maddie. I knew I was smiling like a smitten schoolboy, just thinking of her, but I didn't care.

Madelyn had come a long ways in the last few days. I could

feel our bond growing closer. She had told me she had no wolf spirit, that it had died, but I could feel it. My wolf could feel it, and she had shown signs that it too was strengthening as my own wolf called to it from within her.

I couldn't let myself think of the future. I wanted too much and I knew she wasn't fully ready for that commitment, but I had hope that maybe someday she would. Oscar had taken quickly to me once we made our peace and he didn't feel as threatened with me around his mom. I could even touch her without being growled at now.

I made my way across the room to the balcony doors and stepped outside for a breath of fresh air. The ballroom continued to fill. If there had been any other shifters present, I'm not sure I could have told with the amount of stench the humans covered themselves in. Maddie and Oscar lived in the human world. I couldn't understand how it didn't bother them more. I wasn't sure I could ever fully adjust to the unnatural smells humans used.

I watched them mingle and dance through the windows. A hush and stillness came over the crowd and a man walked up on stage. I knew from pictures it was Stephen Daniels. I quickly headed back inside just in time to hear him welcome everyone and thank them for coming.

I looked around the room, trying to gauge where he was headed. I needed to at least introduce myself and place my contribution before I could bail. Spotting him heading for the bar, I made my way over and ordered a root beer ahead of his arrival.

"Hello, Mr. Daniels," I said as he finally worked his way across the room to where I was standing next to the bar. "Wonderful party tonight. Appreciate you having me."

He eyed me suspiciously like he was trying to place me, then recognition shone in his eyes and his face morphed into a big smile. The scrutiny with which he looked me over set my wolf on edge.

"Liam Westin," he finally said, shaking my hand and clapping me on the shoulder. "I must say I was quite surprised to hear you were coming. In all the years of balls and celebrations, I don't think your father or brother ever made a single one."

"The Foundation certainly keeps us busy, but I am making an effort, sir, and we do appreciate your business."

As he waved his hand in gesture as he spoke, I couldn't help but notice a large ring on his right ring finger. It had an odd insignia on it I had never seen—or maybe I had and just couldn't place it—but it drew my attention and I couldn't stop staring at it.

"Liam, let me introduce you to a few of my friends," he said, interrupting my curiosity over his ring. I tried to shrug it off, thinking it must be a family symbol or just something of special meaning to him.

He introduced me to three men, all around his age and stature. I didn't pay close attention to names after the first one who went to shake my hand was wearing the same ring. In fact, all three of the men wore the ring. I had a fraternity ring back home. It wasn't something I just wore, especially on formal occasions, unless I knew my brothers were present. This ring didn't look like any frat symbol I recognized, but I figured it must be something similar.

One of the men, I think his name was Kent something or another, kept staring oddly at me. It creeped me out and my wolf was getting restless. If I didn't get away and settle him soon, I'd be looking for places to change tonight in order to calm him, and it wasn't safe to do that in the city.

Spotting familiar faces in the crowd, I politely made my exit. I headed right for Jacob and Annie, grateful though surprised to see them. Jacob looked uncomfortable and his eyes kept scanning the room ahead of my approach. I didn't miss the shared look of concern between the two.

"Liam," Jacob said, hesitantly offering his hand.

"What's wrong?" I asked, lowering my voice. My wolf was on full alert at this point.

"Not here," Annie whispered with a smile planted on her face.

"It's good to see you again, I didn't realize you'd be in attendance tonight," Jacob said in a normal voice. He looked over his shoulder and something akin to fear flashed in his eyes.

"Winthrop," Daniels interrupted. "I didn't realize you and Mr. Westin were acquainted."

Something in me told me to lie. "We're not really," I started. "But we are staying here at the hotel and struck up a conversation a couple mornings ago over breakfast. It's nice to see a familiar face in a crowd such as this." I was oozing charm and I knew it, but I didn't know why. Jacob seemed to relax some, though Annie was still very tense. I could hear her heart beating erratically.

"Ah, yes, I suppose it is," Daniels said, sounding a little disappointed.

My brain was spinning with questions. How did a renowned geneticist connect to a business tycoon such as Stephen Daniels? And then I saw it.

The ring.

Jacob was wearing the same ring I had spotted on the hand of every notable mention in the room. He was clearly somehow connected, and it was obvious he did not want our friendship or whatever it was to be found out.

I politely excused myself and wandered about the room. I could hear whispered conversations and suddenly felt like eyes were on me everywhere I turned. A part of me cursed myself for letting my imagination and paranoia run wild, but my wolf was also struggling to maintain his composure among these people.

The ring was everywhere; almost every man present wore one and several of the women displayed similar pendants around their necks. It had to mean something. But what?

I wanted to pull Jacob aside and ask him so many things, but I knew that was a very bad idea. I made my way back across the room and out onto the balcony, which overlooked the Bay. There seemed to be fewer eyes on me, and breathing in the fresh air helped to calm my nerves somewhat. I couldn't help but wonder just want Jacob and Annie were into, though I suspected it was nothing good.

I startled at an approaching man I hadn't noticed until he cleared his throat. I tried not to visibly react. "Keep looking forward," he whispered from where he stood ten feet away, keeping to the shadows. "There's no one else out here but us. If you can hear me, and I know you can, run your hands through your hair."

I took a deep breath and did as he asked. From my peripheral vision I watched him take a long puff off of a cigar and blow it out in the shape of a ring. I waited anxiously for him to speak again.

"I'm a friend of Jacob's. It wouldn't be safe for him to speak to you directly again, so Annie asked if I could do it instead. Your kind isn't safe here. You need to make an excuse and leave quickly. I'll make certain you aren't followed. Then get in your car and go home, Liam."

"What do you mean 'my kind?"

"Don't play games, Liam Michael Westin. Everyone here knows exactly who you are and what you are. You're a bit of a celebrity actually—the first of your kind to ever accept one of Daniels' invitations. It was stupid of you to do so. Things are changing. The Order is dividing and we don't want to see you caught in the middle of it."

"What do you mean by The Order? And how do you know about my kind?"

"We are the Order of the Verndari—The Guardians. We've taken our vows seriously to protect your kind for many millennia. The Order is as old as shifters, but there've been recent changes within. There are those that wish to study you, for the betterment of humanity so they say. They are pushing a new agenda, one that many of us cannot support. Things have been done that I'm ashamed of, but the opposition is strong. The medical benefits they've supposedly found through this unsanctioned research, is making others reconsider the principles that we have always stood on."

Humans knew of our kind? How? Why didn't we know about them sooner? Verndari. I had never even heard the word before, of that I was certain. Even when studying the history of shifters, and nothing about guardians had ever come up.

"I've been here too long, and I've said too much already. We aren't supposed to interact directly with you, only watch, observe, and intercept any human interest as needed. I must go. You should, too."

"Wait. Jane and Oscar. Are they in danger?"

"Jane? Jacob's daughter?"

I stared at him. I needed to see if he was telling me the truth. I wasn't prepared for the look of complete shock that crossed his face.

"I-I never suspected," the strange man said. "You're certain?"

I neither denied nor confirmed, unable to put them in further danger and cursing myself for ever asking.

"As far as I know, they are safe. No one knows of them, if you're saying what I think you're saying. I'm not sure how that's possible, but Jacob and Annie love them and would never intentionally let harm come to them."

That wasn't good enough for me. I worried that I had

unintentionally given away their secret and my wolf roared in fury. I needed to get to them and I needed to do it quickly. The man slinked further into the shadows. Without another word I turned and headed back in, much more in tune to the whispers and stares than even before.

Stephen Daniels was once again standing by the bar. I headed right for him with my biggest smile possible.

"Order you a drink?" he asked on my approach.

"No, thank you, sir, I just wanted to give you this check," I said, producing the large sum I had written and signed earlier. "Unfortunately, I have a very early morning drive back. Now something's come up, and well, its work, work, work all the time these days."

"No sleep for the weary."

"Exactly. But it's been wonderful to meet you, Mr. Daniels," I said, offering him my right hand and the check in my left. He took both and we said an amicable goodbye. I was already beginning to second-guess the strange man outside, but as I passed by Jacob and Annie, I saw the fear in her eyes and watched them turn away. I didn't even so much as nod in their direction before making my exit. I knew I was being watched. I could feel their eyes on me.

Once back to the elevator, I punched in the number to my floor, which I knew was two below Maddie's. No one had got in to ride with me, but if they were watching the elevator lights, they'd hopefully believe I went right back to my room. After arriving on my floor, I found and entered the stairwell taking two steps at a time as I raced up the two flights of stairs.

Once on Maddie's floor, I walked as quickly as possible, trying not to draw any attention and knowing there were cameras watching the hallways. I banged on her door until she opened it.

"Liam? What's wrong?" she asked sleepily, and I realized she and Oscar had gone to bed early. There was no time to waste.

"Look, I need you to trust me right now. Absolute trust, Maddie. Can you do that?" She slowly nodded, but I could feel the anxiety starting to build in her. "Is Oscar asleep?"

"Yes."

"Okay, I need you to pack your things. Whatever you can fit into a bag as quickly as possible. I will get Oscar. I don't have time to answer a lot of questions. We'll talk in the car, but it's not safe here and we have to leave now."

To my shock and relief, she did exactly what I told her to do. I gently picked the boy up and he never even woke. We stopped off in my room and Maddie quickly grabbed my things, threw them into my bag, and within minutes we were heading for the elevator.

"Wait, there'll be too many people in the lobby, and it could draw suspicion. There's a staircase at the other end of the hall. It goes straight to the parking deck, so we need to take that."

We walked to the opposite end of the hotel and decided to chance the elevator there instead. The ball was on the other side of the complex, and I prayed we'd put enough space between us and The Order to get away safely.

Uneventfully making it to my car should have been enough to calm me down, but it wasn't. I gently laid Oscar across the back seat. Maddie looked at me and then back at him. "He needs his car seat, but it's in Annie's car."

"He'll be fine."

"Liam, it's illegal and it's not safe."

"We're not safe. I promise you, I will stop and buy him the best car seat on the market the second we are away from here."

I felt close to having an anxiety attack of my own. Why wasn't she freaking out? As my anxiety grew, I felt a calm come over her. It was the strangest thing. Maddie got anxious over every little thing, so why not now?

She gently wrapped her arms around me and hugged me close. My body shuddered at her touch and I started to relax. She stared into my eyes and nodded. In that moment I knew she trusted me one hundred percent. She was doing exactly what I'd asked of her without question. I could suddenly breathe again knowing that.

We got in the car and I quickly sped away. The entire time we were in the city and even many miles later with nothing but darkness surrounding us, I obsessively watched my rearview mirror, just waiting for the boogieman to jump out or something. That guy had scared the shit out of me.

Maddie

Chapter 14

I didn't know what I was doing. I didn't even know why. Liam had come to my door and looked so terrified, I couldn't tell him no. I just couldn't. I hoped Annie and Jacob would understand. I would call them later and make arrangements to meet up with them. Right then all I knew was that Liam needed me. He needed me to be strong as he struggled not to fall apart. He had been there for me through several panic attacks already. It was the least I could do for him, especially once I saw the desperation in his eyes.

"Do you want to talk about it?" I finally asked, breaking the silence that loomed between us.

"Did you know about the Order of the Verndari? Did you know Annie and Jacob knew all along? What you are? Who you are? They've been lying to you, Mad."

His words didn't make any sense. There was no way they knew who or what I was. I was just their Janie. "That's not possible," I whispered.

"Sweetheart, please don't argue with me about this. I'm telling you the truth. You know I could never lie to you. The Order of the Verndari, it's some sort of shifter watch group of humans. I went out to the balcony to get some fresh air, 'cause you know the smells were driving me crazy and starting to hurt my head from the way humans like to douse themselves in stench. Anyway, I was alone until some creepy guy came out and joined me. He said Annie sent him to tell me who they all were, and that some of them were done with watching and wanted to do research on us. He said we weren't safe. I don't know for sure if they know about you and Oscar, but Maddie, we can't take that chance. They know about shifters. They were all there—so many of them all in one place."

It sounded absurd, but I could tell he was really freaked out. I asked him how he knew they were all part of this secret society group and he told me about the ring. He described it, and I knew exactly what he was talking about. Jacob wore one frequently. He had even promised it to Oscar one day. If he knew about shifters, did he truly not know about me? Or was it all a front so he could observe and study us up close?

I thought back to everything that had been said and done over the last eight years. Anything at all that stood out. Did I say or do anything to alert them to what I was? No. I couldn't have, because I wasn't really a shifter. I couldn't shift. I never had, so aside from a few lingering quirks like my intense sense of smell and really good hearing, there wasn't anything for them to see.

"I know the ring you're talking about," I finally confessed

"They all had them, Mad. Nearly every single person in the room was wearing one, and then the look on Annie's face as I approached them—I'm telling you, looking back she was terrified I might say something to alert the others. The guy told me point blank that they all knew what and who I was. And they just whispered while staring in my direction. I didn't focus in on what they were saying, but on my exit I did key in to several things that verified what he told me. Like, 'I can't believe Liam Westin is actually here.' Or, 'Have you ever been this close to one?' There is no doubt in my mind that the guy on the balcony was telling the truth."

I watched him shiver and I knew it had to be true since he couldn't lie to me. I had felt our bond growing over the past few days. I wasn't sure how that was happening, but it definitely was. Aside from the obvious tells of someone lying like a spike in heart rate and nervous twitches that shifters are more in tune to notice, I would feel the lie on him. He had never lied to me, but I knew I would. I could feel all his emotions at this point. It was the reason I didn't completely freak out when he banged on my door and demanded I pack up and follow him.

He was still obsessively looking in the rearview mirror, though we had gone several miles without seeing a single car. We'd been driving for hours already and I wasn't sure what I was going to do yet. I couldn't let him take me and Oscar back to Westin Pack. Oscar didn't even know about our kind.

"There's a town just up ahead. Can we stop and see if there's a place to buy a car seat?"

"Are you sure? He's sound asleep and we could have been followed. I'm not sure it's safe. I don't think I'll breathe again normally till we're in pack territory."

And that's what I was most worried about. I did manage to convince him it was for the best. We found a twenty-four hour megastore and I asked him to stay with Oscar while I ran in to buy it. Despite having my own money, he whipped out his money clip, handed me some large bills and insisted I take his cash to pay for it.

The moment I was through the doors and safely out of earshot, I grabbed my phone and called Annie.

"Thank God, you're safe. Where are you? We came back to the hotel and all your stuff was gone. Is Oscar okay?" She sounded so upset, it broke my heart.

"Janie, sweetie," Jacob started. "Are you okay? Did something happen?"

"Apparently a friend of yours at the party said some things that totally freaked out Liam. He needed to get away from there and asked that we go with him. We'll be okay, and Oscar and I will be back home before you know it."

"We had asked Jeremiah to warn the boy, not scare the living daylights out of him."

"Wait, so it's true?" I asked, still unable to accept what he was telling me. "You know? You've known all along?"

"About his kind? Yes. I know all about Liam Westin. He's a bit of a celebrity among my friends. The question begs, how do you know about him?"

"I told you, we grew up together." I kept it simple. Could they really not know who I was?

"Oh no, Jane! Are you saying what I think you're saying?"

I started to cry. I couldn't confess something like that to a human. It was a sacred vow among shifters. I couldn't reveal who I was, who I may have been, or who my family was to this man. I could no longer trust him. He had been like a father to me for so long. My heart was breaking.

"It can't be," I heard him say just before Annie grabbed the phone.

"Jane, please come home. Jacob looks like he's seen a ghost.

What's going on?"

"I don't think it's safe for me to come home again, Annie. I'm so sorry."

"Wait," she yelled, just as I was going to hang up the phone. "You're our daughter. We love you. I don't care what or who you once were. I know you, baby girl. Please don't shut us out."

"Did you know? Did you know all this time?" I cried into the phone. I never really cried in front of them, always alone and into my pillow. I knew it would kill Annie to hear it now, but I couldn't care about that.

"I swear we didn't. I think maybe we suspected after Liam came around. I mean, of course we knew what he was. He's a Westin. Also, there had been a pack of out-of-control tigers stalking young girls in the area, back around the time you were"—she hesitated—"injured. So we thought, maybe Oscar was . . ." Her voice trailed off.

I couldn't breathe. I could feel a panic attack coming on. It couldn't be true. The boys who had raped me may have been shifters, too? Where did that leave Oscar? What was he? I had never suspected anything like that. I couldn't fully comprehend it now.

"Janie? Janie?" Annie frantically yelled through the phone. "We didn't know, I swear to you, we didn't know. And we would never hurt you. You know that. It's part of our most sacred vow as guardians, to protect your kinds. Janie, please!"

I pulled myself together and steeled my voice. I had to be strong now, for Oscar. Liam was right, we could never go back. "My name isn't Janie. It's Madelyn. Madelyn Collier."

I heard the sharp gasp confirming that they recognized the name as easily as Westin, and I hung up the phone.

I grabbed the first booster seat I saw and headed to the register. At the counter I loaded up on chocolate and grabbed two root beers. I knew it was Liam's favorite. I didn't think Oscar would wake before we got home.

Home.

I was going back to the pack, not my pack, but the next best thing. I'd be with my kind again, and they'd know I lived. I didn't have a choice now. While the thought terrified me, it also brought me more peace than I had realized it could.

Liam jumped from the car and grabbed the car seat from my

hands. He tossed it on the ground and pulled me into a hug. We just stood there holding each other while I cried some more.

"You called them, didn't you?" He didn't sound upset or surprised that I had done that and I just nodded against his chest. "Ah sweetie, I wish it weren't true."

"They-they said they didn't know about me. They never even suspected. They-they were tracking a pack of out of control tigers. They-they thought maybe Oscar had been fathered by one. Is that possible? What will happen to him? What is he?"

"Shh," he comforted me. "It's going to be okay. Whatever he is, whoever he turns out to be, it's going to be okay. He's a great kid, with a fantastic mom. Wolf. Tiger. It doesn't matter."

I looked up at him in confusion. "What do you mean? What happens when shifters of different species mate? Is it even possible?"

He growled at me and I shrunk back. My head dropped and I immediately submitted to him. He took a deep breath before speaking. "First, that wasn't mating, Maddie. I will be your only mate. What they did to you was the furthest thing from that."

I nodded. I knew what he meant was true. I hadn't meant to upset him.

He softened and brushed a hand through my hair as he pulled me back against him. "It's not impossible for different species to mate. I'm sorry I growled, but it's just hard for me to think of any other man touching you. I just want to track them and rip out their throats every time I think about it."

I smiled against him. I liked that he went all protective like that. It made me feel safe, and cherished even.

"Second," he continued, "it's my understanding that interspecies mating doesn't produce some weird hybrid or anything. God only places one animal spirit in each of us, so there will be a fifty-fifty chance of Oscar being wolf or tiger when he comes of age. Only time will tell. We don't even know for sure that's the case. He could just as easily be half human. And it really doesn't matter. He's just Oscar, and we'll love him unconditionally no matter what he is."

I started to cry again in his arms. My mate loved my son. I had never even dreamed it would be possible. I didn't think I could ever return to the pack because no one would ever accept a half human child, but Liam was telling me he already had. He would protect me and my son. It was so much more than I had ever hoped for, more than I deserved.

For too long I had felt like a shell of myself, only existing and never really living. The last few days with Lily and Liam had already begun to change that. They were changing me, or maybe they were helping me just find myself again. I felt like Maddie Collier, not the weak, broken Janie Winthrop, and I liked it.

"Come on," Liam said. "I won't fully relax until we're back on pack land. Hate to wake Patrick up this late, but I really think I need to warn him."

"Patrick? Not Kyle?"

"Well, Kyle will need to know too, but Patrick's his security Beta. He'll be the one that needs to know first about the Order of the Verndari."

"Annie said they were some sort of shifter guardians, that they protect our kind, not harm them."

"That's what the creepy guy told me too, except he also said that there was a group of them changing things up and wanting to research on us to better humanity."

"What?"

"Yeah, that's why I freaked out and had to get you and Oscar out of there so fast. He told me it wasn't safe for us, that we couldn't trust those people, and I don't know if that includes Jacob and Annie or not. I hope not. I mean, Jacob did send the guy to warn me, but still. I don't know if we can trust them, Mad." He lifted my chin till my eyes met his. "I know you trust them, but right now I really need you to trust me."

I nodded without hesitation. I did trust him and I wasn't sure if I should trust Jacob and Annie. They had been good to me, and my gut told me I should, but I was so confused. I didn't even notice Liam's head descending towards mine until it was too late.

His lips lightly brushed mine, like he was testing the waters. When I didn't pull away he increased the pressure. Hot need burst through me and I wrapped my arms around his neck, guiding him closer, urging him to take more, and he did. I opened my mouth to him and his tongue swept inside, slowly memorizing every crevice he found there. He was delicious and made my mouth water and beg for more. The intensity of the kiss increased and I didn't shy away. When he finally pulled back, grinning like the young boy I once knew and loved forever ago, we were both breathless.

"Can we go home now?" he asked softly, and all I could do was nod.

We got back in the car and drove in silence. There was really nothing more left to say. The lull of the road had my eyes drifting shut and I fell asleep into a blissful, empty void that wasn't filled with demons and nightmares for once.

When the car came to a full stop, I stretched and slowly began the process of waking up. My body was stiff, but I felt rested. I wasn't sure how long I had been out, but thought for a moment I should offer to drive some and give Liam a break.

"Hey, sleeping beauty, it's time to wake up."

I smiled without opening my eyes. I yawned and stretched again, taking in a deep breath. Familiar smells surrounded me and put me on full alert at the same time. Wolves! I shot up, fully awake, and looked around.

"We're here? Already? How long was I out? Did you drive through the night?"

The sun was bright and high in the sky. Oscar giggled from the backseat and I looked back to see him safely strapped into his new booster seat. He wouldn't need it much longer, but it gave me comfort that he was safe and he never seemed to mind, but when? How?

"Was I really out that long?"

"You were snoring so loud, Mommy. Liam and I were laughing at you. You even drooled a little. Even with Mimi's pills you don't sleep that hard."

Liam grinned as I turned horrified eyes towards him. "What? It was cute."

To my embarrassment he leaned over and gave me a quick kiss on the mouth. I know my face was a brilliant shade of red as my cheeks heated in memory of the last kiss we'd shared. I really hoped I hadn't dreamed that kiss. Since we were very obviously in pack territory I knew everything had to be true. Oscar made a sound of disgust from the back seat.

"Eww, you kissed my mom!"

Not helping any.

Liam took it all in stride, as he seemed to do with just about everything. "Better get used to it, kid. Come on, let me show you around and introduce you to everyone."

Suddenly I started to panic. We were here. We were really here, and I hadn't told Oscar a thing. We needed to sit down and have a long serious talk. Why hadn't I told him all along? He deserved to know his heritage, but I couldn't risk a small child in the human world talking too much.

"Um, Liam, before that, Oscar and I need to have a talk. There's, uh, some things he really needs to learn before we introduce him around."

"You mean about the wolves?" Oscar asked. Nothing ever before that had come out of his mouth had shocked me this much.

"You know about the wolves?"

"Yeah, isn't it cool? Liam says someday I might be able to turn into a wolf, too."

I glared at Liam. Furious. He was grinning proudly until the moment he felt my anger. How dare he tell my son about that? He had overstepped a line and it needed to be sorted out quickly.

"Oscar, hon, can you step out of the car and give me and Liam a few minutes to talk?

"What did I do?" Liam asked the second the door shut.

"You told him? You just told him all about shifters and the wolves? Just like that?"

"I'm sorry, I thought he should know. He's in pack territory, and I didn't want him to freak out or anything. He's a smart kid—he accepted it and was pretty excited about it all."

"That wasn't your place, Liam. I'm his mother. If I wanted him to know about shifters, don't you think I should be the one to tell him?" I was still furious. He hadn't done it to undermine me. I knew he was just trying to help, but it should have been me to explain things to him. "I should have been the one to tell him. He's going to be confused and have lots of questions that need answering."

"Oh, trust me—we've exhausted nearly all of them while you slept. For the past four hours he's been asking questions and demanding answers. I even had to let my hand shift just enough to convince him I wasn't bullshitting him."

I knew how Oscar could be and I tried not to laugh at the picture Liam portrayed, but I couldn't keep the smile entirely off my face.

"This is a big deal, Liam."

"I do hear you. I understand. I didn't mean to step on the mommy toes or anything. I'm sorry. I really was just trying to help."

"I know you were." I sighed, letting go of the anger. "It's just...he's my son, Liam. Mine. And I have to do what's best for him, including making some life-changing decisions like explaining things about shifters and other stuff. You need to talk to me before talking to him about stuff like that."

"Okay," he said, resolutely. "I'm still new to all this. I'm going to make mistakes along the way, but I only want what's best for you and the kid." He grinned at me sheepishly and I knew he was up to no good. "And in another, say five or so years when he starts hitting puberty, I'm going to remind you of this conversation and let you explain *that*!"

I punched him, laughing. "Not funny, I'm serious." Though even I knew I didn't sound convincing of that anymore.

"I know. I'm listening and I'll try to remember in the future."

I leaned over and gave him a quick kiss. It was the first time I'd initiated anything like that, but it just felt so right. Natural. My heart was soaring. He was talking of five years down the road. I hadn't even begun to consider the reality of an actual life with him.

We got out of the car and found Oscar kicking a rock as he tried to patiently wait for us. I could feel the excitement ready to burst from him.

"You have any questions?" I asked him, still unsure what Liam had actually told him.

"Nah. Well, okay...just one. How come I've never seen you turn into a wolf?"

My heart sank. I could never tell him that the night he was conceived they had hurt me and killed my wolf spirit. I would not put that on him. Whoever had fathered him was a bad man, but I had come to terms long ago with that fact that that was not a genetic trait that he would inherit. Oscar was a great kid and I couldn't believe him capable of what his sperm donor had done to me.

"My wolf never emerged, bud. It happens sometimes. I can't shift. Never have."

"Liam says sometimes wolves show early, like Kelsey was only ten when hers came out!" I looked at Liam quizzically. That sounded like more than a slight exaggeration.

"I swear, it's true!" Liam said.

"Maybe yours is just late, Mommy. Maybe she was scared to come out with all the humans around. Maybe she will now." He looked at me with such hope in his eyes I had to let my fingernails dig into the palm of my fisted hand to keep from crying.

"Maybe," I said sadly.

"Hey, you ready to go meet my family? Lily will be there," Liam said, changing the subject quickly for me as he turned apologetic eyes my way. I didn't want his pity. I didn't need him to feel sorry for me.

He wrapped his arm around my shoulders and took Oscar by the hand, leading us both into the house. I had been to visit Lily in San Marco on numerous occasions. I knew the Alpha's house well. I knew the Westin family well, or I had. But I was a nervous wreck walking through that door. Had he called ahead and warned them? Had Lily broken her promise and told them? I didn't know what to expect and it made me very nervous.

"Mom!" Liam yelled as soon as we walked in.

"Kitchen," she yelled back.

"Come on. She's in for quite a shock," he laughed, and I knew he hadn't warned them about me.

Butterflies swirled in my stomach as he led us to the back of the house.

Mary Westin was cooking in the kitchen with her back toward us. I hung back as Liam went to hug his mother. Oscar hid behind me, suddenly bashful and unsure of himself. I watched the two embrace and she kissed his cheek.

"Let me look at you," Mary said. "So, how was San Francisco? Anything exciting? You left in such a hurry, and never even called. What was that all about? Did you bring me back something good?"

He laughed patiently, letting her interrogations flow.

"Actually, I did bring home something rather interesting."

"Well, come on, you know how I love surprises. What is it?"

"My mate," he said, and I knew my cheeks pinked. I looked down at Oscar, seeing the surprise in his eyes as he stared back at me. I was certain Liam had covered that part already, too.

"Mom, this is . . ." Before he could finish, she turned and then gasped as her hands flew to her mouth in shock. "Madelyn?"

I started to cry and nod as she descended on me, wrapping her arms around me and pulling me into the comfort only a mother could provide. She broke away and stared up at me in wonder.

"You're alive? You're really here? Does your family know?"

Questions kept bumbling out of her and I was reminded of Oscar when he was excited about something. Oscar. I looked around. He was hugging up next to Liam, just quietly observing it all.

"No, I haven't spoken to my parents," I confessed, feeling the full weight of the guilt I had carried for the last eight years.

"Liam, how?" She paused, looking at her son and noticing mine for the first time. With hands on her hips in true Mary Westin fashion as I remembered as a child, she asked, "Now who do we have here?"

"Hi, I'm Oscar," he said bravely. "Are you Liam's mom?"

"I am, and you know what? I just baked some cookies this morning and I haven't had a tester yet. Would you like to help me?"

He hesitated, but the thought and the smells from her kitchen were too alluring and he nodded happily. "I can help."

"Well alright then, come on." She took his hand and walked the short distance to the counter to retrieve two large chocolate chip cookies and a napkin before escorting him to the kitchen table. They both sat.

"Now tell me, Oscar, how old are you?"

"I'm seven," he said with a mouth full of cookie.

"Oscar, don't talk with food in your mouth," I scolded without thinking.

Mary's quizzical eyes flew to meet mine. I could see her brain working out a puzzle, doing the math. It wasn't what she thought, but I couldn't tell her that in front of my son.

"Sorry, Mommy," he said after swallowing, confirming what she already knew.

"Kelsey and Zander will be by shortly." Then she turned to Oscar. "Zander's my grandson. He just turned one, but he'll be excited to have someone to play with if you think you can handle a toddler."

"Yes, ma'am," he said. "I can teach him how to play basketball. Did he like the gift Liam got for his birthday?"

Mary continued to struggle to put the pieces together. "How do you know what Liam got him for his birthday?"

"It was my suggestion," Oscar admitted proudly. "I knew he'd love it. He did, right? He loved it?"

"He sure did. You are a fantastic gift picker-outer."

"I know," he said before shoving the last of his cookie into his mouth.

"Mary?" A woman's voice came from the front of the house as I heard the door shut behind her. "Up or down?"

"Kitchen," Mary responded back. I smiled, remembering the Westin house had never been quiet. With three rowdy boys and two girls, one of whom was Lily, need I say more? There was always something exciting going on in this home.

Mary rose and went to meet her guest. Kelsey. That was Kyle's mate, if I was remembering correctly. Liam came over and took my hand, squeezing it reassuringly.

"Oscar, come here and meet Zander and Kelsey," Mary yelled from the next room. He hesitantly started to walk, checking back over his shoulder to make sure it was okay. I nodded encouragement, but in the end Liam went with him and I slowly followed behind.

"Hey, Kels," he said, hugging the pretty blonde.

A loud growl bubbled up and out of me. I quickly covered my mouth and blushed in embarrassment. I didn't understand why that happened, but whenever he was intimately close to another female, I felt territorial. Oscar had the audacity to laugh at me.

Kelsey smiled, and elbowed Liam in the ribcage, putting some distance between them. It calmed my nerves some. "Looks like you brought back more than souvenirs," she teased him before turning her attention fully to me. She extended her hand and closed the gap between us. "Hi, I'm Kelsey."

"Ja . . . Maddie," I said aloud. It felt strange yet familiar rolling off my tongue. *I am Madelyn Collier. Maddie*, I reminded myself. After so many years of being Jane, it was going to take a little getting used to. "I'm sorry I growled at you."

Kelsey laughed. "It's still early, girl. You have a lot more growling to do before it's over."

She was talking about us mating. I hadn't let myself seriously consider all that. Could we even mate? To seal the bond, I'd have to bite him, and how could I without a wolf? I still didn't understand fully what was happening to me.

"I've not seen you around here," Kelsey added. "Where are you from? How did you guys meet?"

I didn't want to answer all those questions, but I knew I'd have to . . . again and again. Too many in Westin Pack did know me and when word got around, everyone would know. Word would soon get to my father, my family. There was no way to avoid it now.

"Um, Liam and I have known each other since childhood. We ran into each other again in San Francisco."

"Are there packs in the city? I thought they tended to stay more remote."

"No, we were there for vacation." I said, keeping it simple. I was interrupted by a loud squeal and before I knew what was happening I was being tackled into a bear hug.

"You're here! You changed your mind!" Lily yelled so loudly it left my ears ringing.

"Hi, Lily," Oscar said, taking a second away from the little boy he was playing with to run over and quickly side hug her while she was still squeezing the life out of me, before running back to his spot.

"Hey, O-Man. I'm so happy you and your mom are here."

He just smiled and nodded before turning his attention back to his new small friend.

I stepped back to take in my dear friend. Her pink striped hair was fluffy, rocking the bed-head look, and she was still in her pajamas. It had to be pushing noon already and she was just rolling out of bed.

"Kels, this is my best friend in the entire world!" Lily started, quickly filling in gaps I wasn't ready to talk about.

Mary took the distraction as time to get away. Prying me away from Lily, she explained we'd be in Kyle's office talking for a bit. Then she escorted me down the hall. Liam followed behind. He was grinning, relaxed, and clearly happy.

As soon as the door was closed, she motioned for us both to sit. I knew a full-on interrogation was coming.

"Maddie, do your parents know you're here?"

This woman was ready to cut to the chase. No pleasantries or small talk was going to happen here. I shook my head. "No, ma'am. I haven't talked to my family in eight years."

She nodded. "Is it because of Oscar?"

"Mom, it's not what you think, and she doesn't have to explain herself to anyone. It's really none of your business."

I loved that he quickly came to my defense, but if we were truly considering a life together, this conversation was going to happen many times over. I knew there was no getting away from it.

"Liam," Mary laughed. "When are you foolish, misguided kids going to learn? Everything is my business." I wanted to laugh at her audacity, but Liam tensed and I could feel his rare aggressive side spike.

"It's okay," I told him, placing my hand on his thigh and reveling in the fact that it visibly calmed him.

"Yes, it does have to do with Oscar, but not in the way you think," I said honestly, answering her previously asked question

She let that slide, but moved on to equally hard ones. "So where have you been for the last eight years? Do you have any idea what it has done your family? Your mother? They still mourn your loss all the time. It changed each of them. Collier Pack wasn't the only one affected either. It dimmed Lily's spirit and Liam took to drinking for a while," I glanced at him and he cringed. "Don't think I don't know about those things, son."

I wondered if it were possible? Did my leaving affect Liam so drastically? We weren't mates back then. We were barely friends. Aside from being his obnoxious twin's best friend, I didn't think Liam Westin had really noticed me. Lily had made a few comments otherwise, but I hadn't really believed her. Heck, Liam had all but confessed to crushing on me as kids and I still hadn't believed him fully, either.

I took a deep breath and decided to get this conversation over as quickly as possible. Just rip off the Band-Aid. I smiled, remembering that was an old saying Jason Westin would tell us when we were in trouble. "The truth is hard sometimes, but it's best to just get it out there, like ripping off a Band-Aid. Quick and it's over and you'll feel much better." It amazed me, all the little moments that kept popping up in my mind.

"The night I left, I was raped. By six guys. I was left broken and alone to die in a dumpster, but I survived. It was really . . . hard. I was ashamed and embarrassed and couldn't come home. I found out a few months later I had conceived Oscar that night." I paused to let that sink in. I had done it. I told her without breaking down.

Granted, I had steeled my nerves and determination and shut off my emotions to do it, but I did it. The rest of my story flowed easily as I explained how I'd met and gone to live with Annie and Jacob. That was almost harder at the moment, given the fresh sense of betrayal I felt towards them. I didn't tell her about that, though.

I hadn't mentioned that my wolf spirit had died. Being here, with the familiar woodsy scents, I couldn't bring myself to say it. It was my breaking point, so I left it out.

Mary had very few questions. I could tell my story overwhelmed her. Her eyes were puffy and red-rimmed, fighting back tears by the end of our conversation. She hugged me tightly, but didn't press me for anything more. My instinct at her touch was to flinch away, but I didn't and it didn't take long until I relaxed into her, the loving arms of a mother I had missed so much.

Liam

Chapter 15

Seeing Maddie relax into my mother made my heart overflow with pride. I had a list a mile long of things I needed to do. It was Sunday, but I wasn't expected back in the office till Tuesday, so I didn't need to worry about work right away. I did need to talk to Patrick as quickly as possible. I didn't want to leave Maddie alone, though.

"Mom, we really need to go. Would you mind if Oscar stayed and played with Zander? They seem to be having fun and I need to talk to Patrick without little ears around."

"Why? What's wrong?" she demanded.

I knew better than to make a rookie mistake like that with my mom. I leaned down and kissed her cheek. "It's nothing concerning. He asked me to report back when I got home. You know, after everything that happened with E last year." It wasn't entirely true, but it worked.

"Oh, yes, yes, that's a good idea. You should get right over. Of course, as long as Madelyn is okay with it, Oscar is welcome to stay here. Though I won't promise not to spoil him while in my charge."

I smiled. I wouldn't expect anything less, and the kid could use a little spoiling.

"Thank you," Maddie told her, as we prepared to leave. "That would be wonderful if you are sure it's no trouble?"

"Don't be silly. I've got Zander all afternoon, and Oscar can help me entertain him," she assured us as she shooed us out of the room and out of the house. Maddie left for only a moment, just long enough to tell Oscar we were leaving.

Once in the car I took her hand and squeezed. "I know that

was hard. I'm sorry."

She smiled back at me. "Honestly, it wasn't so bad this time. Telling you was the hardest, mostly because it was the first time I had ever talked about it, but also because, well, it's you. Telling Lily wasn't as bad, and this time was even easier. I might as well get used to it. It's not like I can hide the fact I'm here."

Everything she said made sense, though a part of me that only wanted to protect her hated putting her through it over and over again. We drove in comfortable silence to the cottage Patrick and Elise lived in on the edge of San Marco.

When we arrived and got out, she stopped me as we walked to the door.

"Um, maybe we should let your mom spread the word about me after all. I think it's going to get really awkward fast, having to explain myself to everyone." She looked so uncomfortable it stirred my wolf.

"You don't have to tell anyone anything, Maddie. I will make sure no one makes you uncomfortable here."

"You can't protect me from everyone, Liam. You can't protect me from any of this."

"The hell I can't." I was never so determined about anything in all my life. My mate didn't want to be harassed about her past, and it was my job to see that she wasn't. I kissed her hard on the mouth. "No one is going to bother you. I will protect you," I told her, never meaning anything more in my entire life.

I wrapped my arm around her and kept her close to my side as we made our way to the door. I knocked and waited. I saw Elise peek out the side window.

"Crap, Liam's home and he brought company. Go get dressed," I heard my sister demand in a whisper.

I shook my head. "Sorry, we really thought they'd be over this stage by now. Seriously, from the moment they mated, it's been call ahead or beware of what you're walking into." I laughed. "They're pretty disgusting to hang around, can't keep their hands to themselves. It's bad."

The door swung open and Maddie jumped back, caught off guard.

"Hey," Elise said, giving me a quick kiss on the cheek. Maddie stiffened next to me but I could tell she was fighting to hold back a growl. “I didn't think you were coming home till tomorrow.” She turned to Maddie. “Hey, I'm Elise, Liam's sister. I don't think we've m—” Recognition and shock flickered across her face. “Maddie?”

“E, can we come in or are you going to make us stand here all day? I need to talk to Patrick,” I interrupted her before she could start. I knew by the way I walked ahead, shielding my mate and being far more protective than my sister was used to. I knew the smell of testosterone was filling the air.

Elise's eyes widened as we passed her and sat down on the couch in their small living room. She wouldn't stop staring at her.

“Elise, stop staring,” I warned. “You're making her nervous.”

Elise glared at me. I knew I was going to get an earful later, but I could take it. “Come on,” she finally said. “I feel like I'm looking at a ghost. Just tell me I'm not going crazy, or introduce her to me already and stop being rude.”

“Elise, this is Jane. Jane, this is my sister Elise,” I said spitefully.

Maddie laughed and shook her head as Elise looked disappointed.

“It's a long story, Elise,” Maddie said. “But yes, I'm Madelyn Collier.”

Elise jumped up and ran to hug her. I tried to warn her off, but she ignored me and embraced Maddie anyway. My sister was crying and my mate was starting to cry when Patrick ran into the room to see what the commotion was all about.

“What is going on here?” Patrick demanded.

“Does Lily know?” Elise asked, ignoring her mate.

“Yes, she does. I spent some time catching up with her this week,” Maddie told her.

“But how? When? Where have you been?”

“Enough!” I said, louder than I intended.

Elise sat back and stared at me like I had two heads. Maddie smiled, reassuring me she was okay, but I had promised to protect her from stuff like this and my wolf wasn't backing down. My blood was pumping as my wolf surged forward to protect our mate.

Patrick started laughing. “Bloody hell, look at you. Found your mate, did you?”

Elise looked back and forth between the two of us before bursting out laughing.

"Oh, you lucky dog! What are the odds that your one true mate would turn out to be the only girl you've ever cared about?"

Lily had told her the same. Heck, I'd even confessed as much, but still Maddie looked confused, like she just couldn't believe what she was hearing.

Elise leaned in and sniffed my mate, frowning. "Seriously? Liam, you've been in love with her since you were like eight years old. Why haven't you marked her to start the bond yet?"

Patrick laughed. "That's rich coming from you, love." Then, turning to Maddie, he added. "This one gave me the go-around for months. Of course, she's worth it, but put me through bloody hell first, she did."

Elise rolled her eyes, but the love between them now radiated throughout the room. It began to calm Maddie, and therefore my wolf, too.

"It's complicated, E, and back off. She doesn't like people in her personal space," I said, grabbing my mate by the wrist and pulling her closer to me and away from my sister.

"It's just so natural and you only ever get one true mate, so why are you fighting it?"

Patrick snorted and gawked at her in disbelief. I'd had a front row seat for their mating period and she had no room to judge anyone on such things.

"Elise . . ." Patrick started, but she interrupted him.

"I know what you're thinking, but they've liked each other practically their whole lives. It's not the same as it was for us."

"I told you, it's complicated." I tried again, hoping she'd just shut up already.

"What could possibly be so complicated?"

"Oscar," Maddie said swiftly.

"Oh shit, there's another man? But you're not mated to him, right?"

"No, Oscar's my son."

"You have a son?!?"

Maddie nodded.

It wasn't quite the complication I was thinking of, but seemed like it may be enough to ward off Elise for a while.

"Is his dad still in the picture?" she asked.

"No," I said through gritted teeth, remembering what I knew of Oscar's sperm donor. I could feel my wolf getting more agitated. We hadn't even come over to see Elise. I still needed to talk to Patrick, but at this rate I'd have to go for a run to calm down first.

Maddie must have felt my irritation because she snuggled a little closer and patted, then squeezed, my upper thigh. I think it was meant as comfort but all it did was send blood flowing hard down south. I had to shift uncomfortably in my seat to hide the physical evidence of what her touch was doing to me. Right then I was very grateful my infatuation with skinny jeans was a thing of the past.

"Patrick." I decided it was best to just change the subject. "We actually came to talk to you. Some things came to light in San Francisco that you need to be aware of." I looked at my sister, knowing she wasn't going anywhere, and also knowing that he wouldn't keep anything important from her anyway, but I still had to ask. "Is it safe to talk here?"

"Yeah, sure, but how serious are we talking?"

"Life altering serious," Maddie said, only half joking. What we were about to share with him had certainly altered the path of her life.

He took a deep breath and nodded. "Okay, then, that sounds very serious. Let's head downstairs. Kyle had one of those cool soundproof devices installed there."

We all got up and followed him downstairs. Elise, of course, followed me. It shouldn't have bothered me, but it did, mostly because she had annoyed me by putting Maddie on the spot the way she did. I understood that it was like a ghost had just walked into the room, and that everyone was curious to know where she'd been and why. But it didn't change the way I felt about it, or my insatiable need to protect her. Irrational? Maybe, but then no one ever claimed that a mating male was rational.

The downstairs had been converted into an office, but part of the old den feel from Kelsey had still remained. It was woodsy and soothing, and I'd always liked it here. Kelsey had lived in this cottage for a couple of years, before finally mating to my brother Kyle. She had used the space as her wolf den when not allowing her wolf out to run, for fear her secret would be exposed. At that time, she didn't know that she lived among other shifters. Heck, she didn't even know she was a shifter. It had been a strange situation, but they had all overcome it, and were happier now than ever.

Looking around, I noticed the old couch from upstairs had been brought down, as well as a new big screen—even bigger than the one upstairs—and Patrick's video games, too. I hadn't been over in a while, but had noticed the new furniture upstairs, and wasn't surprised. Patrick had been rocking the coolest bachelor pad ever before Elise moved in, so it was only a matter of time before my control freak of a sister took over. I was thrilled to see it had all been moved downstairs. I made a mental note to set up a boys' night soon with Patrick and my brothers like we used to have.

"So, what's this all about?" Patrick asked, interrupting my thoughts as he motioned for us to sit on the couch.

I looked at Maddie, suddenly unsure of what and how much to tell them. To my surprise she just smiled back at me, took a deep breath, and started from the beginning—the very beginning. To say I was shocked was an understatement. It was difficult for me to sit there and listen to it all again, but I somehow made it through and remained sitting the entire time.

She told them about the gang rape, and getting pregnant with Oscar. She explained her anxiety and depression, and how Annie and Jacob, two humans, had taken them in. I knew the majority of it was more for Elise's sake than Patrick's. He had to hug E close and rub her back a few times to calm her. Mad's story wasn't an easy one to take in.

When she reached the part about me finding her in the midst of an anxiety attack, Elise couldn't take it anymore. She reached over and hugged my mate tightly.

"I'm so glad Liam found you. Everything's going to be better now. I promise!"

"So you've been living in the human world?" Patrick questioned. "Why do I feel like there's a whole lot more to this story?"

"Because there is. That was just the backstory so E would stop peppering her with questions," I said as my sister hauled back and punched me in the arm.

I ignored her and focused on what Patrick needed to know. "So, obviously, I thought I had seen a ghost and I may have stalked her, and then found out who she was with and where they would most likely be in San Francisco. Made arrangements to include a work commitment and left. I found her the next day and I met Annie and Jacob. Nothing seemed off about them, and they genuinely seemed like good people." I skipped through the details of the week; honestly, they didn't matter to pack security. "My cover for getting away with sneaking off was a charity ball hosted by Stephen Daniels." I paused, seeing recognition flicker in his eyes.

"I know the name," he confessed. "I've researched all the Foundation's top supporters. He's clean."

"He's not," I assured him.

"What exactly are we talking here?"

I took a deep breath. This wasn't going to be easy for him to digest. "The Order of the Verndari. Have you ever heard of it before?"

He shook his head no. I hadn't expected he would have. I got up and walked to his desk, taking a piece of paper and a pencil. I sketched a quick replica of the emblem on the rings they all wore and showed it to him.

"Have you ever seen this mark?"

He hesitated before shaking his head yes. I was surprised. Why was he hesitating? He didn't speak, so I continued.

"This is the symbol of the Order of the Verndari. They are a secret society of humans who know all about shifters. They watch us, they supposedly help us, and if the guy who told me all of this at the ball where I was surrounded by dozens of them was telling the truth, then a group within has taken to researching and studying our kind, too. I was warned they are very dangerous."

"Larry isn't one of them. Patrick, you know he isn't," Elise said.

"E, he wears their symbol. I think he is."

"Who's Larry?" I asked.

"Larry, Dave, and Martin are three allies of mine. They are friends. Humans. They give me heads-ups on pack movements. They are the ones that alerted us to the Bulgarian traveling with my brothers during our mating challenge period. Remember?"

I nodded my head. I did. Patrick's asshole of a father actually sent one of Patrick's own brothers to challenge him for Elise during their mating period. It was the most disgusting thing I'd ever heard of. When a small group of immigrants arrived here, there had been a Bulgarian spy among them. Westin was already at war with the Bulgarians. Kelsey, whose given name had previously been Elena, didn't know she was originally from the Bulgarian pack. She's been one badass Pack Mother for us, but the Bulgarians were still hell-bent on finishing what they had started so long ago. It led to a war between the packs. Patrick's father, Alpha of the Irish Clan, had sided with the Bulgarians.

"They also helped me save Elise. They had been monitoring the Bulgarians that kidnapped her last year. That's how we met. I knew they were part of some secret society, and that they have been terrified that their people would find out they broke their law and interacted directly with a shifter. It's apparently part of their greatest code. I didn't know what the faction was called or even how many there are. They refuse to share any details, only information that can help with security for our pack."

"So this guy just approached you at some party and told you all of this?" Elise questioned in disbelief.

"Jacob sent him."

"Jacob? Wait, Maddie's Jacob?" Patrick asked, trying to keep up.

"Yes. Jacob and Annie are part of the Order of the Verndari," I said.

"They never knew about me," Maddie said. "Apparently around that same time there was a pack of out-of-control tiger shifters on the loose stalking young girls, so they assumed that might have been what had happened to me. They even wondered if Oscar was half tiger, but they never suspected I'm a wolf."

"How is that even possible? You lived with these people. They had to have known. You couldn't have just gone all those years without shifting. How did you do it?" E asked skeptically. "'Here, hold my baby. I need to go for a few hours walk in the woods?'"

I glared at my sister.

Maddie shook her head. "I've never shifted, so it's never been an issue."

Elise's skepticism turned to complete shock.

"I told you, it's complicated," I said.

By "complicated," I hadn't meant Oscar. I already loved that kid and as far as I was concerned I'd be the only father he ever knew. I paused for a minute in that thought. Father? I let it hang in the air of recognition. Yes. I already considered him family. My kid. I was a father. The thought gutted and elated me at the same time.

When I had said complicated earlier, though, it wasn't about Oscar, it was about Madelyn. If she truly had no wolf, then how could we possibly complete the bond? Her human teeth wouldn't be sharp enough to pierce my skin in the exchange of blood that came from marking each other and beginning the lifelong bond between mates. I hadn't begun to push the issue because a part of me feared it wasn't physically possible for us. I knew I would still be committed to her and Oscar in the same way for the rest of my life, but I still wanted the full package. Right now, I just didn't see how it was ever going to work like a normal mated pair.

I hadn't even noticed that I wasn't the only one who had fallen quiet, lost in my own thoughts, until Patrick cleared his throat. "So, aside from being aware of the Verndari and now knowing the sign they wear that identifies them, what further knowledge do we have from this?"

"Yeah, we've known about them, maybe not their name, but about them, for the past year."

"And you never thought to tell anyone?" I questioned.

"Kyle and Kelsey are aware. We decided it was best not to alarm everyone unnecessarily. If they are truly just observing, and have for done so for thousands of years, what difference does it really make?"

"Not even the council knows?"

Elise and Patrick both shook their heads as I tried to absorb it all. I wasn't sure how I felt about my siblings keeping such a massive thing to themselves. I could sort of understand, I guess. I mean, I had chosen to come straight to Patrick with the information, instead of alerting every packmate I crossed paths with on my return home.

"The way he spoke, and warned me of danger, I can't help but think there's more than just observation going on. He made it sound like there was a divide among his people: those holding to the old ways and watching and helping—he called them the guardians—and those wanting to research us to better humanity with modern technology."

Elise gasped. "Raina! Patrick, you don't think?"

He shook his head no in reaction, but slowed it to a

questioning shrug.

"What about Raina?" I knew she was Kelsey's Bulgarian aunt, and the only Bulgarian allowed in Westin territory.

Patrick filled us in. "Raina was supposed to arrive in time for Zander's birth. Larry warned us a small group of Bulgarian women arrived in San Francisco and were thought to be heading this way, a few months ago and before his due date. Raina was confirmed to be in the group, but they never arrived."

"Kelsey's been sick with worry. It's been over a year since anyone's heard from Raina. You don't think...?" Elise questioned.

"I don't know, but by the way he spoke, I wouldn't exclude the idea that the Verndari have her."

Maddie

Chapter 16

I couldn't reconcile what Elise and Patrick had said about the Verndari, with the loving parental figures I had lived with for the majority of the last eight years of my life. There was no way that Jacob and Annie could be involved in something like that. Kidnapping shifters? Experimenting on them for research? That's basically what they were talking about. I tried to contain my fury at the insinuation that my loved ones could be involved in something so sinister.

I knew the moment I could get away by myself, I had to call Jacob and Annie. I had to get to the bottom of this and I couldn't believe hearsay. I needed to hear it from them. I needed them to explain to me what was going on. They had admitted to being guardians, Verndari, but they said they could never hurt our kind, so this didn't make sense.

I sat quietly while Liam finished talking with Patrick. Elise had finally stopped asking a million questions, though I could still see them churning inside her. I had been open and honest with them, even confessing what Oscar most likely was. It had been even easier this time. I didn't cry once. I was becoming numb to telling the story and in a way, that felt good. It wasn't controlling me anymore and now I was feeling stronger after each time telling it.

As the conversation moved into small talk, I reminded Liam that we shouldn't leave Oscar for too long. It wasn't right to just drop my kid off on his mom like that, so we said our goodbyes and headed back to the Alpha house. As we pulled up I was suddenly struck by a thought that hadn't yet hit me.

"Um, Liam," I said, biting my lower lip, unable to broach

the subject without completely embarrassing myself. “What's the plan for tonight?” I finally blurted out.

“What?” He looked confused.

“Oscar and I need a place to sleep tonight.” I tried to sound sensible.

Inside I was a bundle of nerves. Did he expect me to stay with him? Did I want to? What kind of impression would that be for Oscar? Where would Oscar sleep? We had always shared a room. I mean, we didn't have to, there were plenty of other bedrooms in the house, but even when he was still in the nursery, I had slept on the floor beneath his crib. From the second I decided he was mine and I was keeping him, I’d always struggled having to be away from him. The guilt from those early days when he first came home and I was terrified and struggling to connect with him, still weighed heavily on me.

“I don't have a place for us yet. I still live at Mom's,” he said apologetically, looking embarrassed. “But there're plenty of rooms there, especially since Kyle and Elise have moved out. Of course, you're welcome to stay in mine,” he said, grinning from ear to ear at the thought and causing me to blush. “But I understand if you're not ready for that yet. Whatever you're comfortable with is fine with me.”

I always knew he was one of the good guys. Not feeling pressured to take things to a level I didn't know if I was ready for meant the world to me. I knew it wasn't because he didn't want me in that way. When we were sitting on the couch upstairs at Elise's and I had touched his leg, he had twisted in his seat, and there was no mistaking how badly he wanted me.

“Hey,” he said before getting out of the car. “Why don't we grab Oscar and go for a drive? I'd like to show you something.”

“Okay,” I said, wondering what he was up to.

He didn't get out of the car as I exited and walked up to the house. I turned to question him but he just smiled and waved me on from the driver’s seat. I knocked on the front door. Lily opened it and laughed.

“Girl, you do not need to knock around here. Mi casa es su casa.”

I followed her inside and back to the living room where Oscar was happily playing with the baby and watching cartoons, something I'd rarely ever let him do. He couldn't have been happier.

"Hey, Mommy," he said with barely a glance.

"Hey, buddy. We're going for a ride around town, want to come?"

"Nah, I'm good."

I stared at him with the mom face, but it only met the back of his head as he went back to playing. Mary walked in just in time to see the exchange.

"Go on, he's fine," she encouraged. "Zander is staying the night and I already made up the twin bed in the nursery because they want to room together. I do hope that's okay?" She asked, but I didn't really feel like it was a question.

"Oscar, come here a minute."

He huffed but obeyed. "You okay sleeping with Zander in the room without me?"

"Mom," he said incredulously. "I'm seven, I'll be okay. Can I stay here, or do I have to go with you?"

I smiled and hugged him, kissing the top of his head. "You can stay. Just do me a favor and stop growing up so fast."

"Never gets any easier with that problem," Mary assured me. "All you can do is hope and pray that they are truly ready to fly when they leave the coop and that they always know they can come back home."

Guilt shot through me. I knew she meant me. I would have to face my parents. I nodded and thanked her again for watching him before heading back outside to find Liam still sitting in the car waiting.

"Where's the kid?" he asked. I knew he knew his name, but he had been affectionately calling him "the kid" or "the boy" since he'd met Oscar.

"We've been ditched," I said sadly.

Liam laughed. "Well, okay. Wanted his opinion too, but guess it'll wait."

He didn't explain further as he backed up and drove off. We were only on the road for about two miles before he veered off on a side road, followed by a couple more turns. The last one ended in the middle of a large field surrounded by woods. He got out of the car and walked around to lean up against the hood. I joined him.

Liam wrapped his arm around me and leaned in close,

practically whispering in my ear and causing the butterflies to take flight in my stomach again. My heart raced from his nearness.

"What do you think?" he asked.

"It's beautiful," I said, and he smiled happily.

"Okay, now you'll have to use your imagination a little," he said, pulling out a piece of paper from his back pocket. He released me long enough to unfold it and pass me a hand drawn sketch of a house. Two stories, a large garage, and a big wraparound porch. Off to the side he had even added a swing set. I didn't need to use my imagination to know it would be an amazing house.

He used his left arm to point out exactly where he thought everything should be. "So," he finally asked. "What do you think?"

"It's gorgeous. Who wouldn't want to live in a place like this? And the lot is so isolated, but only a few miles into town. It's perfect."

"But would you want to live in it? Is it perfect for you and Oscar," he asked and I felt his nervousness for the first time, "and me?"

He looked so hopeful and I finally realized what he was asking.

"You want to build this place? Here? For us?" I said "us" so effortlessly, like it was the most natural thing in the world.

"I don't want us to live with my parents forever. Hell, if I'd known finding my mate would feel like this, I'd have built it a long time ago in preparation of your arrival."

He was still nervous and I saw the vulnerability in his eyes. He was nervous about me. Somehow that thought breathed new life into me. He wanted me and Oscar in his life. We weren't going to be some obligation to him. He was choosing us. Before I could speak, he was talking again.

"I'm not going to pretend to know everything. I don't know how we will ever be able to fully bond without your wolf, but I don't care." He was standing in front of me now, his hands on either side of my face, caressing my cheeks. "Maybe our life won't be normal. Maybe our son will be a tiger." He said "our son" and my heart nearly leapt from my chest. "Those little details don't matter. What I do know with absolutely certainty is that I love you. I want to spend the rest of my life with you and Oscar. I want to help erase all the bad you've faced in your life and fill it with nothing but happiness.

And the rest doesn't matter. We'll figure out the details as we go along."

He paused, staring into my soul, making me feel complete and vulnerable at the same time. "Madelyn, I've loved you my entire life, for as long as I can remember. You are my one true mate. So, I'm asking, will you and Oscar move in with me? Build this house together? Stay with me and share a lifetime here?

He was holding his breath, awaiting my answer as I stared at him in awe. The only boy I'd ever loved was confessing to loving me. There was no way I could pass up on a lifelong dream in the arms of Liam Westin. I nodded as happy tears fell from my eyes.

He relaxed, looking happier than ever. He kissed me, but it wasn't the passionate kisses we had shared earlier; it was a hopeful kiss filled with love. He picked me up and swung me around. We laughed.

"You've just made me the happiest man alive. Now come on, show me where you want your front door. I plan to have them break ground this week. The sooner the better."

We ran around hand in hand, dreamed aloud while we lay in the grass staring at the sky as the sun started to set and planned for a future together. It was arguably the greatest moment of my life. When I started to yawn and my stomach began to rumble loudly, we decided to head back. Realization struck that we hadn't really eaten all day, and I was suddenly famished.

Liam called his mom to check on Oscar without me even asking him to. It was the little things like that that made him truly exceptional. We swung by a place called the Crate for dinner. There were a lot of people there, but few gave me a second glance. We made it through dinner and were waiting on dessert when that started to change.

A tall, dark-haired man with bright-blue eyes approached us. He was strong and handsome, his arms covered in tattoos. I had no doubt many women swooned over this guy, but he didn't hold a candle to Liam, for me.

"Liam," the man said, approaching us and shaking hands with my mate. I held in a giggle, letting it sink in. Yes, he was definitely my mate. All mine.

"Cole. It's good to see you."

"Thought Patrick said you wouldn't be back till tomorrow."

"That was the plan, but plans change." He grinned, reaching across the table and taking my hand. "Cole Anderson, this is Maddie Collier, my mate."

I blushed, unable to believe he'd just broadcasted it so clearly. A quiet fell across the room as people strained their necks to get a look at me.

"Collier? As in Madelyn Collier? The girl who's been missing for . . ." He seemed to struggle for the timeline.

"Eight years," I filled in for him.

Whispers started up throughout the room. It wouldn't get any easier trying to hide from it. I was going to have to put my big girl panties on and own it. I could feel my nerves rebelling as I fought back the panic trying to settle inside me. Liam squeezed my hand, helping to ground me and not let me succumb to the darkness threatening to pull me back under.

I liked Cole Anderson immediately, because the next thing out of his mouth wasn't "Where have you been?" or "What happened to you?" No, he turned his attention off me entirely and back on Liam. Clapping him on the shoulder, he said, "You lucky son of a bitch. She looks like a keeper."

"Says the man who prays every night to never meet his true mate." Liam affectionately joked with him, and I couldn't help but wonder if it were true. He definitely had the love 'em and leave 'em vibe going on with a hint of bad boy, or maybe it was just the tattoos that gave him that wicked appeal.

He shrugged with an effortless ease that just gave him a certain unquestionable "it" factor. "Just 'cause I have no desire to find mine, doesn't mean I can't be happy for you to have found yours."

A young woman approached us. She looked to be in her early thirties, maybe. It was hard to tell for sure. She wouldn't stop staring at me. I gripped Liam's hand tighter.

He looked up and took notice. "Hello, Kara."

"Hi, Liam. I'm sorry, I didn't mean to overhear, but did you really say you're Madelyn Collier?" she asked me.

I nodded slowly. Her hands flew to her mouth in shock.

"I'm Kara. You probably don't remember me, but I was roommates with your sister Lizzy in college."

"Lizzy?" I said softly, as memories of my oldest sister filled me, and I vaguely recalled the girl from trips to visit Lizzy on move-in day and visits. She was eight years older than I was, and studying for her masters when I left home.

"I just spoke with her the other day. She was preparing for your memorial. Have you spoken to her? Does she know you're alive?"

I shook my head. I hadn't called them yet. I knew I would have to, but I hadn't found the courage to face them.

"She'll want to know. You have no idea what your disappearance did to her. To all of them. They will hold the biggest celebration ever when you return home."

"She's not returning home, Kara. Sure, we'll visit her family, when she's ready, but until then, I'd appreciate it if you didn't tell them. Let her do it on her terms," Liam told her.

"Not tell them? Are you serious? Lizzy would kill me if she knew I had information on her sister and didn't tell her."

"It's okay," I interrupted, feeling Liam's anger surfacing. I loved how he was always coming to my defense, and I knew he always would. "I guess I knew this was sort of inevitable. It's why I didn't want to come back with you to begin with," I told him.

"Please," I said, appealing to Kara, "wait to call her until tomorrow. It's something I should do myself. I promise I'll call home tonight."

Liam
Chapter 17

I shouldn't have taken her to the Crate. It was stupid. Of course someone was going to recognize her, and I'd just blurted out her name for all to hear and gossip over. What was I thinking? She had handled herself well, though, and Kara seemed to have backed down.

I knew calling home and facing her past was not going to be easy on her. I decided it would be best if we got back to my parent's house and put Oscar to bed, then borrowed Kyle's office to have some privacy to make the call. I knew I wouldn't leave her side through any of it.

Thinking about it, I shot off a text to Kyle.

LIAM: hey, need to borrow your office this evening. Okay?

KYLE: why?

LIAM: Maddie and I need it for a few minutes.

KYLE: Kels told me about you and MC. So NO!

LIAM: Ass. Why not?

KYLE: Already lost one chair to Elise, not happening again.

LIAM: ???

KYLE: What do you need it for?

LIAM: Calling her parents tonight.

KYLE: Oh.

KYLE: Yeah sure.

KYLE: But no sex in my office

LIAM: Thanks . . . I think.

I put the phone away and it hit me. Gross! I suddenly realized I knew exactly which chair Kyle was referring to. It now sat in the corner of the living room at E's place. I started laughing out loud, causing weird looks my way. Maddie gave me a quizzical look and I shook my head. “Tell you later.”

We quickly finished our dessert, paid the bill, and headed home.

“So what was that all about back there?” she asked, still curious about my outburst.

“I was texting Kyle, asking to borrow his office to call your folks tonight after Oscar goes to bed. He said no.”

“Why?”

“He was worried we wanted to have sex in there. Apparently, E . . .”

She cut me off mid-sentence. “Eww! Don't finish that statement.”

I laughed and she joined in.

“Apparently there was a chair involved that now sits at Elise’s place.”

“The red and brown one in the corner that looks out of place for the décor upstairs?”

“Yup, that's the one.”

“That's terrible,” she said, laughing.

“I did not want to ask how he knew about it!” We both laughed harder, and were still laughing and joking about it when we walked into the house. Dad was in the living room when we arrived. He stopped. Frozen, he stared at Maddie, causing my arm to tighten around her protectively.

“Hello, Mr. Westin,” she said politely.

“Jason,” he said, as if on autopilot. He looked her over much in the same way her own father would before ripping her from my arms in a big embrace. I growled at him. “Simmer down,” he told me. “Madelyn. I can't believe it's really you. Mary told me, but seeing you here, now. You're all grown up. Your parents must be ecstatic.”

“Actually, they don't know she's here yet. We're calling them tonight.”

He looked confused. “You haven't called them? They don't know you're even alive?”

Maddie looked sad at the accusation and I glared at my dad until he backed off some.

“No, sir.” She sighed. “It's a long story. I really don't want to go into again right now.”

"Mommy!" Oscar yelled, running into the room to hug her.

I bit back another growl that was trying to surface, reminding myself it was only the kid. I had to admire the irony. Wasn't it he who had warned me off not that many days ago? I didn't know this crazy protectiveness would continue to worsen.

I closed my eyes and ran a hand through my hair, trying to calm myself and my wolf. *It was just family. No threat,* I tried reminding myself.

Kyle had walked into the room while I was lecturing myself. When I opened my eyes, they met his. I expected to get a wrath of shit from him, but he just gave me an apologetic smile. I knew he understood what I was going through.

Chase was away at college. At least I didn't have to hear it from him.

"Look at you," Kyle said, addressing my mate. "Little MC all grown up. Z-Man hasn't stopped talking about Oscar since I got here. He seems like a great kid. You've done a wonderful job with him."

Maddie beamed with pride and I wanted to thank my brother for his kind words to her. He didn't make a big fuss over her sudden appearance like others had, and I know she appreciated it as much as I did.

"And you," she said. "Alpha. Wow. I mean, we knew one day, but it's just crazy, right?"

Kyle gave a worried look to our dad. We were all still a little concerned about him, but he looked unaffected.

We spent the remainder of the evening playing games and hanging out in the family room. Kyle hadn't stayed long; he had just come to grab his mate for a kid-free night. Zander was staying and Oscar thought it was super cool to have a sleepover with the tyke. Despite the age gap, they seemed to get along and entertain each other well.

I could tell Maddie was extra nervous the closer it got to bedtime. "Are you sure you're okay with this?" she kept asking him.

"Mommy, I'm fine. Are you going to be okay?"

"I'll be fine, buddy."

"Grandma Mary says Liam's room is just across the hall. Could you sleep there tonight, you know, just in case?"

I heard her intake in breath and tried to fight back a smile. I knew I liked that kid.

"Yes. I have a few things to do before bed, but if you need me tonight, I'll be just across the hall."

"Okay, good night, Mommy. Good night Liam."

"Night, Unkie Leem. Night, Aunt Maddie," little Zander said. I could see Madelyn turn to mush. The squirt was going to have her wrapped around his tiny finger any second.

"Come on, Aunt Maddie," I teased. "These boys need sleep to grow big and strong."

"Just like you, right Liam?" Oscar asked excitedly.

"You got that right, kid." I fluffed the hair on his head and told him good night, but he grabbed my hand and pulled me down towards the bed. Before I knew what was happening he had his arms wrapped around me tightly.

"Thank you for taking care of Mommy today so I could play with Zander and Grandma Mary. I had a lot of fun," he whispered to me.

"Anytime, kid." It bothered me that he felt so strongly that Maddie needed to be looked after. She was far stronger than any person I had ever met in my life, yet her own son seemed to find her weak and fragile. "We'll be right across the hall tonight if you need anything."

I quietly closed the door to the nursery and found Maddie staring at the adjacent door, looking more nervous than ever. I wanted her. God knew I wanted her, but I would never push her for more than she was ready to give. I figured that was an issue we'd deal with later. First up was probably an even harder one. It was time to make the phone call I knew she dreaded above all else.

Without a word, I took her hand in mine, gave it an encouraging squeeze, and led her down to Kyle's office. He had left it unlocked for us, so we quickly entered and closed the door behind us. We were completely alone, and for a brief moment I could appreciate why Elise would choose this room to, uh, pick out her new chair. I struggled not to laugh just thinking of it.

"I can't do this, Liam," Maddie said, reaching for the doorknob and ready to bolt.

"Hey, hey, hey, come here," I said, wrapping my arms around her and holding her close to my chest. "I'll be right here. We'll do it together. I know it's hard, but do you really want them to find out through the grapevine? They'd be en route the second they heard."

She shook her head. "No, I'm not ready for that. I can't see them yet."

"I know. I know," I said, kissing the top of her head. "That's why we have to make this call, and you know it."

She nodded, but when I pulled back and really looked at her, she looked terrified.

"Mad, they're going to be thrilled. They've missed you so much." I said, trying to be reassuring.

"Don't you think I know that? Don't you think the guilt of that has eaten me alive every day of the last eight years?"

I hadn't thought about that. I really hadn't considered why she was so purposefully staying away from her family. I knew she had always loved them, and I also knew they still very much loved and missed her.

"I'll be right here with you. You can do this."

Her eyes begged me not to make her and I had an internal battle over what to do. In the end, I knew we had to call them. I put the phone on speaker and dialed the number to the Collier Alpha house.

"Hello?" A woman's voice came across the phone.

Maddie shook her head no and ended the call. Tears filled her eyes and my heart broke watching her. She was trying hard to breathe, but I could feel her headed for a panic attack.

"That was my mom," she said.

"I know, I know. And you can do this, sweetheart. You are so much stronger than you know."

She nodded, but I knew she was borderline hysterical.

"Ready?" I asked, as she shook her head no. I tried to give her an encouraging smile as I dialed the number again.

"Hello?" I heard Cora Collier say again over the phone. "Hello?" she said a little harsher when we didn't immediately respond.

I watched Maddie staring at the phone with tears running down her cheeks. It was clear that she wasn't going to speak right away, which put it back on me. I couldn't completely protect her from this, but I could help as much as she needed.

"Mrs. Collier? This is Liam Westin."

"Liam," she said, clearly surprised. "What can I do for you? Is everything okay with your family? Is your mother okay?"

"Never better, and she is fine, thanks for asking." I pulled Madelyn into my arms as she continued to cry softly.

"I'm surprised to hear from you, especially at this hour. Is there something I can do for you?"

"Actually I need to speak with both you and Zach. Would it be possible for him to come to the phone? Perhaps you could put me on speaker so the both of you can hear," I advised.

I knew Zach Collier well. He was a tall, stoic man, with a quiet, commanding manner. I liked him a lot. Over the last year, since working at the Westin Foundation, I'd had the opportunity to really get to know him. Collier Pack had unanimously agreed to invest in Westin Foundation and we had spent months working closely on the details.

"Hello? Liam?" Zach Collier's deep voice came through the phone, filled with concern.

"Hi, Zach," I said.

"Cora said you needed to speak with the both of us? Is everything okay with your family?"

"Yes, sir, they are all fine."

"And the investment? Did something happen?"

"No, sir. I promise your money is safe with me. This isn't a business call. It's personal."

"What's going on, Liam?" Cora asked.

I looked down to find Maddie staring at the phone, lost inside herself.

"There's really no easy way to tell you both this. I suppose I should start with letting you know, I found my true mate."

"Oh, Liam, that's fantastic!" she gushed. "I know your mother must be so relieved."

"That's great news, son, but you didn't need to call us for that. I would have seen the announcement come out."

"Well, that's a bit complicated still," I laughed.

"Mating always is, but so worth it in the end." Cora said.

I could hear the love in her voice, and knew she was thinking of her own mate, not mine.

"Wait, is she from Collier Pack? Is that what this is about?" Zach questioned.

"Actually, she is, or was. Is," I finally decided.

"Come again?" he asked.

I took a deep breath and let it out. There really was no easy way to say this, so I just blurted it out. "It's Maddie. My one true mate is Maddie. Your daughter and I've found her."

Madelyn's eyes flew to mine, larger than I'd ever seen them. I gave her an uncertain face and shrugged. I didn't know how else to say it. There truly is no way to say, "Hey, remember that daughter of yours that ran away and was presumed dead? Yeah, she's here and she's my mate!"

"Could you repeat that? I'm not sure we heard you right," he said cautiously.

"No, sir, you heard me correctly. I found Madelyn. She's alive and doing very well. I brought her home to San Marco with me. She has a son. You have a grandson. It's our Maddie, Zach."

I could hear Cora crying through the phone. "Maddie?" she wailed. I feared she might become hysterical from the news. "Maddie's there? Zach, we have to pack, we need to go to her."

"No," Maddie said aloud, shaking her head with eyes pleading me to stop them.

The line went quiet. "Madelyn? She's there? She's listening in? Right now?"

"She is," I confirmed.

"Madelyn, we love you so much. I am so sorry. I'm so very sorry. Just come home. Please, come home," her mother begged.

I heard some noise in the background and could make out that Zach was trying to comfort his mate. "Shh, Cora, it's okay."

"Zach, it's Maddie, that was our baby girl. She's there, right now." Speaking directly to Maddie, she spoke a little louder. "Baby, please, talk to us. We need to hear your voice. Are you okay? Please, I just need to know you're okay."

"I'm okay, Mama," Maddie finally said. "I miss you guys."

"Oh, Madelyn, we miss you too. So much, every day. Not a day goes by we don't think of you," her mother assured her.

"I'm okay. I'm okay," she said, as if trying to convince herself as much as them.

"When will you be home?" Zach asked.

"I'm not coming home, Daddy. Not yet at least. This hasn't been easy on me. I'm still trying to adjust to being around wolves again. I'm not ready to come home."

"Then let us come to you!" Her mother was practically begging. "We can be there tomorrow if we drive through the night."

"Mama, please, no. I'm sorry. I just need some time. Please, just know that I'm okay. I'm safe, and I love you."

Maddie turned and walked out the door. I knew her parents could hear the click of the door behind her. I didn't know what to do. Should I run to her, or console her grieving parents?

"Liam? Liam, please?" Zach begged.

"I'm here, Zach."

"Tell me she's okay. I want your word that she's truly okay and no harm will come to her."

I pulled out my phone and texted him a picture of Maddie on the boat ride over to Alcatraz. She was smiling in the sunshine and looked truly happy.

"Oh my God. Thank the heavens, it's her. Look Zach, it's really her!" Cora exclaimed, telling me they received my text. Next I shot off a picture of me and Oscar we had taken on our outing the day Maddie and Lily caught up.

The line went quiet and I knew the questions were about to come.

"That's Oscar. Your grandson," I informed them.

"H-h-how old is he?" her mother stuttered.

"He's seven." I heard the gasps of astonishment.

"Is this why she left? She got pregnant and thought what, that we wouldn't care? That we wouldn't take care of her and our own grandchild?" I could hear the anger and hurt laced in Zach's tone.

"Zach, I promise you it's not what you think." I battled internally on what to tell them, and decided it was best they knew. "The night Maddie disappeared, you know she snuck out of the house and went to a concert and that she was separated from her friend and disappeared, never to be seen or heard from again. What you don't know is that she was assaulted that night, brutally so, and left for dead. You don't need all the gory details to understand what I'm saying. She survived, but in a lot of ways it killed the Madelyn you knew. She's been living with humans under a different name. They took her in when she found out she was pregnant with Oscar."

Her mother was openly crying through the line. It made me

sick to have to share Maddie's story, but it was better this way than for her to have to keep repeating it over and over again.

"She's been through a lot, but she's strong, and beautiful. She's a wonderful mother. I'm telling you, that kid is the best. You'd be really proud of her. And I don't know exactly why she never called to let you know she was okay. She told me once she thought it was best if you all just thought she was dead and moved on. I don't think she realized how impossible that would be for any of us left behind."

"I'll try to get her to come around, but please, she just needs time. Too many people here know who she is now, and I just didn't want you to find out through the grapevine. Of course none of them know the details of what happened to her, but even just hearing she's alive and here, it needed to come from us. She wasn't ready but I pushed her into it. I'm sorry. I don't want to hurt either of you any more than you've been."

Zach's voice was filled with emotions. "There's no other man on this Earth I would want for my daughter's mate, than you. Thank you. Thank you for taking care of her and bringing her back home. Thank you for telling us and"—he had to take a moment before he continued—"thank you for sending the pictures. They mean a lot to Cora and me. We've waited eight years in hopes of hearing anything, anything at all about Madelyn. I can't tell you what it means to know she is safe and with you, and hear her sweet voice even if only for a moment."

"She'll come around. I know she will. She loves you guys, but she's been through a lot, so I really feel like we need to do this on her terms."

"Okay, son. Okay. We're going to trust you on this, but do me a favor and try to get her to at least talk to us." The door opened quietly and Maddie walked back in while he was talking. "We don't care what happened or why she stayed away. We don't ever have to mention it again if that's what she wants. We just want to be a part of her life. A part of Oscar's life, too."

She looked at me with big questioning eyes.

"I'll see what I can do, Zach. And I'll call you in a few days and let you know how she is even if she's not ready yet."

"Thank you," he said.

"Thank you, Liam," Cora added as they hung up the phone.

"Did you tell them?" she whispered.

"Yes. They needed to know and I didn't want you to have to relive it all again with them."

She cried as I held her. "They still want to speak with me? They still want to see me? Are you sure you told them everything?"

"I told them enough, and of course they want to see you. They're your parents, and they love you, Mad."

"And Oscar? They said they wanted him in their lives, too?"

I laughed, wondering how she could be so blind. "Of course they want to know him. He's their grandpup."

"It's all so much. Too much."

"I know. Shh, come on, let's go to bed."

I led her back to my room. Her bags were already waiting inside. I noticed she'd changed into her pajamas while she had been away and I grabbed a pair from the bottom of my drawer and went to the bathroom to change, too. I didn't usually wear pajamas, but figured tonight was probably not the night for her to find that out, and I sent up a quick thanks to my mother who insisted on buying me a pair every Christmas despite knowing I didn't use them.

Maddie

Chapter 18

While Liam went to change in the bathroom, I pulled back the covers on his bed and climbed in. I should have been a nervous wreck. Any other night I would be freaking out at just the thought of spending the night alone in the same room with him, let alone the same bed, but I was numb from the emotional overload.

I wasn't sure how to feel about my parents. I had tried for so long to bury them in my past and not think of them and how they were feeling about my absence. Hearing Mom break down nearly broke me, too. I was grateful Liam had shared stuff with them. Stuff I didn't want them to know and doubted I could ever tell them. Part of me wanted to be angry at him for doing that, because I still felt ashamed and didn't want them to know, but I knew it was for the best.

He walked out of the bathroom with nothing but a pair of PJ bottoms on. I had only truly seen him without a shirt twice, at least as an adult. The first had left me mesmerized and drooling and that had been mostly from across a pool. Now he was about to climb into bed next to me like that. The room suddenly felt very hot and I fought not to toss the covers aside in an attempt to cool down. My mouth was suddenly very dry and my palms sweaty with anticipation.

He walked over to a small mini fridge in the corner. Why did he have a fridge in his room?

As if reading my mind, he chuckled. “Left over from my college days. I've got some cold water in here. Want one?”

“Yes, please,” I said, and even I could hear the husky modulation of my voice.

Liam stilled, like he was trying to compose himself, then reached in and grabbed two water bottles and headed to the other side of the bed. He climbed in and slid under the covers, but remained sitting. He handed me a bottle. The cool liquid helped my dry throat, but it did little to cool me off.

"How are you holding up?" Liam asked, watching me cautiously. I hated thinking he was waiting for me to break. I had my moments still, and I got that he had seen me at some of my lowest points in years, but I had been doing really well and getting stronger before he showed up and turned my life upside down. I sighed knowing it was true, but also in the best ways possible.

"I'm stronger than you think, you know," I told him stubbornly.

He looked confused for a moment. "Sweetheart, I think you are the bravest, strongest woman I've ever known." He said it with such conviction and awe that I knew he was telling the truth. "I know today was a long, hard one, though. I mean, twenty-four hours ago I was walking into a charity ball expecting a boring evening." He laughed. It had truly been a long day. "You faced a lot of demons today and I did pretty much kidnap you and Oscar. You faced both your families today. It's been a lot."

And you told me you loved me, I wanted to add to his recap of the day. All the rest didn't matter because of that. He had said it didn't matter what Oscar was, or that I couldn't shift. He was all in, and looking up at him, I knew it was time he knew I was, too.

I sat up beside him trying to calm my nerves. My hands were a little shaky at first, but when I reached up to caress his face, they calmed instantly. I was amazed at how our bond affected me like that.

I pulled his face down to meet mine, pausing when our foreheads bumped. I stared into his eyes and smiled. He smiled back, then I kissed him. It wasn't the first time we had kissed, but it sure felt like it. Instant need shot through me, a raw primal kind I had never felt before. I had experienced phantom needs before. Everyone thought I would shift early, so I had been taught of the wolf's primal urges at a younger than usual age. It was exactly as they'd described, minus the wolf, so I always thought of them as phantoms, ghosts of what would have been still lingering within me.

I deepened the kiss and gave in to my desires. Here with him,

I felt free. I groaned against his mouth then he maneuvered us to lay side by side, as we explored one another. His hands started to roam and when they found the hem of my nightshirt, he stopped. Pulling back, he stared at me with uninhibited lust clouding his eyes, but he still thought first of me.

"You're sure about this?" he asked in a deep, sexy voice.

I bit my bottom lip and nodded. I was sure. I wanted him. I needed him.

His hands slid up my back, sending shivers through me. His mouth found mine once again. This was my mate. There was no reason to be shy or hold back, so I skimmed my hands over his naked chest, memorizing every inch, every ridge and muscle.

When his hands found my breasts, I moaned against him from exquisite pleasure. He shifted our positions, so I was now lying on my back with him next to me, giving him better access as he stripped off my shirt and tossed it to the floor behind him before resuming his exploration.

I didn't know it could feel like this. My head rolled back and my eyes closed in ecstasy as his mouth left mine to follow the paths his hands had just taken. It was so much, yet I craved more. I wanted him, all of him. My desires surprised me. It was more than I had ever hoped for.

Everything was perfect. I was hot and buzzing with need when his hands moved further south, removing my bottoms and igniting a new kind of frenzy in me. The pressure kept building and I begged him for more. He didn't stop until my head fell back and I screamed out in pleasure.

His mouth covered mine to silence me, as his hands slowed and my body shook, coming down from a high I hadn't known existed. I could tell he was smiling against my lips. I had expected him to pick up the pace, thinking we were just getting started, and I knew I was ready for more, but he pulled back and laughed, kissing my forehead.

I didn't know what was so funny. Had I done something wrong? My cheeks flushed hot and I wanted to crawl under the covers in humiliation.

"I'm sorry," he said, trying not to laugh; "it was really bad timing."

I tried to roll away from him. I needed to cover myself.

"Shit, I guess I blew that moment, didn't I? It's all Kyle's damn fault. Hearing you moan and scream out, knowing it was for me," he said, with desire still evident in his voice, "made me want to go punch every other person in this house who may have heard you, and then I thought . . . Kyle's office!"

I should have been mortified, but I started giggling instead. "No, we can't."

"Oh, yes, I think we can. We are going to need furniture in the new house," he teased, and I started laughing so hard tears sprang to my eyes. In hindsight it might not have been so funny, but we were both so exhausted at that point that it seemed hysterical. By that time we'd been up well over thirty-six hours straight, or at least he had, and me minus the nap I take in the car.

I smiled up at my mate as he lay next to me. "Thank you," I said, suddenly feeling vulnerable and changing the mood between us.

"Sweetie, you don't ever have to thank me for 'that!'"

I blushed and tried to hide my face. I was tired and it had been an emotional day. I didn't want to cry anymore, but it was there just under the surface. I hadn't known for sure I could ever be intimate with a man. Not even my mate, but with Liam, it felt good. So good. I had told him yes when he'd asked me to stay and build a life with him, but until that moment, I wasn't confident in what our life would be like. As I lay there naked for the first time since the night Oscar was conceived, I no longer felt like Jane as a weak shell of the person I'd become, I just felt like me. Madelyn Collier, the real thing, and for the first time in my life, I felt like a woman.

"We probably should try to get some sleep, even if that's the last thing on my mind right now," he growled, nipping at my neck and pressing himself into my thigh, causing me to gasp and my body to heat up.

He pulled back, grinning, "Sleep, I said, you dirty-minded woman."

I laughed at that knowing there were no clean thoughts in my head and watching him roll off the bed. I frowned, realizing that while I lay there naked as the day I was born, he had remained in his pajama bottoms. I vowed to rectify that quickly next time, but also knew that the moment was over, and exhaustion was quickly settling in.

He gathered my pajamas from where he'd thrown them and tossed them at me.

"You want me dressed?"

"Want? Hell no! But I didn't think we should traumatize Oscar quite so soon, should he come in before we wake up."

My heart felt like it was going to explode. Despite everything that had happened between us— and somehow I knew it was just as big a deal to him as it had been to me—he was thinking of my son first. I was overcome with emotion, with love.

By the time I dressed again, he was back in bed and pulling me close to him so that my back aligned perfectly against his body. He threw the covers back over us and contentedly sighed. He kissed the top of my head and squeezed me even closer.

"I'm really happy you're here."

"Me too," I confessed.

"Good night, Maddie. I love you."

"I love you, too," I whispered, as I fell into the most blissful sleep I could ever remember.

Liam

Chapter 19

I groaned as an elbow jabbed me in the chest, then an arm whacked my shoulder. I wasn't ready to get up, but when I was nearly kneed in the balls, I started the slow process of waking up.

"Good morning, Liam," Oscar said, mere inches from my face.

I was so shocked I jumped and nearly fell out of the bed. It took me a moment to realize where I was and what was happening. Maddie was still fast asleep as Oscar attempted to wedge himself between us.

"Shh," I said, putting my finger to my mouth. "We don't want to wake Mommy, okay?"

He nodded.

"Too late," she said in a sexy morning voice. She rolled over to the other side of the bed, freeing up enough space for Oscar to stretch out between us. "Good morning," she said happily as she planted a kiss on his nose. "Did you sleep well?"

"Yup. And I made it the whole way through the night," he said proudly.

She reached for her phone that she had set on my nightstand beside the bed and checked the time. I glanced over Oscar's head and saw that it was nearly ten in the morning. Late enough that I should have been up, but I really just wanted to curl back into bed and sleep some more. I groaned.

"I rarely get to sleep in this late, yet it doesn't feel like it's been long enough."

Maddie readily agreed.

"Maybe you guys should go to bed earlier next time, like me and Zander," Oscar said innocently, causing his mother to blush as she no doubt remembered the night before.

I knew it wasn't something I was going to forget anytime soon. I thought back to how it felt watching her fall apart, laying naked in my arms, and I shuddered. *Shit, think about anything but that!* I didn't need to sprout any more wood than I already had in front of the kid, and I definitely saw a cold shower in my very near future.

“So, what are we going to do today?” Oscar asked, settling in between us. I suspected he wasn't going anywhere anytime soon.

I sat up, propping my pillow behind my back. Oscar leaned into my side, making himself right at home. I hadn't been around a lot of kids. I mean, I liked them and they seemed to like me, it's just that Zander was the first grandkid in the family and Chase was only a few years younger than me. None of my friends had kids, especially not actual kids—maybe a baby, or a toddler even, but definitely no seven-year-olds. I wasn't entirely sure what was going on. It felt a little awkward having him squished there between us, and yet a part of me really liked it, too.

My family. This was my family. They were a package deal. I'd known it all along, yet something about the intimate moment with the three of us crammed into my bed made it seem suddenly real. I was going to be the only father figure this kid ever had. I really hoped I didn't screw it up, or screw him up.

“Grandpa Jason says I can watch the shifters change at the pack run tomorrow. I'll bet it's so cool. I can't wait!” he said excitedly.

“Um, maybe we should start off a little smaller for your first time,” Maddie told him.

“But Mom, please! I want to see the wolves,” he begged.

“Tell you what,” I said. “If it's okay with Mommy, we'll head out to the house site and I'll change for you. You can see what happens and we can answer any questions you have.”

“I think that's a very good idea,” Maddie approved.

“Okay, that's awesome! Thanks, Liam,” he said, turning around and hugging me. “Where's the house site?”

“Just a few miles away. You can pick out where you want your swing set to go while we're there.”

His eyes got huge as he looked back and forth between us before standing up and jumping excitedly on my bed. “You mean it's going to be our house? We're going to live there?"

"Well, it's not built yet, but it will be," I told him, seeing no reason to keep it a secret from him, though I glanced towards Maddie just to make sure I hadn't overstepped some invisible maternal boundary again. I was relieved to see her smiling and happy.

"But I mean, we're going to live there? All three of us? You, me, and Mommy?"

"Yeah, of course, that's what I mean," I said.

He stopped and his mouth opened. "You mean you and Mommy are getting married and we're going to be a family?!"

Married? What was he talking about? Shifters didn't care about things like that. Marriage was just a legal bond for tax purposes. Mating was far stronger than the so-called bonds of marriage.

"Why would we get married?" I asked him. It didn't make any sense to me.

"You don't want to marry Mommy?"

"I don't really see the point," I told him, noticing a second too late that Maddie was trying to shut me up, and I had clearly said something wrong.

Oscar looked at me with big tears in his eyes. "I thought you said we were going to live together. I thought you were going to marry Mommy and be my daddy and we'd be a real family."

He jumped up and ran from the room as Maddie moved to follow.

"Hold up," I said as she was reaching for the door to go after him. "What the hell just happened?" I honestly had no idea why the kid was upset. And what was that nonsense about being a real family. We were already a real family, or at least well on our way in that direction.

"Liam," she started, biting her lower lip as she gathered her thoughts. "I understand what you were saying. I do, but you have to understand where he's coming from. He doesn't know the ways of the shifters. He's only ever lived in the human world, where people fall in love, and get married and start a family and live happily ever after. Marriage to him is the commitment of family. He doesn't know anything about bonding. So, you pretty much just told him that you want to live with us, but not commit to us."

"Maddie, that's bullshit, you know that. I'm already committed to you. Both of you."

She walked over and wrapped her arms around me and planted a kiss on my bare chest. "I know that, but he doesn't. We just uprooted him from the only family and the only home he's ever known. It's not going to be easy on him. He has this image in his mind based on what he does know, and you kind of just shattered it."

I sighed and stared at the ceiling. If this was parenting, I really sucked at it.

"I need to go talk to him," she told me and I just nodded silently, wondering how I was going to fix this, while hoping Maddie was just able to clear it up and explain to him that as a mated pair we were already a family. Once we completed the bond, then that was it. There was no divorce in the shifter community. We mated for life, stronger than any marriage the humans could even fathom.

I wasn't entirely sure what had just happened. One minute life seemed pretty damn perfect. The next, I'm being blindsided by a now-upset kid. Marriage? It wasn't something I had ever even thought of. Shifters didn't marry. I didn't even see the point. I got what Maddie said, but Oscar was just going to have to learn our ways, and I knew he would in time.

I tried to shake it off, and went to the bathroom to take a much needed shower. Patrick was coming over this afternoon so we could update Kyle and Cole Anderson on the Verndari. I could already tell it was going to be another long day.

To my surprise, the morning went by faster than I expected. When I'd gotten downstairs to breakfast, Mom and Lily had informed me Maddie had taken my car and gone out with Oscar. I knew they'd been through a lot and needed some time together, and clearly they needed to talk about this morning.

"You're okay with that?" Lily had asked me hesitantly.

I was a wolf, and wolves tended to be territorial. I didn't like people messing with my stuff, and if it had been anyone but Maddie, I would have freaked out over someone taking my vehicle. Somehow, it really didn't bother me. She was my mate, so what was mine was hers. It surprised me too, but that's how I felt. Simple as that.

By lunchtime they still hadn't returned, but Kyle and Patrick showed up with Cole in tow, so we took the sandwiches Mom had fixed and headed for Kyle's office.

"How are you holding up?" Kyle asked. I wasn't sure what he meant and must have looked confused because he continued. "Kels told me about MC. That can't be easy on you."

"Not sure what you mean," I said honestly.

"Elise and Lily filled her in on the details. He knows everything," Patrick said.

My mind was all over the place. "What are you talking about?"

"Everything that happened to her? A kid? Your lifelong crush back from the dead? Dude, it's a lot to take in. I just wanted to make sure you were okay."

"I've got my mate. We have a great kid. I couldn't be better."

"Then why do you look a million miles away?" Kyle challenged.

"Oh, it's nothing," I sighed, still fixated on what Oscar had said that morning. "Really, I'm fine. The kid said something this morning that I can't stop thinking about, is all."

"Well, come on," Cole said. "We can tell by your face that we aren't going to get anywhere today until you spill it, so just get it over with already. No offense, but I really don't want to spend any more of my day off than absolutely necessary with you mutts."

I let out a deep breath. "Fine, it's nothing really. He was just asking if I was going to marry his mom and then got upset when I said no, that shifters didn't marry. I didn't mean to upset him and Maddie explained how he only really knows the human world and will take some time to adjust and learn our ways. I still feel like crap over it. So what do you think? Should I ask Maddie to marry me?"

Kyle looked at me like I had two heads. "He'll come around. Seriously, that's what you're worried about?"

"Yeah, I don't really see the point," Patrick said. "You'll be mated soon, I assume, and then it doesn't really matter either way."

"You're all a bunch of idiots. Don't listen to them, Liam. If it means that much to the kid, just do it. What's it going to hurt? Keep the kid happy, keep his mom happy. Geez, you two are mated, that much you should know by now," Cole added for Kyle and Patrick's benefit.

"Okay, I see his point," Kyle conceded.

"I wouldn't even know where to start," I admitted.

"A ring. Down on one knee. Say 'I do' and then it's done. Humans do it all the time, many multiple times. How hard can it really be?" Cole asked.

"But then what? I don't know the first thing about human marriages, or weddings. Where do you go to make it legal? Do we have anyone here that can even do that?" I asked.

Cole shrugged. "You can get a license online, it's easy."

"Mr. Anderson, sounds like you just volunteered," Kyle teased.

"Fine, if that's what it takes to get out of here quicker, then I will get certified to officially marry the two of you. Crisis over. Now, please tell me that wasn't what you dragged me over here for on a Monday afternoon. You know it's the only day I close the shop."

Patrick glanced my way and the mood in the room instantly changed.

"What's happened, and why do I have a bad feeling about this?" Kyle asked.

I started to talk, but Patrick cut me off. "Kyle, you remember my friends. My *'out of town friends,'* " he said cryptically.

"Yeah, what about them?"

"How much have you filled Cole in on them?"

"Shit, that's been a total need-to-know. I haven't told anyone about your, uh, *friends*." Kyle said.

"Well, you might want to fill Cole in quickly, before I start then," I told him.

Kyle's curious eyes scanned me. "You know about Patrick's, uh, *friends*?"

I nodded.

"Okay, so I'm the only one here who doesn't know about his *friends*, so please, just clue me in already," Cole said, getting frustrated.

Half an hour later he was shaking his head. "I get why you kept this to yourselves, but as Beta, don't you think I should have been included in that 'need to know?' "

"At the time, no. Honestly, I'm not real sure where Liam fits into any of this or why we're even telling you now, so maybe it's time you brought me up to speed too. What do Patrick's human friends have to do with you, Liam?" Kyle asked.

"Too much of a coincidence for it to be different groups, and he's confirmed they wear the same symbol. We just found out that the people Maddie was living with are part of a secret society called the Verndari, an ancient faction, fully aware of the shifter presence and monitoring all activity. Monitor and assist if trouble arose, at least that was supposed to be but, but they're dividing and changing."

I went on and told them everything I knew and even what I suspected. We pieced together they likely had Kelsey's aunt, Raina, and that did not sit well with my Alpha brother at all.

"What do we do about them?" Kyle asked.

"Nothing," Cole said. He took a piece of paper and pencil from Kyle's desk and drew the symbol I immediately recognized. "Is this the symbol you saw?" I nodded. "I do appreciate you guys laying your cards on the table. I hope in the future we can maintain more open communication. Maybe not with you, Liam, but Kyle and Patrick, I do expect to be kept in the loop of things like that. If you can't trust me, then perhaps I'm not the Beta you need."

"I trust you entirely, Cole. This was just a matter of keeping as tight a lid as possible. I admit, I was wrong not to include you."

"Damn straight. If you had you'd know, I've got my own connection to the Verndari. Didn't know their name, but there's a couple regular human tourists that like to come up for fresh tats. And wouldn't you know, they bear that same mark on them. I've even done a few new recruits of theirs."

I looked closely at the emblem. "It's a little off," I said. "This line shouldn't be here."

"Not on the original. I know because I've added it to a few recently. Guy by the name of Jackson brings up people from time to time. I know he knows about our kind. He hasn't come right out and told me, but he's hinted loud and clear. Been trying to determine if I'm a shifter or a potential recruit. I'd say what you're seeing with that line is a coup within this group."

Patrick piped in. "That makes sense, Liam. You told me the guy said there were some who were moving things in a different direction. Researching on our kind and stuff."

"To better humanity," I whispered. It was bad. It was very bad. "These people have been in our territory, they're watching us.

They are taking our kind and doing who knows what with them. We have to stop it."

"We need someone on the inside, eyes and ears that will work with us and keep us informed," Kyle said smartly.

"Martin's supposed to get back to me on his findings on Raina. I can ask, but he won't be happy that I know about any of this. They are very secretive," Patrick said.

"Jacob and Annie. They sent the man to warn me. They love Maddie and Oscar as their own flesh and blood. They'll help us."

It was decided that I would try to reach out and get answers from the Winthrops. We took some time to write out a list of questions we wanted answers for. Now all I had to do was convince Maddie this was the right thing to do, even knowing she never wanted to speak to them again.

Maddie

Chapter 20

Oscar was upset and frustrated when we left the Alpha house (I found it funny they still called it that despite the Alpha no longer living there). His questions regarding marriage had really seemed to freak Liam out, and the more I thought about it, the more it did me, too.

"Oscar, how about some ice cream?" I asked, driving down Main Street, knowing my son would never turn down ice cream.

"Yes! Mint chocolate chip!" he said, perking up for the first time since he'd stomped out of the bedroom.

I parked in front of the Cold Shack and we went in and placed our order. Two cones to go. By the time we got them, I could feel the eyes watching us and I needed to be able to talk and answer his questions without so many ears around, listening in.

"Come on, let's go for a drive while we eat," I said, putting on a brave smile.

I didn't know my way around Westin territory, so I headed to the only place I truly knew, the property Liam wanted to build us a house on. I stopped the car in the empty field. There was a creek running along the back of the property and we got out and went to explore it.

"It's really pretty here, Mommy," Oscar observed.

"Do you like it?" I asked, and he nodded. "Would you like to live here?"

He looked around very seriously, taking in all the sights. He looked up into the trees and frowned. "Where would we sleep?"

I laughed. "Well the house isn't built yet, silly."

"This is the place Liam was talking about?"

"Yes it is. What do you think?"

"I really love it, but don't tell him that, okay?"

"Don't tell him? Why?"

"'Cause it's not right, Mommy. You deserve better."

"Better than Liam Westin?" I snorted, unable to imagine such a man existed.

"He doesn't even want to marry you. He doesn't want us."

I hugged my son tightly. "Buddy, there're a lot of things I should have told you before now. How about we walk around and talk?"

We walked and we talked for hours. He had so many questions and the reality hit me that my son wasn't a little boy anymore. He was brave and smart and intuitive. We talked about things that had never before been mentioned. He wanted to know about his father. He said spending time with Liam made him wonder where his father was and why he wasn't around. I couldn't answer that for him, but I was honest enough that he stopped asking, and I didn't think he would again.

He wanted to know about growing up around the wolves and my family, and I told him everything I could think of. We laughed, we lay in the grass and pointed out crazy shapes in the clouds, and we splashed around in the creek when it got too hot.

I wasn't even sure how long we were out there, but I did know the moment Liam showed up. I could smell that he was in his fur and I knew he was watching us. I chose to ignore it and continue my time alone with Oscar.

"Do you think Liam is mad at me?"

"No, baby, I don't."

"Do you think he'll still show me his wolf?"

I smiled and kissed his forehead before pointing out the beautiful white wolf just inside the tree line watching us. "Why don't you ask him yourself?"

Liam, clearly listening in, walked slowly towards us.

"Liam?" Oscar whispered, in total awe as the large wolf nodded his furry head. He was so beautiful. "Can I pet you?" he asked.

I could see the revolt in the wolf's eyes, but he snorted and lowered himself to the ground, signaling it was okay. Oscar approached slowly, much like he would have a wild animal, but once he touched him, it was like he'd just found a stray dog and made a new best friend.

"You're so soft," he said. "Mommy, come feel how soft Liam is."

I sat down on the ground in front of him and he laid his big head in my lap. I cautiously stroked his fur and Oscar was right, it was the softest thing I'd ever felt. Petting shifters wasn't exactly the norm. Being treated like a dog was the utmost in disrespect, but he seemed content and didn't mind Oscar petting and hugging on him, either.

Oscar jumped up and started to run away. "Come here, boy," he said, clapping his hands together.

Before I could correct him, Liam jumped up and licked the side of my face, before shifting. It was the first time I'd seen my mate fully naked and I couldn't stop staring, until the sound of disgust came from my seven-year-old. I blushed, knowing that the thoughts I was having seeing him standing there were definitely not appropriate for kid company.

"Eww, you're naked!"

Liam just laughed and ran after him, picking him up and risking traumatizing my kid for life.

"You treated me like I dog. Not cool, kid," he said, tickling him all over.

"You need to put some clothes on, Mommy's staring at you," Oscar whispered.

Liam looked back and grinned. I could tell in his eyes he knew I liked what I saw and it pleased him greatly. "Mommy will get over it, I promise."

"But why are you naked?"

Liam laughed easily. "Well, let's see. Have you ever seen the Hulk?"

"Of course."

"And what happens to the Hulk's clothes when he turns all big and green?"

"They tear!" Oscar said excitedly, sharing the answer.

"That's right! So what do you think would happen if I'd left my clothes on before I shifted to my wolf?"

"Oh," he said seriously. "I hadn't thought about that. Wait, does that mean everyone at the pack run tonight will be naked?" He looked enormously disgusted.

"Afraid so, kid. Don't worry, you get used to it. Nudity really isn't something we think about much around here, though we do try to be civil and remember to wear clothes in public."

"Can you shift back so I can watch how it's done?"

"Sure, but then I have to get home. And I suggest the two of you do, too. I don't know about you, but I'm really hungry," Liam told him.

Oscar shrugged. "We had ice cream."

"What? Without me?" He feigned shock, but Oscar just happily nodded.

"Mint chocolate chip!"

"No way, that's my favorite." Liam pouted. "Hey, about this morning. You know I didn't mean to hurt you, right?"

"I know," Oscar said. "Mommy and I talked about it."

"She's a really good mommy, huh?"

Oscar looked at me and smiled. "The best!"

"Can I tell you a little secret?" Oscar nodded. "I don't really think of things like marriage, but I do get why something like that seems really important to you, but we don't need that to be a family. As far as I'm concerned, we already are. You get me? I love your mom, and I love you. You guys are my family now. Just the three of us. Is that okay with you?" He put his fist out and waited for Oscar to pound it.

Oscar looked at me then shook his head and rolled his eyes at Liam. "I got you," he said, giving him a fist bump, "but you really have to stop making Mommy cry."

Liam turned around quickly as I tried to wipe the happy tears from my cheek. He smiled and it made my heart melt. "I think it's okay this time," he whispered to Oscar.

Picking up my son, he walked to me and pulled me to my feet so the three of us embraced in the middle of the field that would someday be our home. He hugged Oscar a little closer, and leaned down and kissed me to the giggles of my son.

Oscar no longer seemed to even notice Liam was still naked as the day he was born, but my body was buzzing and fully aware of my mate. Before things got really awkward, I broke away. Liam gave me a devious half smile and I swore he could hear my thoughts just then. It made me blush all over. He passed Oscar off to me and told us he'd meet us back at the house.

Next thing I knew, there before us stood a beautiful white wolf.

“That was so cool!” Oscar yelled as Liam's wolf winked and took off back to the woods. “Come on, Mommy—let's see if we can beat him home.”

We jumped into the car and drove back to Mary and Jason's house. Much to my disappointment, Liam was walking around the corner of the house, pulling on his shirt as we pulled up.

“Wow, you're fast. I'm going to go wash up for dinner. I could eat a whole cow. I'm starving!” Oscar announced.

“I heard that, and you better be,” Mary called from inside the house.

“We're eating at the pack house tonight before the run. It's always a huge feast. Mom's really excited you're here, and can't wait to show you off,” Liam informed me.

“I'm happy to be here too,” I told him honestly. I wrapped my arms around his neck and pulled him down to kiss me. He didn't hesitate. After last night, I was feeling stronger, bolder, braver, especially where he was concerned.

It was far too short for what I wanted, but when a throat cleared behind me, I knew the moment was gone too soon. Breaking away, I turned to find Lily watching us.

“You two are disgustingly cute, but at least you're not fighting it anymore. And yet,” she sniffed, and examined my neck. “still nothing! Jesus, people, why is this mating thing so difficult for this family?” She threw her hands up in the air and stomped off.

“I cannot wait until the day she meets her mate and we all get to remind her just how easy it really is.” Liam said evilly.

When Oscar came back out, freshly washed, he grinned and told us that the Westins had just headed over for the pack dinner. He was very excited and a little anxious about meeting the pack.

“There's a whole lot of people excited to meet you two,” Liam told us, looking at me with concern. “Are you ready?”

Oscar nodded excitedly, while butterflies swarmed my stomach with nerves. I smiled. I needed to be strong, and next to Liam I did feel strong. I could do this.

He put his arm around me and took Oscar's hand as he led us to his pack. The image of the three of us walking together as one family made me happier than I ever remembered feeling.

Collier Pack always had pack meals together before a big run, too. We only ran together four times a year though: summer and winter solstice, fall harvest, and a spring run. I was surprised to learn that Westin Pack held monthly pack runs.

As we entered the pack house I was taken aback by how big it was. There were shifters everywhere, hundreds of them. I had never seen so many in one place before. My anxiety was starting to kick in. Liam must have felt it, because he gave me a squeeze of encouragement.

As we walked to the line serving food, people stared and whispered.

"Ignore them. They're just curious," Liam whispered in my ear, even knowing they all heard him loudly and clearly. His arm didn't leave my waist until he was given his tray and had no choice, but he walked in front, clearing the way for me and Oscar to follow. It was the small gestures like that that put me at ease.

We hadn't really discussed tonight. I tried not to think about it, knowing my panic would just set in. This was a pack run. I would be expected to run alongside Liam, but I couldn't. The sheer pain that caused inside me was almost unbearable. What kind of mate could I possibly be for him with no wolf?

My eyes were starting to well up with tears and darkness settled into my peripheral vision. *Not here. Not now*, I swore under my breath, trying to regain control of myself.

Lily dropped her tray on the table next to me and sat down. She had startled me, helping to grasp on to something other than the panic I was feeling. Did she know? Had I even told her I couldn't shift? My best friend, and I couldn't share something so deep and personal. How was I going to tell an entire pack?

I steadied my breathing, using some of the coping mechanisms Annie and I had practiced. Liam leaned in and kissed my temple. I smiled back at him and heard the increased murmurs around us. He was publicly staking his claim on me.

Then I smelled it. I smelled him. Wolves, but especially male wolves, carried a unique scent that warned others off. We used it when feeling threatened, or occasionally mating males would use it to mark their females and caution other males from getting too close. We lived in a civilized society now, so it was rarely used for this purpose. Liam and I hadn't started the bond yet, but he was making it clear to everyone present that it was his intention to do so.

My eyes widened and I knew my cheeks were beginning to turn pink. I looked at him and he just grinned back at me proudly and shrugged.

"Really?" Lily asked, crinkling her nose to the smell. "Is that necessary?"

"Yup," he said, unable to wipe the grin from his face.

Despite Liam's not so subtle warning, several—mostly mated—couples came by to introduce themselves. It wasn't so bad. I really liked everyone I met and they helped put my anxiety at rest.

Halfway through eating dinner my arms started to itch. I scratched before noticing the hives beginning to pop up. *Oh no, not again*, I thought, quickly trying to make a mental note of everything I had eaten that day.

"Mommy, are you okay?" Oscar asked.

"I'll be alright. Looks like my allergies are kicking in again," I told him.

"Allergies?" Lily asked. I knew it was rare for shifters, but ever since Oscar was born I'd had issues with them. Unfortunately, shifters were highly susceptible to human medicines. Our bodies required more of them due to our higher metabolisms, but we were also more sensitive to them. I knew what Benadryl did to me. It would be lights out quickly.

"Food allergies," I said. "Though they haven't been able to determine exactly what yet."

"Do you want me to get your medicine, Mommy?" my sweet son asked.

"It's okay. I'm done anyway and will just have to call it an early night. I'm sorry, bud."

He nodded sadly, got up and returned our plates. When he came back I stood and said good night to Lily. Liam, as I knew he would, got up and followed us out.

"There're going to be plenty of other kids hanging out tonight. Oscar can stay with them. I promise, he'll be fine," Liam offered.

I didn't know how I felt about that. I wasn't used to other people watching my son. I didn't know them, though I knew that was irrational. We were in pack territory and Liam was a Westin. No harm would come to Oscar under his protection. Shifters took care of their own, and by association we were now part of that.

"Jessica," Liam called, waving over a woman who looked to be in her early thirties and very pregnant.

"Hey, Liam. How are you?" she said, looking a little confused, and I got the feeling they weren't exactly friends.

"I'm good. Really good," he said, smiling down at me. "This is my mate, Maddie, and this is our son, Oscar."

My heart did a little twirl in my chest when he said "our son." I realized he wasn't just marking me tonight, but Oscar, too. It was so much more than I could have ever hoped for.

She didn't falter once at his insinuation. "Hi, I'm Jessica Moore. It's really nice to meet you," she said, offering me her hand, which I took and shook. "Hi, Oscar. It's nice to meet you, too," she added.

"Hello, Mrs. Moore. It's very nice to meet you."

"How old are you, Oscar?" she asked, making the hair on my arms stand up. I had faced plenty of judgment over the last seven years. Being a teenage mom bore scars of its own. I was prepared to face whatever negative comment that was about to come our way.

"I'm seven," he said proudly.

I held my breath, waiting for the shock and "Wow, you must have been very young when you had him," or, "Is this your mom or your sister?" or just the glare that so many women sent my way, being a twenty-four-year-old mother of a seven-year-old. It was like you could see them calculating the years in their heads.

But there was none of that from Jessica Moore. She just smiled back and said, "I thought so. My son Bobby is just your age. Would you like to meet him? He's going to be so excited to have a new pup in town."

Tears pricked my eyes as he glanced up at me and I nodded encouragingly for him to go on. It gave me hope that he would be accepted into the pack, that I would be accepted.

She made quick introductions and the boys appeared to hit it off immediately. It reminded me of the day I had first met Lily Westin and we became instant best friends.

Jessica returned while I watched them. "I think they're going to be fast friends," she said, sounding pleased. "I'm obviously not going to be running tonight, and will keep an eye out on them.

There're a few other kids that will be joining them tonight. We're having a sleepover at my place. They want to watch the shift and start of the run, then play for a little while before I round them up for popcorn and movies at home. Oscar is welcome to join us."

I glanced at Liam, who smiled and nodded encouragingly at me. My skin was still crawling with hives and the itching was getting worse. I knew I would be dead to the world soon, and Oscar would have nothing to do otherwise, so I let go of my fears and I said yes.

"That would be great. Thank you so much."

"Anytime. It was really nice to meet you. Maybe we could have coffee or something soon."

"I would love that," I said honestly. I sensed no judgment from her and the hope of maybe having a friend, someone with a son Oscar's age that I could discuss things with and who would actually understand, made me excited for a future here.

We said goodbye to Jessica and left Oscar in her care. Liam walked me back to the house and waited until I was dressed and in bed for the night. He wasn't pleased with the human meds I pulled out in search of the Benadryl. I could tell from the look on his face how they disgusted him, but he didn't really know what I'd been through and how they'd helped. I swallowed four Benadryl, knowing the exact amount I needed to get rid of the hives without spending the next day sleeping them off.

"I'll be asleep soon. I'm sorry," I said, yawning, as I could feel them already starting to kick in.

"I won't be out all night, but I am expected to at least make an appearance."

"Will they be upset that I'm not there?"

"Don't you worry about that," he said, kissing my forehead, then my nose, before finding my mouth. The effects of the meds combined with the potent need for my mate filled me with pure desire. It was the most passionate kiss we'd ever shared and I moaned into his mouth, trying to deepen it.

He pulled back, breathless, and I could see the raw need in his eyes that mirrored my own feelings. A blaring sound signaling the start of the run broke the moment. Liam was hesitant even then to leave, and I knew it wasn't out of worry for me, but pure desire.

He groaned in frustration. "I have to make a quick

appearance. I'll be right back."

I sighed in frustration, knowing I wouldn't stay awake that long. "The meds," I reminded him. "I'll be asleep before you return. So go, run. I'll be fine."

I didn't want him to leave, though. I didn't want the medicine to pull me into darkness. I wanted my mate. He kissed me again, unwilling to leave just yet. His hands never left my back as they caressed the bare skin exposed at the bottom of my shirt, but just that simple touch and his taste brought me pleasure. I had been warned at an early age of the sexual frenzy that would come from taking a mate, but I had not been prepared for what that would feel like.

He pulled back and looked into my eyes. The world was starting to turn to a haze around us and I struggled to stay awake. He gave me one more quick kiss and whispered, "Good night, sweet Maddie," before I faded off into darkness.

Liam

Chapter 21

Maddie looked so peaceful and so vulnerable as she drifted off to sleep. I knew I had to make an appearance at the run. Enough questions would come my way over why she wasn't there, but if I missed, too, Kyle would not be happy.

While there were a lot of perks to being a Westin, there was also a high demand of requirements. Missing pack events was not acceptable. My dad always said, to maintain control of a pack this size, the family had to always lead by example, not just the Alpha, but the entire Westin family. It was a lot to bear, but none of us had ever really complained about it either. It was who we were. Simple as that.

I knew I wouldn't stay away from her too long. The drugs she had taken made her exceptionally vulnerable and my wolf was struggling against me to leave at all.

When the second horn blew, I knew what I had to do. I quickly changed into an old pair of sweats. Walking out of that room was one of the hardest things I'd ever done, but it was my duty as a Westin, so I did.

My family was waiting at the front behind Kyle as he spoke and I casually slipped in behind them. I made my appearance. Most of the pack was already naked and waiting for the call to shift. I looked around to find Oscar, who didn't seemed fazed by it at all. I was glad I'd taken the time show him what it was going to be like.

Before meeting Oscar, I had never really given much thought to fatherhood. Now, I couldn't stop thinking about it. The impact of potentially screwing it all up weighed heavily on me. I listened in to the other boys.

"You're staying at the Westin house?" "Do you know Kyle?"

"How does your mom know Liam?" "Is she going to mate him?" "Is he going to be your dad?" "I don't believe it."

The other boys were grilling my kid and it didn't sit too well with me. When Kyle called the run, I stopped him before he took off.

"Do me a favor. Say hi to Oscar before you take off."

"Kids giving him a hard time?" he asked.

"He is the new kid and we are the Westins."

"Tough position to be thrown into. I got you," he assured me.

"Thanks, bro."

Kyle walked over to where the boys were standing and they all silenced and stared up at him in shock and awe.

"Hey, Oscar, thanks for taking care of Z for me."

"Anytime, Kyle," he said proudly.

"M-M-Mr. Westin, h-h-have a good run," Jessica's kid stuttered out.

"It's Bobby, right?" Kyle asked, and the poor kid just stared up in shock, nodding his head slowly. "I'm glad to see Oscar's making friends already. You boys stay out of trouble and have fun tonight."

"We will, thanks, Kyle," Oscar said.

Kyle mussed the kid's hair before taking off to join Kelsey and start their run.

"Whoa, you really do know Kyle?" one of the other boys asked.

"Hey Oscar," I said, not even giving the kids time to recover. "You okay for tonight?"

I could see worry in his eyes. "I'm a little worried about Mommy," he said quietly.

"I know kid, me too, but she is already sound asleep. I won't be out long."

"So you'll keep an eye on her?"

"You know I will. And if you want to come home early, just call me, and I'll come get you, okay?" He nodded, gratitude written all over his face.

I pulled him aside and whispered, even knowing the other boys were listening in to every word. I said, "Don't let the other kids give you too hard of a time. You may be the new kid, but remember, you're a Westin now." He nodded like he even understood a little about what that meant. "Now," I said louder for all the boys, "you were asking why we don't wear clothes when we shift. Ready to see for yourself?"

Oscar grinned excitedly. "You're going Hulk?"

"I'm going Hulk. You ready?"

"Yes!" he exclaimed.

I clapped my hands dramatically, then shifted right on the spot. My old sweats went flying in every direction, shredded, as I knew they would.

"Cool!" Oscar yelled as the other boys agreed and cheered. "Thanks, Liam," he said, giving my head a little pat. I nodded and headed off into the woods.

Normally my wolf and I were at peace on a run, but both of us were too worried about Maddie to enjoy it. I only lasted an hour before I headed back. I shifted at the back door of the house and headed straight for my bedroom. Oscar was gone for the night, so I didn't even bother putting on clothes, though I did lock the door, just in case, before climbing into bed next to Maddie.

She moved slightly, and then rolled into me like she was seeking my warmth. A peace washed over me as I wrapped my arms around her and pulled her closer to me. I didn't fall asleep right away, but as the other wolves headed for home, or moved deeper into the forest, my wolf finally relaxed and I drifted off into a contented sleep.

Having forgotten to turn off my alarm, it sounded much too early. I reached over and hit it until it silenced. Too late, though; Maddie was already stirring. As she stretched up against me, my body responded quickly.

I knew she wasn't fully coherent yet even as her hand glided gently across my abs before heading lower and exploring my body.

"Mmmm," she moaned, the sexiest sound I'd ever heard as she wrapped her hand around me.

I couldn't take it any longer. My mouth sought out hers as my hands cupped her breasts. I gently removed her clothes before her eyes even opened. I expected to see a startled look, knowing she was still in that in-between of dreaming and reality, but she smiled like she knew exactly what she was doing to me and I was lost in her.

As she continued to explore my body, I began worshiping hers. No part was left unattended until we were panting with the need for release. "Mine," I growled as I positioned myself over her.

As I started to let my weight sink onto her, I immediately felt something change between us.

I looked down to meet large eyes filled with fear. It was like a knife slicing my chest open. She was afraid. She was afraid of me. The thought gutted me as she gasped for breath and fought against the rising panic. Our bond was strengthening and I could feel her emotions as if they were my own.

She pushed at me and I quickly rolled off her.

"Maddie? Sweetheart, it's okay. It's okay. We don't have to do anything. I'm so sorry." I just kept talking, not really knowing what to say. How could she think I'd ever hurt her like that?

"I'm sorry," she said, jumping up from the bed and running for the bathroom. I tried to follow, but she slammed the door in my face. I stood there staring at it, unsure of what to do. When I heard the shower come on, I went back to sit on the bed and wait.

She came out wrapped in a towel, hugging it close to her. Her skin was pinked from the heat of the water, and her smell quickly filled the room. Despite what had happened, I still wanted her in every way possible.

She sat down beside me, her shoulders slumped.

"Will it always be like this?" she asked quietly. "Will I always remember whenever we try to get close?" She turned teary eyes my way.

"I don't know. You have to know I'd never hurt you. I'll wait as long as it takes, for whatever you can handle." Anger flared in me over what they'd done to her. They'd taken something that should have been beautiful between just the two of us, and turned it ugly. I needed to get up and move. I had to be in the office later and thought maybe I should just head in early. My head was all screwed up. I didn't know what to think or how to feel.

One more look at Maddie, and all that changed again. It was like being on an emotional roller-coaster. I was dealing with my own feelings, but I could also feel hers so strongly. She was embarrassed, upset, and frustrated.

"You deserve so much more than me. So much more than I can offer you, Liam."

"Don't," I said. "It was our first try. I'm guessing your first try since—since it happened."

She nodded, the tears flowing down her cheeks now.

"We've got some obstacles, for sure, but we're going to make it," I told her, wishing out into the universe for it to be true.

I held her for a while, trying to reassure her as much as myself. I didn't know what the future would hold for us, but I knew I damn sure wasn't giving up on us.

"I have to go into the office today. Are you going to be okay?"

She nodded. "I was thinking of calling Annie today. I didn't like how I left things the last time I spoke to them, and there're so many questions I need answers to. I wasn't going to tell you, because I wasn't sure you'd agree," she confessed. "But I don't want there to be secrets between us. I've had too much of that in my life already."

"Thank you for trusting me with that," I said honestly. It meant a lot to me that she didn't want to keep things from me. "Tell you what, why don't you get dressed, and come to the office with me? We can call Annie from there. My office is buffered with the same device as Kyle's office here."

"I don't know. I really should check on Oscar."

"I'm sure he's still at Jessica's. Drop me off and you can have the car. I'll give you directions to where he's staying. Maybe the two of you could come by for lunch? I'll get one of my sisters, or Christine, to watch him while we call Annie."

"Okay," she agreed.

I went to shower quickly and change for work. I was looking through my ties, trying to decide which to wear, when she walked up behind me and pointed out a blue one.

"That one," she said, pulling it off the rack. She wrapped it around her neck and tied it into a perfect knot. It was definitely one of the top ten sexiest things I'd ever seen. She removed it from her neck and placed it around mine, adjusting it perfectly to the right position and fixing my collar. "What?" she asked as I stared at her in surprise.

"That was incredibly sexy," I confessed.

She laughed and playfully slapped me. "Sorry, I'm used to tying them for Oscar on the rare occasion he's needed one."

"This could become a new daily routine," I teased, making her blush. I loved making her cheeks flush like that. I pulled her into my arms and kissed her. There was no hesitation or fear in her response and it settled my wolf and relaxed me, too.

Mom wasn't even up as we raided the fridge for something quick to eat. All of San Marco would be slow to rise after the pack run. I didn't need to be in the office so early, but there were things I needed to get done, and the sooner they started, the better.

When we reached the Westin Foundation, I invited Maddie in. I wanted her to see where I worked, and to be a part of every aspect of my life. She looked around curiously as we made our way down the halls to my office.

"I knew you couldn't stay away," Christine said, startling me as we entered the reception area to my office.

"Hey Chris, what are you doing in so early?" I asked.

"Well, I heard some pretty crazy rumors about my boss man, and I knew you'd be in early today. Just can't stay away." She glanced over my shoulder where Maddie stood behind me. "Maybe the rumors aren't quite so crazy after all."

I laughed. "Chris, this is my mate, Madelyn. Maddie, Christine Canine, my assistant."

"You're really Madelyn Collier?" she asked.

"Yes," Maddie sighed.

"Well, congratulations, you two! This is all pretty exciting stuff. No worries," she said, holding up her hands. "I've learned my lesson about going after other women's men. I'll never cross the line between true mates ever again."

I laughed. "Chris challenged Kelsey for Kyle during their mating trials." I filled Maddie in. "I'm going to finish up our tour, then I have a few phone calls to make before you hit me up with anything this morning."

"Sure thing, boss. It was nice meeting you, Maddie," Chris said as the two of us walked into my office and closed the door behind us.

"So, this is my office," I told her before swooping her up in my arms and kissing her senseless as she giggled.

"I love it," she finally said, slightly breathless.

I let her go, grinning like an idiot. At my desk, I jotted down directions to Jessica's and hit the speaker on my phone. "Hey, can you get me a number for Jessica Moore, please?"

Chris quickly rattled it off as I wrote it down with the directions and thanked her before hanging up. I handed the note to Maddie.

"Thanks," she said.

"The boys are probably up by now, but if you'd prefer you can call her first. I know you're anxious to see Oscar."

She kissed me goodbye and left.

I watched the parking lot from my office window to ensure she made it safely to the car.

I called Chris, leaving it on speaker. "Hey boss man, what's up?"

"Can you get me Troy on the line?"

"Troy?"

"Yeah, it's personal business."

"Okay, you're the boss," she said, hanging up. My phone rang a few minutes later. "Troy's on line two."

"Thanks, Chris," I said, before changing lines. "Troy? Liam Westin."

"Hey, Liam, kind of surprised to hear from you so early after a run. What can I do for you?"

"You know the plot of land we've been discussing?"

"Sure, sure, you finally ready to build that cabin we talked about?"

"Actually, no," I said. "I'm going to need some new house plans drawn up, and the sooner we can break, ground the better."

"Heard you were taking a mate. I'm assuming that's going well?"

"Never better. So, how soon can we start?"

He laughed. "I'll personally come by with plans this afternoon. Give me some details on what you're looking for to help speed the process. My guys can be out there to get started as soon as you make the final decision on what you want."

"That's perfect, Troy. Thanks so much." I gave him a few ideas I was thinking, the size of the house we'd need, and answered all his other questions before hanging up. Despite the early morning setback, I was feeling quite optimistic about my future with Maddie and Oscar.

Maddie

Chapter 22

Alone in the car, I willed myself not to break down. I felt so much guilt over what had happened that morning. The flashbacks hit the moment I felt Liam's body press against mine. It was like I was trapped, and then panic set in so quickly. I know he felt terrible, and it wasn't his fault. I didn't know how to fully explain it. It wasn't that I didn't want him—I did, in every way imaginable. It had just triggered such a strong memory. I was angry and upset about it. Why couldn't I just be normal? I had the best man in the entire world, and I still couldn't fully be with him, because of the gang rape.

I felt more than saw Liam watching me from his office, so I took a deep breath and pulled out of the parking spot. I didn't want him to know how much it worried me. He deserved better, but I was too selfish to give him up. He was mine. The strong possession I felt over him scared me at times. And I knew he felt it too. The way he had growled “mine” just before we had almost made love, had thrilled me to my very core.

I pulled over to the side of the road to collect my thoughts and call Jessica Moore. I didn't want to just show up. What if they were still sleeping?

She picked up on the first ring. “Hello?”

“Hi, is this Jessica?”

“Yes, it is, who may ask is calling?”

“Hi Jessica, this is Maddie, Oscar's mom.”

“Oh, hey Maddie. The boys are all up. They've had breakfast and are playing video games right now. Oscar's been great.”

“I'm so glad to hear that. He doesn't have very many friends his age.” *Or any*, I thought, but didn't add.

"Well, you wouldn't know it to watch him. He's fitting in just great, like he's always been here. I think those Westin brothers had a bit to do with that."

"Come again?"

"Apparently both Kyle and Liam came by to check on Oscar yesterday. The boys have a bit of idol worship to begin with when it comes to their Alpha, but Liam was apparently the big hit with some Hulk shifting move he did for them. It's all they've talked about."

My heart squeezed with happiness. Liam had done that for Oscar? "Well, I'm glad to hear he's fitting in and having fun."

"You can pick him up anytime, they're playing now and no bother at all."

"Thanks, but we have a few things to do this afternoon. I'm on my way over now."

"Okay, see you soon, Maddie."

We hung up and I drove around for a bit, alone with my thoughts, before pulling up at Jessica Moore's house. I could hear the boys before she opened the door.

"Hi, Maddie, come on in," she said, giving me a friendly hug that surprised me. "This is Tina, Sally, and Vickie. They all have boys Oscar's age too that stayed over last night."

"Hi," I said, surprised to find no judgment in any of them. They were all curious about me and Liam and wanted to know how we had met and what was going on. I gave them a sunny version of knowing him my whole life and running into him in San Francisco only to discover he was my one true mate. They sighed, smiled, and congratulated me.

"Hey, Mommy," Oscar yelled across the room finally noticing I was there.

"Hi, bud, did you have fun?"

"Yes, but I can't talk now, 'cause Bobby and I are about to win this round."

The other women laughed.

"You'd think they'd been friends forever. He just fit right in," Tina assured me.

"We try to get the boys together at least twice a week while they're still on summer break. Could I have your number to include Oscar?" Vickie asked.

"That would be great," I said, genuinely meaning it.

"Where are you and Oscar staying?" Sally asked.

"At the Westins'," I told them.

"The Alpha house?" Sally clarified.

"Yes, for now, though I don't get why everyone still calls it the Alpha house since the Alpha doesn't live there."

They all laughed. "I think it will just always be the Alpha house," Jessica said.

"That's really cool how quickly they took you both in," Vickie said.

"Why wouldn't they?" I asked. "I've known them practically my entire life. Lily and I were best friends growing up."

"You were? But you're not from around here. We'd know," Vickie said.

I looked at them, confused. Was it possible they didn't know who I was? I had expected rumors to fly around faster than that.

"You really don't know? I'm Madelyn Collier. My father is Alpha of the Collier Pack. I spent every summer with Lily and Liam growing up, and visited Westin often."

Tina gasped, and I saw recognition on all their faces.

"Madelyn Collier? You're serious?"

I nodded.

"But, I remember when you went missing. How can that be? I had heard you were dead," Sally added.

I sighed. "I know, it's a long story. Maybe someday I'll tell you."

Jessica hugged me. "If you ever want to talk about it, we'll be here." The other ladies all nodded in agreement, but no one pressed me for more. I felt accepted, and it felt good.

"Thank you," I said. Shortly after, I called Oscar over. He wasn't ready to go, but he listened and thanked Jessica for having him. He and Bobby had made plans for another sleepover in a few days. On the drive back over to Westin Foundation, Oscar couldn't stop talking about all the fun he had.

We swung into the Crate and ordered burgers to go. It was the one thing I knew Liam liked. Then we headed to the Westin Foundation to have lunch with my mate. There were a lot more people at the office this time, but they were all friendly and no one questioned us being there as I led the way to Liam's office without stopping to ask directions or permission.

"Hey, Maddie. Who do we have here?" Chris asked as we entered his outer office.

"Chris, this is Oscar. Oscar, this is Liam's assistant, Christine."

"Hi, it's nice to meet you," Oscar said, shaking her hand.

"Oh, I see you're going to be quite the heartbreaker around here. What a perfect gentleman."

I proudly smiled down at my son.

"Is Liam free?" I asked.

"For you? I'm sure, but let me check."

She called him on the phone before telling us to go on in. Liam was sitting behind his desk, but instantly jumped up. He gave me a quick kiss before picking Oscar up in a hug.

"We missed you last night, so I hope you didn't have too much fun. Don't think we should do that too often," he told him.

"But, I have plans to sleep over again Friday night. Mommy said it was okay."

I actually didn't remember saying it was okay, but I didn't admit that.

"Well, if Mommy said so, I guess I'll survive."

"We brought you lunch. Hamburgers!" Oscar informed him.

"Thanks. I was just going to order here, but hamburgers sound so much better," he confessed.

I sat down on the couch and pulled the coffee table over to set the food out. Oscar and Liam chose to sit on the floor. Watching him, in his suit and tie, sitting on the floor laughing and eating with Oscar, surrounded by his plush executive office, seemed oddly out of place, and yet so incredibly right.

"What are you smiling about?" Liam asked.

"I'm just happy," I said with a shrug.

He reached over and took my hand and kissed it. "I'm very glad to hear that, because I truly hope you aren't going to kill me. We have work to do."

"We?" I asked.

"We." He got up and walked to his desk, bringing back a stack of papers. "You don't have to love any of them, but it's a start."

"What is that?" Oscar asked, and I was thinking the same thing.

"They're breaking ground on the house tomorrow, so we

need an idea of what this house is going to look like, and quick."

"We're building a house?" Oscar asked, again, exactly what I was thinking.

"Well, we don't want to live in Grandma and Grandpa's forever, do we? We need a place of our own. I've picked out ten I liked, but there're a lot more if you guys don't agree."

"I get a say in it?" Oscar asked.

"You plan on living there too, right?" Oscar nodded. "Then yes, you get a say."

I picked up the first of the stack. "Liam, if I'm reading this right, it has six bedrooms." *What in the world would we need six bedrooms for?* I wondered.

"Yeah, I was worried it may be a little small."

"Small! You're insane, that's way too big," I told him.

He frowned. "I figured your family would want to visit now and then. Plus, we don't want Oscar to be an only child forever, do we?"

Oscar giggled. "I'd like a little brother, like Zander," he said hopefully.

I wanted to throw up, but faked a smile for Oscar's benefit. After what had happened to me, I wasn't even sure I could physically have kids again. They had told me Oscar was a miracle child. I made a mental note to set an appointment with the local pack doctor to discuss. I didn't want Liam getting his hopes up when I might never be able to give him kids of his own.

The next house I picked up had eight bedrooms. I groaned. "You realize I'm the one that's going to be stuck cleaning this monstrosity, right?"

"We'll hire a maid," he said without a second thought.

Oscar waved one in the air. "I like this one. It has a huge porch and a big game room."

Liam grinned. "That's my favorite too, kid."

I took it and looked it over. It had a big open floor plan, a full basement with the game room Oscar got excited about, and five good-sized bedrooms upstairs. I looked at the sketch of the full wraparound porch and I loved it.

Liam grinned and high-fived Oscar. "Looks like Mommy loves it, too. I think we found our house."

Oscar attacked Liam and they began wrestling on the floor,

when there was a knock at the door and Chris popped her head in.

"Mr. Westin," she said, smiling and shaking her head. "Troy is here."

"Great, send him on back."

A tall man with graying temples entered. He had a sophistication about him, yet his attire screamed blue collar worker.

Liam stood up with Oscar tucked under one arm as he carried him by the waist, his legs flailed out behind him.

"Troy," he said, shaking his hand. "This is Oscar, and that's Maddie. And I think we've found our house. Right. kid?"

Oscar replied, "Right," and he handed the man the floor plans to the house we had unanimously agreed on.

Troy looked them over and grinned. "I knew you'd love this one. A little smaller than you'd wanted, I know, but we can always convert part of the basement into more bedrooms if needed down the road."

"For now, it's perfect. My girl loves it. My kid loves it. Perfect."

"Well, alright then. We'll break ground tomorrow. I've got my best crew on it," Troy told us.

Tomorrow? I thought. One thing I was quickly coming to understand was that when Liam Westin set his mind to something, he was a force to be reckoned with.

We said goodbye to Troy and he left. As soon as the door closed, Oscar demanded to be put down and he looked Liam right in the eye. "You called me your son," he said in an accusatory voice.

"Do you have a problem with that?" Liam asked him.

"No, but do you mean it?"

"Well, first, there's something I've been wanting to ask you. And I haven't run this by Mommy yet, so I really hope she doesn't kill me for asking."

Okay, he had my full attention. *What was he up to?* I wondered as he shot me an apologetic look.

"Oscar, you know I love your mom, right?"

He nodded. "I sorta figured that out already."

"And I love you too, kid."

Oscar hugged him. "I love you too, Liam."

Liam pulled him back to look at him again. "How would you feel about me being your dad?"

"I guess if you and mommy are together and we're building a house to all live in, you kind of are?" Oscar asked with a hopeful voice that made me want to cry.

"I mean, how about we make it official. I'd like to adopt you. How would you feel about that?"

"You mean it? You really mean it?"

"Yes, I do. I want you to be my son. A real Westin. Would that be okay with you?"

Oscar threw his arms around Liam with tears in his eyes. "I love you, Liam."

"I love you too, kid. And before we get too crazy celebrating, I have something else I need to ask."

"There's more?" he asked. I was thinking the same, still trying to wrap my mind over what just happened. Liam wanted to adopt Oscar and give him his name. It was more than I'd have ever asked for.

I wiped my damp eyes and looked up to see Liam kneeling before me. "I want you to know, I heard you. Both of you"—he included Oscar—"and I want to do this right in every way. So, Madelyn Amanda Collier, will you make me the happiest man alive—be my mate, and my wife?" He held out a beautiful diamond ring between shaky fingers.

I was so overwhelmed I couldn't speak, only nod and smile as the tears fell. He kissed me as Oscar cheered us on.

"I love you, Maddie. I've always loved you. For better or worse, I'm all in."

It amazed me how quickly life could change. One week. It had been one week since the moment my eyes connected with Liam's and my whole world changed. It was all happening so fast, and yet it didn't scare me one bit. I was excited for our future and knew it was exactly right.

Liam
Chapter 23

I called E and asked her if she'd mind watching Oscar for about an hour. She said she didn't, and both she and Lily arrived at my office to pick him up.

"Guess what?" Oscar announced the second he saw them, before even saying hello. "I'm getting adopted!"

Both girls looked at each other, confused, then turned their attention to me and Maddie, but Oscar was quick to fill them in further.

"Liam wants to be my dad. My real dad. He's adopting me to make it official," he said proudly.

My sisters looked at me. "Really?" Lily asked.

"Really," I told them.

"And he's marrying Mommy, too!" Oscar finished the announcement for us.

Elise snorted. "You're getting married?"

"Yup," I said.

"Why?" Lily asked. "I mean, I don't have anything against marriage, but you're mated, you'll be bonding soon, you don't need marriage."

"Wait, like white dress, flowers, party...the whole deal?" Elise asked.

"That's the plan," I told her. "And why, Lil? Because it's important to Oscar. He's new to our ways and if it's easier for him to understand, then we're going to do it." They looked at Maddie to see how she felt about it. "Oh, she already said yes, no take-backsies."

Maddie giggled. "It'll be fun."

I knew the moment it sank in and Lily heard what we were telling her. She squealed and clapped, jumping up and down. "I get to be the maid of honor!"

I didn't think it was really a question. "Dork, you can't nominate yourself for something like that."

"Wanna bet, little brother," she said with a smirk. I groaned and rolled my eyes.

"Yes, you are going to be my maid of honor," Maddie said, and the three girls sat down on the couch in my office and began planning it out.

"Wait," Elise said. "Where are you having it and who's officiating?"

"That's up to Mad, but I was thinking the new house. Oh, and Cole Anderson is officiating."

"Cole?" Lily asked. It was no secret she'd always had a huge crush on him, even though he was far too old for her, and definitely not her one true mate. The entire world would have known about it long before now if that had been the case.

"Yes, Cole is getting certified so he can perform the ceremony."

"When did you plan all this?" Maddie asked, laughing.

I shrugged. "Yesterday."

I sat down at my desk and tried to get some paperwork done, knowing they weren't going to leave anytime soon. After awhile the distractions and the giggling became too much, and I would have been lying if I wasn't getting a little stressed from all the plans they were quickly making over this wedding.

"Hey, I called you to take Oscar on a tour, not bore him to death with your babbling, and don't you two have work to do, too?"

Lily rolled her eyes at me. "Come on, Oscar, I'm thinking someone wants a little alone time with your mom."

I wish, I thought. What we were going to be doing was nowhere near as fun as what Lily was thinking.

They finally left. Maddie was beaming with happiness. They had done that, and for that I was thankful. No, I had done that. Who knew a wedding would mean so much to a girl? I noticed she kept looking down at her hand that was now wearing my ring. I didn't think anything could wipe the smile off my lady's face. I hated to bring Annie and Jacob up, fearing it would burst her joy, but it needed to be done.

"You ready to call Annie?" I asked anxiously.

"Yes! I can't wait to tell her, she's going to be so excited." Then it hit her. Life with Annie was very different now. She looked a little sad, but determined not to let it get to her.

I put the phone on speaker, and she dialed the number she knew well.

"Hello?"

"Annie, it's Maddie," she said.

I could hear Annie crying. "Janie—er, Maddie, whatever you want, I'm so happy you called. Jacob and I weren't sure we'd ever hear from you again."

"I was upset at first, but I'm trying to let it go. I know it's only been a few days, but honestly it feels like a lifetime ago," she told her.

"I know exactly what you mean," Annie exclaimed. "Is Oscar there? Can I speak with him? We miss you both so much."

"Miss you too. Oscar's not here right now though. And Annie, I have some questions I really need answers to. Can you do that?"

She sighed. "I'll try."

I sat back and just listened, taking in their conversation.

"You really didn't know what I was, even after all you know?"

"We really, truly didn't. I don't think either of us had ever been more shocked in our lives. I mean, of course we recognized the Collier name, and vaguely remembered hearing the youngest daughter went missing, but never once did we ever suspect that was you."

"How much do you know about people like me?"

"Everything. The Verndari have been passing down the knowledge from generation to generation since the beginning of time. I told you, our job is to protect you. Almost all legends and lore exist as ways to protect your kind. The Verndari did that."

"What do you mean?" I asked, forgetting she didn't know I was on the line, too.

"Liam?" she asked hesitantly.

"You're on speaker, Annie. It's just the two of us. If you truly know anything about our kind, you know I can't keep any secrets from him."

"Because he's your mate?" she asked.

"Yes and soon-to-be husband." Maddie beamed.

"You're getting married?"

"We are, and I'd really like you and Jacob to be here for it."

I quirked an eyebrow at her and she shrugged, giving me a sheepish look.

"Is that really what you want?" I mouthed to her. She stared at me for a moment and then nodded. I sighed. "Okay," I mouthed again. Whatever Maddie wanted or needed this wedding to be, I was damn sure going to give it to her.

"You really mean it?" Annie said.

"I do," Maddie confessed. Both women began to cry, and plan, so I sat back in my chair, knowing we weren't going to get any further anytime soon. They talked for nearly an hour before things started to turn serious again.

"Annie, I have a few more questions for you. I'm not sure you're going to like them though," Maddie said, drawing my attention back. She walked around my desk and sat in my lap. It was clear she needed my touch to get through the next part. I wasn't sure that simple gesture should have brought me so much joy.

"My friend, her aunt is missing. It's been alluded to that the Verndari are researching, perhaps even experimenting on our kind. Is that true? Plus, we think they may have her aunt Raina."

Her quick intake of breath through the phone was heard loud and clear. "I-I can't talk about that, Janie."

"So it's true then?" she demanded.

"It's not safe to discuss that here, Janie."

"Annie," I said, "what did you mean about the legends and lore? Can you answer that?"

There was relief in her voice when she responded this time. "There are so many, I don't even know where to begin. Nearly every myth or legend in existence was created as a cover-up by the Verndari to protect some shifter or another."

"Can you give me an example?"

"Okay, how about werewolves. A silver bullet will kill a werewolf. Have you ever touched silver, Liam?"

I laughed. "I have actually. We are entirely immune."

"Exactly!" she said, like that was precisely the answer I was looking for. "Do you know that your metabolism runs seventy-five percent faster than a human's?"

"I'll take your word for it."

"During the medieval period, shifters were struggling. It was a hard time for everyone and it was easier to find food as a beast than as a human, if you get my point. So more and more began appearing and the humans were taking notice. Several wolves were even killed. What we observed was that the lead from the bullets would enter your body, and because of your high metabolism, would speed through your circulatory system at an alarming rate, causing severe lead poisoning. Many died from this. Silver, on the other hand? Nothing, so the Verndari began the story that the only way to kill a werewolf . . ."

"Was to shoot it with a silver bullet," I finished for her.

"Exactly. Therefore, in reality, it saved the poor creature from a miserable death."

"Are you aware that, even to this day, we rarely keep silver around? It's almost a rite of passage with young men to handle it since they are so fearful because of that myth. Now, I know it was bullshit, because I have touched it and even swallowed some on a dare, but it is still a common fear."

Annie laughed. "I promise, that was never the intent."

"What else?" I asked, growing more curious.

"Um, how about vampires?"

"Don't tell me vampires are real?" I said, smelling the bullshit on that one.

"No, not at all. But, well, you're aware of the bonding practices of shifters." Her voice softened. "You and Janie will be experiencing it firsthand soon, if you haven't already."

"I'm aware," I said, neither confirming nor denying her real question.

"So, anyway, during the age of exploration, people—shifters too—were traveling about more, spreading out across this planet. Now, wolves are pack animals and largely moved together, but that's not the case with most shifters. Many had dispersed, leaving others desperate to find a mate. In the search for their mates, there became a practice among some that would leave them biting anyone they could find. A small few took it too far and humans began to notice as bodies were found drained almost entirely of blood at times, and so began the legend of the vampire as a smokescreen to protect the shifters."

Everything she was saying made so much sense, and yet it was unbelievable to fathom at the same time.

"Wait, I thought the vampire legend came from the *Dracula* book, didn't it?" Maddie asked.

"Well, yes, there's some truth to that. It didn't actually come from the book, but he certainly heightened our cause with that one, didn't he?" Annie said with a smile in her voice.

"So you're saying he was Verndari?" Maddie asked.

"That's exactly what I'm saying," Annie confirmed.

"So, if what you're saying is true—and the Verndari have been protecting our kind for all these generations—why the change to testing and researching now?" I asked.

"Hold on, someone's at the door," Annie said. I heard some commotion in the background coming through her line. Hushed voices I couldn't make out. "Janie, sweetie, I'm so happy you and Oscar are enjoying your vacation. We can't wait to see you both soon. Miss you. Love you. I'll be in touch again soon."

"Goodbye, Annie," Maddie said.

"What just happened?" I asked.

"Someone was there. She warned us it wasn't safe to talk on the phone. I just hope we didn't get them into any trouble."

"You think their phone was tapped or something?"

"I don't know what to think, Liam, but she said she'd be in touch, so we have to believe they'll find a way."

That was the last we heard from Annie and Jacob. Weeks went by and we settled into our new life. Oscar had his friends he spent a great deal of time with. Maddie and the girls were busy planning the wedding, which was coming up quickly. The house was on schedule to be completed in another month. They were knocking it out in record time. And Maddie and I still hadn't bonded. With each passing day I worried we never would. I feared it wasn't physically possible.

Love, desire, and intimacy certainly weren't our problems. We were growing closer and more comfortable and confident with, and in each other by the day, but I still couldn't bring myself to try having actual sex again. Every time I even thought of it, I'd remember the fear in her eyes the day we'd tried and it made me sick. I had no problems pleasing her and loved how responsive she was to me, but for me, I'd taken to handling things myself in that department. It was never the same and seemed to be lacking more and more each day.

Just last night, Maddie had caught me jacking off in the shower. To my surprise, she'd stopped me and taken care of things herself. If I couldn't have her, that was definitely the next best thing. It made me hard as a rock just thinking about it. I wasn't sure which of us had been more shocked by her boldness, but I had loved it.

She was still asleep next to me as I grew harder and more uncomfortable from the memories of that shower. I tried to ease out of bed without waking her, but when she was using my chest as her personal pillow, it made it a little difficult. I felt guilty touching myself with her right there, but I was getting desperate and needed relief.

I started stroking myself and closed my eyes, willing back the groan wanting to escape. I was startled and my eyes flew open as I felt her soft hand wrap around mine and join me. She was watching me closely and I'd never felt so exposed. I wasn't exactly used to being vulnerable, not even in front of my mate.

She kissed me and increased the pressure as I groaned.

"I want to try something. I don't know if it will work, but it's worth a try."

I couldn't talk. I was raw with so much need, and simply nodded. She smiled, looking a little relieved. As if I'd ever tell her no.

She sat up and moved to straddle me. I was once again surprised by her boldness but I just watched as she rubbed herself against me. I had to grip the sheets in fists to keep from reaching for her. I wanted her so bad. She seemed to be testing herself, or maybe me; I wasn't sure, but I could feel how hot and ready she was, too.

She grabbed hold of me and started to lower herself down on me. She froze and I thought she was going to panic again, but she didn't. She smiled and began to move, searching for a rhythm that felt right. I only lasted another minute before I had to touch her. I had to move with her.

Our breathing increased. My heart was pounding in my chest. Sweat shone on her body, giving her a beautiful glow as she rode me to her release and I followed her into ecstasy.

She collapsed onto my chest. I thought she was going to cry, but she didn't. She looked up and grinned. She was so unbelievably beautiful. “We're going to be okay,” she said.

“I'd say okay is a huge understatement.”

Maddie

Chapter 24

Liam and I had been together a full month already. Oscar had begged to go to school with his new friends at the start of the new semester. I was skeptical at first, and by far it had been a harder transition on me than on him, but he seemed happy, and was fitting in famously. Overall life was good.

I had done a lot of soul searching and growing since coming to San Marco. I came to the realization that the boys who raped me had stolen my control. No matter how much I loved Liam, feeling him press down above me, pinning down my arms, or any movement that made me feel trapped, was a trigger back to that night. It wasn't that I didn't trust him. I knew he would never hurt me, but the irrational fear from the memories always seemed to surface. Sometimes I was better at hiding it than others and I'd gotten good at changing positions when I started to feel the panic.

The thing was I wanted my mate. I wanted a normal relationship without the fears from my past. I didn't know how to fully explain all of that to him, so I began exploring opportunities to take control myself. When I was in control, I felt invincible and free to explore myself and my mate. It had worked, and I couldn't keep the stupid grin off my face, which probably wasn't a good thing since I was having a late lunch with Lily.

Lily was meeting me out at the new house. The foundation was done and the framing was complete. When I arrived a little early, I was excited to see we even had floors now. Troy kept reassuring me it would all be complete before the wedding in just four weeks. I could not wait to start our life together.

Lily's car pulled up and she eyeballed me suspiciously the

moment she got out of the car. She hugged me and took a deep breath, inhaling my scent. She pulled back, frowning.

"Really? I thought the grin on your face meant you finally bonded with my stupid brother. What is taking you guys so long?"

"It's complicated," I told her for the millionth time.

"That's all either of you ever say, 'it's complicated,' but there's nothing complicated about it. He bites you, you bite him, done."

I was grateful we were interrupted by a new vehicle arriving. I had expected to see Troy, since he spent a lot of time at the house overseeing his guys, but it wasn't, it was Patrick O'Connell, Elise's mate.

"Hey, Patrick, what are you doing out here?" Lily asked.

"Liam asked me to come get Maddie," he said, sounding casual, but something in his stance didn't make me feel very comfortable.

"Well, we have plans, so that dork can wait," Lily said, pouting. I didn't want to miss out on some girl time, either. I saw Lily a lot. We even lived in the same house, but we rarely got any time for just the two of us.

"Sorry, it's important. Something's come up," he said.

"Fine, I'll come along, too," Lily said stubbornly.

"That's not possible, I'm afraid. Maddie and I have some mutual friends we need to speak with." He was being cryptic, but I could only imagine that mutual friends would be of the human variety. I hadn't heard anything from Annie since she had hung up on me weeks ago. If there was news about her or Jacob or from them, I needed to hear it.

"It's okay Lily, we can reschedule."

Her jaw opened and then closed. "We will not. I've been looking forward to this for days. We have plans to make, things to do. You"—she turned on Patrick, poking her finger into his chest—"do not get to disrupt that."

"I'm sorry, Lil. It's important, and it's Kyle's orders. Take it up with him if you have a problem. Come on, Maddie," he told me.

"Madelyn Amanda Collier!" Lily started and I knew she was furious. I wasn't too pleased with how this, whatever this was, was being handled either, but I gave an apologetic shrug.

"I should go and see what he needs," I told her. Lily didn't know about the humans or our connections to them, and I couldn't just tell her now. "I'm sure it's important if Liam and Kyle sent him to get me. We'll talk soon, okay?"

I could see the hurt in her eyes and I hated it. I turned quickly and followed Patrick. "This better be important," I warned him, upset that Lily had been hurt by his actions.

We drove, mostly in silence, heading out of town and down the mountain. We didn't go to the city at the base of our mountain, though; instead, about halfway down Patrick stopped and carefully watched for cars in both directions before turning right onto a dirt path I could barely make out. He drove to the tree line where we met a bunch of fallen trees blocking the path.

Great, just great, I thought. He got out of the car and moved enough trees out of the way to drive through. He stopped on the other side and replaced the mess behind us. It gave me a momentary panic of being trapped.

"You're fine," he told me, getting back into the car. "Liam warned me you might start to panic, but everything's fine. It's just a precaution."

At the end of the little road, if you could even call it that, was a small cabin. I immediately recognized Kyle's car and as we exited the vehicle I could smell my mate. He was close by. So was another all too familiar smell.

I ran towards the house and opened the door. Annie and Jacob were standing next to a table talking to Liam and Kyle and two other men I didn't recognize.

"Annie! Jacob!" I cried, running into their open arms. I hugged Annie close and Jacob wrapped his big arms around us both. "I've been so worried about you both, but you're okay, right?"

"We're fine," Jacob said.

"And we miss you and Oscar so much," Annie added.

They both had tears in their eyes when I pulled back to look at them. Liam rose and came to stand by my side.

"You knew about this?" I challenged him.

"Not until about an hour ago. Kyle picked me up and we came straight here. Patrick agreed to go get you while we talked some things out." He ran his hand through his hair and looked stressed. "There's a lot to catch you up on."

"I still don't like you dragging her into this," Jacob said.

"But they know her, and they won't suspect anything strange

with Janie coming to visit you, even at the office," one of the strangers said.

"Maddie, this is Dave and Martin, my *friends*," Patrick said, with enough emphasis for me to understand these were his human contacts from the Verndari.

"Hello," I said. "What are we talking about?"

"Take a seat," Kyle told me, speaking for the first time. I looked over to Liam, who smiled and nodded, letting me know I should do what Kyle said. I sat in the chair Liam had abandoned and he stationed himself behind me, close enough for his presence to relieve some of the anxiety starting to build.

"There're some things you need to know about Jacob Winthrop," Kyle said.

I glanced at Jacob, who cringed.

"Let me explain it to her," he practically begged. "She's my daughter."

Despite it all, they still looked at me the same, like a mother and a father. I loved them, despite what they were a part of. I knew they were good people and I didn't think anything could change that perception, until Jacob began to speak.

"Janie, baby, I've done some things I'm not proud of. I have my reasons. I never wanted to hurt anyone."

"Jacob, what's going on here?" The calm in my voice shocked even me.

"You know some things about the Verndari?"

I nodded, but didn't speak.

"Well, for many generations we've watched and protected the shifters, silent guardians over your people. We've done everything in our power to ensure the humans stayed unaware. The duty of the Verndari was passed down from parent to child from the beginning of time, as far as we believe. But about a decade ago, a new leader rose up in the Verndari. He was young and modern, and his father was dying of cancer. Modern medicine wasn't helping, and he was determined to seek any aid possible if it meant saving him. That was the first trial run on the shifters."

"They rounded up a few rogues at first, shifters known to cause problems anyway. It started out with good intentions. They were taking out human threats, and were only running tests on them, then rehabilitating and releasing them back into the world. That was the plan, at least, but he gained popularity quickly and a small group of rebel Verndari began experimenting on shifters, looking for cures to human ailments with no regard to the shifter." Annie continued his story.

Martin took over next. "I remember when Jacob and I were brought into the loop. We were both horrified at what we found there. We agreed to stay, and implemented humane procedures for the experiments. This man"—I noticed none of them were giving up his name—"he was changing the minds of the youngest of our society, in secret. I reported back to our council, but was given orders to observe and report. For almost a decade I've been observing and reporting, and I'm done. What they're doing, it's not right." He looked at Jacob. "What you're doing isn't right either, and you know it."

"Jacob went in to protect the shifters, to make sure the lines of ethics were not crossed, and he stays, giving each of them the best life possible in there," Annie defended her husband.

"But they have crossed that line. What they're doing is unethical. They've started locking them in cages, like wild beasts. They aren't animals, and it's just wrong," Martin said.

"It's true," Jacob confessed, "and they are getting bolder about their tactics, no longer taking just the troublesome shifters. They go after any lone shifter they can find. Wolves are harder because you are such a dominant pack animal."

"We had gotten word of the Bulgati brothers and were told to pick them up. The boys and I stood down when Elise showed up, and then you Patrick. We certainly didn't know the two of you would be there, but if our superiors had known, they'd have ordered us to grab the two of you, too," Martin told Patrick.

"So the Bulgati brothers, you have them?" Patrick asked.

"Yes," Martin confirmed.

"Are they dead?"

"Not yet."

"Good, because I want to be the one that kills them," Patrick told them with such vengeance it frightened me.

"Raina?" Kyle asked.

"Raina was travelling with three other women. They tried to stay under the radar and made for an easy target. She's still alive," Dave assured Kyle.

"And how do we get her out of there?"

"Death is the only way they leave," Jacob told them. It made the hairs on my neck stand up. How could the loving man I knew have anything to do with this? "I can arrange it," he confessed.

Kyle growled and jumped from his seat.

Jacob held his hands up in peace. "I can give her a sedative that will lower her heart rate enough to declare her dead. It will be a short window of opportunity, but I can toss her into the crematory and eject her before igniting it. In theory no one would ever know, but she'd be a ghost on the run from there."

"Or she can come here, permanently. We can protect her, Kyle," Patrick assured him.

"Why would you do this?" Kyle asked Jacob.

"Despite what you may think of me, this is not the ways of the true Verndari. I have been undercover with them since nearly the beginning. I've done things I'm not proud of." He looked at me with tears in his eyes. "But the thought of them ever getting their hands on Janie and Oscar makes me sick. I will do anything to protect them. This has gone on long enough. The Order will not intervene. The Coven, which is what this small segment of the Order is calling itself, has found enough value in their research both for humanity and the protection of shifters to be overlooked. As long as they are keeping a low profile, many see no harm from it. They are wrong. This is not the job we were given. This is not protecting your people. Maybe I could go along with it for a while. I'm sorry to say many of those research developments came at my hands, but I always cared for those shifters. I never used any practices that I would not use on my own mother. Still, wrong is wrong. Every time I think of them getting their hands on Janie or Oscar—" He shivered at the thought, unable to finish the sentence. "I can't do it any longer."

I was numb and shocked by his words and what he was confessing. Liam rubbed my tight shoulders. "With the packs at war, it leaves us all vulnerable, Kyle. We need to take what we know to the Grand Council and start restoring the peace between the packs," Liam said.

"You cannot tell them of the Order of the Verndari," Annie said adamantly. "To do so could mean the deaths of hundreds. If the Verndari learned the shifters were aware of their presence it would change everything. The Coven would kill off everyone in their labs and start over, or I fear they'd become more vocal about it and start rounding up shifters in larger quantities. Plus, we don't know how the others of your kind would take to the news. It's too much at risk. The packs are already at war, you can't afford to be at war with the Order as well."

"No one is talking war here," Patrick said.

"What I absolutely know is we want Raina out of there. I'm trying to keep it to myself, but Kelsey is going to freak when she finds out about this," Kyle said.

"So don't tell her," Dave said, like it was the simplest solution in the world.

"They're fully bonded, that's kind of impossible," Patrick told Dave as the rest of us all glared at him. It was quite obvious they may have been watching us for thousands of years, but they didn't know everything.

"What does that mean?" Dave asked.

"It's a shifter thing, you couldn't possibly understand," Patrick said, trying to play it off.

"It's true then? Of course I've heard the rumors, but you're talking about telepathy, aren't you?" Jacob asked, and we all awkwardly stared at the ground, refusing to make eye contact with him.

"Jacob," I finally said. "What you've done has already put us in a really bad position." I saw the pain in his eyes at my accusation. "I don't say that to hurt you. I love you, and Annie, and am so grateful for all you've done for me and Oscar, but there are things about our kind that we just can't talk about or share, and you're going to have to respect that."

He nodded slowly.

"Kelsey is very"—I fought for the right word to explain—"strong," I finally decided on. "She is Pack Mother to the Westin wolves and she is not someone you want to piss off. I need you to get Raina out safely. She belongs here, with us, not locked in a cage in your research lab."

He nodded. "Like I said earlier, it won't be easy and there will be only a brief window of opportunity. And Janie, we're going to need you."

Liam
Chapter 25

"Like hell," I growled at Jacob. "She will not go near that place. It isn't safe." I was so fired up I knew I was starting to sprout fur, and I didn't even care. They were not going to put my mate in jeopardy, I didn't care who they were.

"Shit," I heard Kyle say through the roaring in my ears.

I vaguely felt the pressure of Kyle and Patrick trying to hold me back. The fear in the human's eyes only encouraged my wolf as he surged forward to take control and protect our mate.

"Madelyn!" Kyle yelled. "Calm him down, now!"

I felt the Alpha power pour off Kyle as he barked his orders at Maddie, but instead of submitting, my wolf pressed on, even more irritated than before. Never in my life had I lost control of my wolf, but I was on the verge of doing just that when I felt her soft hands on my cheeks.

"Hey, look at me. Liam, look at me," she spoke softly. "I'm okay. They aren't going to hurt me. I'm right here. Look at me. Focus on me, and breathe. In and out, like you always tell me. Just breathe."

My whole body shook as I started to regain control. I reached out and crushed her to me, kissing her forehead. "Mine," I growled.

As the shock wore off and my wolf started to calm at her touch, the reality of what had just happened started to set in. I got up and left without a word. Outside, I gulped in deep breaths of fresh air and tried to calm my nerves.

"That was a mating cry, Maddie," Kyle told her. "I don't know what you two are waiting on, but if you don't complete the bond soon, he's going to lose it. The possession will only continue to worsen. Trust me, I fought mine for a long time, but I was used to battling my wolf. Liam has never shown any Alpha signs, until now. He's not used to fighting for control like that."

I tried not to listen to the details as they began to plan, details that included Maddie going to work with Jacob and helping to smuggle Raina out. I knew we had to get Raina out safely. When Kelsey heard about it, she was going to lose it. While she had remarkable control of her powers, her mothering instincts had kicked in with Zander's birth, strengthening her even more, and no one wanted to test the limits of her powers now.

I paced back and forth in the yard, kicking rocks and refusing to go back inside, despite the desperate need insisting I protect Maddie from everyone inside.

At last she came out of the cabin.

"You're going through with it, aren't you?" I accused more than asked her.

"I have to, Liam, but it's okay. No one there knows about me. They are used to me practically disappearing for long periods of time. Jacob and Annie have kept that cover—that I have been ill and battling depression again. They don't suspect a thing. Martin and Dave were the only two Verndari assigned to monitor Westin territory, and they never reported me being here. It's okay," she tried to assure me.

"There's nothing okay about any of this, Maddie," I told her. I wanted to beg her not to do it, but I could see the resolve in her eyes. She'd already made up her mind, without even discussing it with me. "Didn't you see what happened in there? I'm not safe. I can't control him. If you try to go through with this, they're going to have to lock me up in a cage, because my wolf will want nothing more than to protect you and I'm going to lose control if we feel you're in danger."

"Don't you get it, Liam? I have to do this. For years I had lived scared of my own shadow, hollow inside, and as a ghost of who I once was. You've given me my life back, my spirit. And I can't just sit by knowing what's happening in there and not help. What if it was Oscar? Or Lily? I can't live knowing I could have helped and didn't. I don't expect you to understand, but it's something I need to do."

I wanted to beg her not to go through with it. Just the thought of her in danger was killing me. I wanted to rewind back to that morning, and this time we weren't leaving that bed, but that was just wishful thinking. The thing is, I was proud of her for wanting to take a stand, but I just couldn't handle the repercussions of knowing how I would feel when she did.

I wasn't scared of my wolf, but we weren't in sync for the first time in my life. It was like there was already a second war being waged...only this one was taking place within me.

"I can't be a part of this, Maddie," I said, and turned to leave.

I knew Kyle was watching me closely from the shadows of the cabin. "I'm just going for a run. See that she gets home safely," I commanded my Alpha. His eyes registered the shock, and if it had been anyone but me, he probably would have disciplined them on the spot, but as my brother and knowing it was out of character, he let it drop and simply nodded.

"Come on MC, back inside," Kyle told her as I stripped and shifted. Leaving my clothes and my heart behind, I ran full speed into the woods.

I ran clumsily at first. My wolf was still battling me for dominance, and being in wolf form gave him a stronger advantage. I pushed on and stubbornly refused to fully submit to him. We dodged around trees and ran through streams. I needed to get as far away from that cabin as possible, but my wolf wanted to return and protect our mate.

Maddie had to make her own decision on this. I had made it clear how I felt about it. If she decided to push forward, I wouldn't stop her, but Kyle and Patrick were going to have to stop me, because I wasn't sure I was strong enough to contain my wolf.

I ran for a while, enough to tire out my wolf, but eventually was pulled home. I expected to find Maddie there, too, but instead I only found Oscar sitting on the back porch, alone.

"Liam? Is that you?" he asked, seeing my wolf approach.

I nodded my head, then shifted before him.

"That's so cool," he whispered under his breath.

Sniffing the air around me, I knew Maddie wasn't around, but I had the next best thing and that seemed to satisfy my wolf. The kid was my pack, too, my family.

"Kid, do me a favor and go grab some clothes. Tell Grandma Mary we're going out for a bit."

"We are?" he asked as I felt his excitement begin to bubble.

"We are if you hurry. I don't know about you, but after the day I had, I could use some ice cream."

That had him moving quickly and soon he returned with a pair of jeans and a T-shirt. Not my usual attire, but it was a casual kind of afternoon. There was no way I could concentrate on work right then anyway.

Mom stepped out on the porch looking a little worried. "Everything okay?" she asked in that way that she did when she knew the answer but wanted you to confirm it. I didn't.

"Everything's fine. Oscar and I are just going to hang out for a bit."

"In the middle of the afternoon? On a work day?" she questioned, giving me the all-knowing mom eyes.

"Yup," was all I said; "Come on, kid, let's go."

We got out to the driveway and Oscar stopped. "Mom has your SUV," he said, sounding disappointed.

"I know," I assured him.

"Are we walking all the way to the Cold Shack?" He didn't sound too happy about the thought.

I led him over to a large garage at the back of the property. His interest piqued. I knew he had never been inside and the windows were all tinted so you couldn't even see in.

"Pick one," I said as I opened the door and escorted him inside.

His mouth dropped open and his eyes were wide in shock as he looked at my collection of vehicles. A large, black, dually diesel truck; a brand new Jeep I hadn't even really broken in yet; a silver BMW convertible; a sleek green Jag that I rarely took out; and a classic 1965 Stingray in Vette yellow. I had a thing for cars.

"That one," he said, pointing to the Corvette.

"Good choice." I grinned down at him, grabbing the keys off the hook on the wall.

"Are all these yours?" he asked.

"Yup."

"Cool! So, why do you share the SUV with Mommy then? She always has to take you to work so she can use it and all, but you don't really need her to do that with all these."

I laughed. "I know." I shrugged. "Guess I just like the extra time with her."

He grinned. I knew it made him happy that I loved his mother so much, even when she was breaking my heart and stirring up my wolf with that mission nonsense. He would never know about that, though.

I kept things upbeat. The 'Vette only had two seats, so he had to sit in the front. I knew Maddie was going to freak out, and he did, too.

"Mommy's not going to be happy about this. Are you sure it's okay?"

"Of course I'm sure," I said. "Here." I grabbed one of my motorcycle helmets off the shelf and shoved it down on his head. "Now, buckle up, and you'll be good to go."

"I'm still supposed to be in a booster till I turn eight," he warned.

"I know, I know. Remind me to check while we're in town and see if anyone has one. In the meantime, this works, right?"

He giggled, and I liked that he was happy. His laughter made me crave more of it, so I went to the cabinet and grabbed my old football shoulder pads. I took off the helmet and shoved the pads on him, then replaced the helmet.

"There," I said, checking him over thoroughly. "There's no way she can say you're not safe now."

Oscar laughed harder. "You really want me to wear all of this?"

"Riding in the front seat is very serious. Just making sure you're absolutely safe." I opened the door as he climbed in, still laughing. I strapped him down, satisfied of his safety, even if he did look ridiculous. I needed a little ridiculous just then.

I opened the bay with the remote in the car and we drove off, closing it behind us. I knew I was speeding as we flew around curves and over hills. Oscar cheered me on the whole time. Sometimes boys just needed a little danger in their lives.

We arrived safely at the Cold Shack. I unbuckled him and removed the gear before we got out. He was in second grade now, so I didn't want the others to pick on him because I was over-exaggerating things.

We headed inside hand in hand. He ordered a cup of mint chocolate chip and I got a banana split. We sat in the booth and chatted about everything. He told me school was going great. He was making lots of friends. We talked about the new house. He hadn't seen it in a while, so I promised to stop by on the way home.

Jessica came in with Bobby and two other boys. I recognized the one that was giving Oscar shit the night of his first pack run, but by the way they'd greeted each other and Oscar begged for them to join us, I knew they had already become fast friends.

We pulled over some extra chairs and Jessica and the boys sat down. I was suddenly out of the picture and forced to talk to her. I really wasn't in a social mood, though, so I first checked my phone. Several missed texts from Christine popped up.

There was some paperwork she needed my signature on before end of day. I checked the time. I could give him a few more minutes.

"So, Liam, how is fatherhood going? Oscar seems to be adapting nicely and I hear the new house is almost complete," Jessica started, obviously just making casual conversation.

We chatted for a few minutes. I was surprised at how much information I had garnered from her on Oscar and how he was settling in. Jessica Moore was obviously in the know with the second graders of San Marco. It was reassuring to hear how well he was doing, not that I expected anything less.

As we stood to leave, Jessica did too, and I noticed for the first time just how very pregnant she was. A longing to see Maddie's stomach swollen with my child washed over me. I grinned despite the trials of the day. I couldn't wait to see it and know that was my child she was carrying.

We said a quick goodbye and headed back to the car. Oscar got in and buckled, but didn't move to put the safety equipment on. I looked past him to the Cold Shack and saw the other boys watching. I didn't say a word as we drove off.

We headed for my office and as we walked in, Chris immediately began doting on Oscar. The kid was a bit of a charmer, I had to hand it to him. By the time I had gone in and signed the stack of papers she'd left on my desk and returned, that boy had Christine Canine wrapped around his little finger. Promising her he'd visit again soon, we left.

"Can we still stop by the house? Or do you think Mommy will be worried by now?" he asked.

"Mommy will be fine," I assured him, and we headed to the

home site.

I knew, before I even saw my SUV in the driveway that Maddie was there. I pulled up next to her. She and Lily were standing in the middle of the field in obvious discussion. I could only assume it was wedding plans, knowing Maddie would never discuss her mission and the Verndari with my sister.

As Oscar jumped out of the car, it drew Maddie's attention. I could feel the confusion and frustration rolling off her.

"Tell me you did not run out and buy *that*," she emphasized, pointing to the Corvette; "just because we argued?"

"You and Mommy are fighting?" Oscar questioned and I saw the immediate regret on her face.

"No, just a little disagreement. Mommy and I are fine," I assured him.

Lily snorted. "About time you disagreed on something. It's not normal for two people to be so...so agreeable all the time. There's joy in makeup sex," she whispered low enough that I hoped the kid didn't hear, but his questioning eyes told me he did. I shook my head, telling him not to ask, and was happy he didn't.

"I did not just run out and buy that because I was upset. I picked Oscar up and we went for ice cream. That's it," I told her, not really feeling like I needed to justify myself.

"If you've had that all along, why have I been waking up before the crack of dawn to take you to work and feeling guilty about monopolizing your vehicle?"

Oscar said matter-of-factly, throwing my words back in my face, "'Cause he likes the extra alone time with you. He has plenty of vehicles, so you don't need to feel guilty. If you want something different, I'm sure he'd let you choose. I got to pick which one to ride in today." He had a momentary look of panic. "Liam made me wear a helmet, and football pads, and buckle up. I was perfectly safe." Then he ran away, finding Troy as they headed into the house for a tour.

Lily was laughing. "You made him wear a helmet and pads to ride in the 'Vette?"

I shrugged. "I didn't want Maddie to freak out over him being in the front seat and riding without a booster."

"But he wasn't in them when you got here," my sister challenged, and I wanted to smack her.

I sighed. “Yeah, I'm sorry about that,” I said, speaking only to Maddie. “We ran into Jessica and a few of his friends at the Cold Shack, and it wouldn’t have been cool to do that in front of his boys. I was careful driving, though.”

I tried to give her an innocent smile. There was still tension between us and I knew it had nothing to do with me taking Oscar for a ride without a booster seat. Lily must have sensed it too, because she excused herself to join Oscar on his tour inside.

“Are we okay?” Maddie asked sadly, and sounding a little unsure.

I nodded and hugged her close to me, stroking her hair and inhaling her scent. “I understand why you feel you have to do this. I don't have to like it to respect that. And I really don't need the details. Just promise me you'll be careful. Don't take any unnecessary risks and come home safe and sound with all of this behind us.”

She nodded against my chest. “It's not happening for a . . .”

I cut her off. “Maddie, I really can't handle the details. I was barely keeping control of my wolf today, and poorly at that. I've never lost control like that before. The more I know, the worse it'll get. I know mates aren't supposed to have secrets, but for all of our sakes, please keep this to yourself.”

She wrapped her arms around my waist and hugged me tightly. “If you're sure that's what you really want.”

“It's not, but it's what I need,” I told her honestly.

Already in my thoughts was the one place I dreaded most. I knew I would know when the day of her mission came. I knew that I wouldn't be able to handle it, or control my wolf from stopping her without serious intervention. I knew she was going to hate what it did to me, but I didn't see much choice. I started calculating a plan. I couldn't risk her or blowing her cover and endangering her further because I wasn't strong enough to control the beast.

Thinking through the details, I planned to talk to Kyle, make him swear that, when the day came, he'd lock me up in the place we feared the most, because it was the right thing to do.

Maddie

Chapter 26

I didn't like keeping things from Liam, but I tried to do as he wished. It was making things a little awkward between us and I constantly second-guessed if what I was doing was right. I couldn't sleep at night thinking of all those shifters stuck in cages. The mission was to get Raina out safely, but could I really leave the rest behind?

I had secretly spoken to Patrick about the possibility of rescuing others. His friend Dave worked in the clinic where they were holding them, alongside Jacob. Patrick and Dave had another human friend named Larry who was the third Verndari assigned to the region along with Martin, whom I had already met. Larry was apparently a bit of a computer whiz, and we were able to coordinate Raina's escape with their system's patching window, though Jacob wasn't aware of that. The servers running the camera system in the building would only be down for three minutes and it took another two minutes to get the system fully back online. A five-minute window wasn't much, but it was hopefully enough for what I was planning.

There was absolutely no room for error if we were to pull it off. I had to be in Jacob's office when the computers went down and back before they came back online. He would be busy taking care of Raina's supposed remains, and as far as he was concerned, my only role in the day would be to park next to the trash compactor with Patrick safely hidden inside. Patrick would retrieve Raina and hide her with him inside the trunk of my car while the cameras were down, and then I'd simply drive home afterwards.

The plan was simple, it just wasn't enough. For my enhanced

plans to work, everything had to go perfectly.

The night before the mission I dropped Oscar off at Jessica's for another sleepover at Bobby's. Since school had started back, Oscar was thriving with other kids his age. They typically only did sleepovers on the weekends now. A Wednesday night sleepover was unexpected and apparently super exciting for the boys. I had thanked Jessica profusely. All she knew is that I needed to leave early the next morning and would be out of town for the day. I could have left him with Mary, but didn't think he'd ask as many questions or draw too much attention towards my plans if he was distracted by Bobby Moore.

"So tomorrow?" Liam asked, noticing Oscar was not around for dinner or to say good night to.

I simply nodded. He had asked me not to tell him the details. He didn't want any part of it, but I wouldn't lie to him to maintain that request, either. My admittance made him very possessive. I headed to bed early, knowing morning would come quickly, but he had followed me and there had been little sleep that night. When he had lain over me, something he hadn't attempted since the first time we had tried to have sex, the panic began, but I pushed it aside, knowing he needed the control more than I did for once.

It was arguably the best sex we'd ever had. I found I really enjoyed the aggressive side of Liam in the bedroom, even if I was a little sore and a whole lot tired on this very important day. I could have sworn I even felt my canines sharpen as a result, and wondered if I had just imagined it or if nature would find a way to truly bond us. I blushed and smiled thinking about it. We had gotten very little sleep, but he woke long enough to claim me once again before I headed out.

"You look very happy for someone who's about to cause mass chaos on an already dangerous mission today," Patrick said when he picked me up. We had a couple hours of driving to reach Jacob's office and there was no real point in him riding in the trunk the entire way.

I was surprised to find Patrick O'Connell very easy to talk to. He didn't pry into anything too deeply. We talked about how Oscar was adjusting to school, the wedding plans, Elise—basically anything but the mission ahead of us. I was grateful for his company, but it didn't stop my nerves from increasing the closer we got.

Just before we arrived at Jacob's office, I stopped at an abandoned gas station that I knew would not have any cameras watching, and helped Patrick into the trunk. Apparently, there was already a release button from the inside so a person would not actually get locked in there. Who knew?

It was a rental car that Jacob had somehow managed to get to Patrick beforehand. A cover story had been fabricated so no one would question why I was driving it. It was supposed to help us remain untraceable, and that no DNA could ever be pulled from it, showing our part in the escape. It had sounded a little paranoid to me, especially since the plan was for everyone to believe Raina was dead, but Jacob had insisted.

I pulled up next to the dumpsters at the side of the building, exactly where Jacob had told me to park. The lot was largely full, so it didn't even look odd for me to park there.

"Ready?" I asked Patrick in what appeared to be an empty car.

"Just breathe, Maddie. You can do this," he told me.

"I know. I know. I'm just nervous. We left absolutely no room for error."

He chuckled. "It's just a good thing humans don't have heightened hearing. You need to try and slow your heart rate. You're going to freak out every shifter in there."

I laughed. "Okay, okay, I can do this. Here goes. Good luck."

"Good luck, Maddie."

I got out of the car and walked around to the front desk. By all appearances, it looked like a small, elite research facility. That's what I had always thought it was. I just didn't know that the research being performed involved my kind against their will.

"Janie!" the receptionist greeted me, sounding a little surprised.

"Hello, Helen," I said, trying to remember what the old Janie would have said and how she would have acted. I wasn't that scared, fragile girl anymore, but I needed to act like I was.

"Jacob said you've been struggling some lately. I hope this is a sign you're doing well?"

"Yes, thank you," I said, barely making eye contact with the woman. "I'm here for lunch with Jacob."

"I suspected as much," she said, nodding to the food I was

carrying with me. "I'm sure he'll be thrilled to see you out and about. Just sign in here," she said, pointing to a visitor log on the desk. "You remember how to get to his office?"

"Of course," I said politely.

"It was really good to see you, Jane."

‘You too, Helen," I said as I turned and headed down the hall I knew would take me to Jacob's office. I was a nervous wreck. My hands were even a little shaky. Fortunately, that only confirmed the severe depression stories and anxiety attacks Jacob and Annie had told people in light of my absence. It wasn’t that I was really ever around these people, but I supposed they at least asked about me and kept up through Jacob.

I knocked on his door and waited for him to welcome me in, but as the door opened a young man I didn't recognize stepped out, shaking hands with Jacob.

"You sure you can't do lunch? We could finish this discussion once and for all," the stranger said.

"Sorry, Trevor, this is my daughter, Janie. I don't believe you two have met before. Janie, this is Trevor Daniels, Stephen's son. You remember him, don't you? He's one of the proprietors of the clinic. I'm afraid I have to decline your lunch offer. As you can see, I already have plans," Jacob told him.

"Hello, Janie, it's so nice to finally meet you. I've heard so much about you," Trevor said shaking my hand. It gave me chills all the way to my bones. He couldn't have been much older than me, but the vibes coming off him were pure evil.

"You as well," I said quietly, not making eye contact with him.

"We'll talk soon, Trevor. Janie, come on in. I'm so happy you could make it."

It sounded like a perfectly normal conversation for a perfectly normal visit, but as soon as I stepped into the office and the door closed behind me, I let out the breath I had been holding.

"Be strong, Jane, it's almost over," Jacob reassured me.

I presented him with a box of fried chicken with all the fixings I had picked up at the drive-through. He cleared his desk and I laid out the spread. We both were well aware of the camera in the room watching us. We didn’t talk much, just ate, or at least pretended to in amicable silence.

At exactly 11:20, his phone rang. I jumped a little, thankful that these people wouldn't think anything of it. We both knew it was the call telling us Raina was dead. Martin would have already administered the necessary dosage to make it appear so.

"Yes . . . okay . . . which one?" He sighed sadly. "Not Raina . . . Okay, I'll be right down." Hanging up, he addressed me next. "I'm so sorry, dear, one of my patients has just passed away and I need to go and tend to a few things. Please eat. I won't be long."

"Are you sure?" I asked him.

"Of course. I'll make it as fast as possible." He left and I stared at the food ahead and pretended to eat, despite the fact that my nerves had my stomach rolling. I took out my phone and opened a game. I wasn't sure if the cameras could see me or not, but it allowed me an excuse to watch the time.

Eleven-thirty rolled over and I knew Larry was kicking off his patching of the security monitor's feed. I waited, trying not to look around for the camera to check the light. At 11:37 a text came through, causing me to jump.

"Now or never," was all it said.

I looked around the room. Spotting the camera in the corner, confirming the light was off, I hit the four-minute countdown on my phone, pulled out the access badge Patrick had given me earlier, and I headed out the door. Seeing it was all clear, I ran to the end of the hallway and peeked around the corner. Finding it clear also, I ran to the end of the hall and used my badge to get in. Even with the systems down, the access panels worked; they just didn't log in any data from whenever and whoever had accessed them.

I entered the room and came to a shocking halt. I knew I didn't have much time, but I was not prepared at all to see shifters in human form crammed into four foot cages stacked five across and two high. There were seven rows in all and they were all full but one.

"Help me," a lady cried hoarsely.

That was enough to spur me back into action. Checking my phone, we only had two minutes remaining. I quickly hit the emergency release button that opened all the cages at once.

"You never saw me. This is your chance to escape, but the rest is up to you," I told the room, loudly enough for all to hear.

I quickly scrambled for the door, checking that the hallway

was clear, and let myself out. The shifters didn't hesitate even a moment. A few practically plowed me over as I made my way back to Jacob's office, letting myself in and sitting in the exact spot I had been when the cameras went down. Before the door fully closed behind me, I saw several of them start to shift into various animals as they ran through the halls in search of their freedom.

The noise and the chaos resumed. A few gunshots were fired and I prayed no one got hurt. It made me cringe, and I cowered behind Jacob's desk. When the door finally opened Jacob entered, pale as a ghost.

"What's going on? I heard a gunshot," I said, bordering on hysterics. It wasn't exactly a show just for Jacob. I hadn't predicted the humans would fight back with weapons. I was scared for both sides and questioned if what I had done was the right thing.

Sensing I was going into a panic attack, Jacob began soothing me and speaking in calming tones. His phone rang and I jumped.

"My daughter's here," he finally said. "I need backup to ensure she gets out of the building safely." He hung up and to me he said, "I'm so sorry, Janie. There's been a breech in the facility. Security is on its way to escort you out."

"Aren't you coming?" I asked.

"No, I'm afraid I have to stay and clean up the mess. We're not sure what happened."

"Is it safe?" I demanded.

"I'll be fine, dear. Go home and tell Annie and Oscar I'm okay, and I love them."

I nodded and when the security guys came for me they were fully armed. Three of them surrounded me and escorted me to my car, never suspecting once that I harbored two shifters in my trunk. We didn't see a single animal or shifter anywhere. I wondered what happened to them all. There had been so many.

The second I was away from the last security tower I started crying. By the time I reached the old abandoned gas station we had stopped at on the way in, I could barely see the road and I was shaking all over. It suddenly dawned on me that I hadn't heard anything from Patrick. Terrified he didn't make it, I started screaming.

"Patrick?!"

"I'm here, Maddie. I have Raina, we're both okay."

I slammed on the brakes and jumped out. Opening the trunk and seeing Raina's wide, shocked eyes as she was nestled against Patrick was my breaking point. I sat on the ground and just cried.

Raina got out, still looking confused. Patrick followed and tried to comfort me, but I was inconsolable and quickly losing my internal battle as panic rose within.

"Come on, it's not safe out here. We need to keep moving. I'll drive," Patrick said as he tucked Raina into the backseat before helping me into the front.

Just before the door closed, a smell so memorable and strong hit me, crippling me in panic. I looked around and just at the edge of the woods I saw them . . . all six of them. They smiled and nodded at me in appreciation and my entire body began to shake violently. Tigers!

"What's wrong?" Patrick asked, sounding very concerned the moment he got into the car.

"Drive. Quickly, just drive," was as much as I could say before the full realization of what I'd done began to sink in. I had freed the shifters. I had freed the six men that had raped me so violently. What had I done?

In a fog, like I wasn't really myself, just watching myself, I picked up my phone and I called Jacob.

"Janie, are you okay?" he asked, sounding very distracted.

"No," I said in a far too calm and eerie voice. "The six men that raped me—I just saw them by an abandoned gas station, approximately three miles from your office."

I heard him inhale sharply, knowing I had never once confessed to being raped to him or Annie, before covering the receiver and yelling out some orders.

"We'll get them, Jane. I promise you, they won't be allowed to wander free for long. If it's the last thing I do, I'll get them. I'm so sorry. I don't know how this happened."

Guilt. That's what I felt, sheer guilt. I had done this.

"Shit. You fecking let them all out, didn't you?" Patrick asked.

I was still in that daze outside of myself. "You didn't see them, Patrick. They were in cages like animals, stacked two high and five deep. Seven rows, all filled but one."

"That would have been mine," Raina said softly. "They'll come for me now, too."

"They won't," Patrick assured her. "We went to great lengths to ensure they all believed you were dead. They think you were already cremated. No one will be looking for you, especially with all the others on the run now."

"Wow! Who are you people? And is that why I can't remember anything? How did I even get here? Where are we going?"

I supposed Raina's fear and questions helped distract me from my own. I was still very shaken up, but I had something to do as I tried to tend to her.

"Relax, Raina," I started.

"See, how do you even know my name? We've never met. I've smelled him before, but I can't place where, but you, I've never even seen you before. Why did you do this?" she interrupted me.

I smiled in spite of it all. "Kelsey sends her love."

"Elena? She did this?" Raina asked, using Kelsey's given name that she hadn't gone by since she was four years old.

"Perhaps more like Kyle, on Kelsey's behalf. He's been working hard to keep this entire mission from her. Not so easy for a fully bonded couple, but I don't believe she knows, yet," Patrick filled her in.

"You're Westin then?" Raina asked, looking confused.

"Patrick O'Connell. Originally from the Irish Clan, but I've been a Westin for a while now. I'm mated to Elise Westin. This is Maddie. She's mated to Liam Westin and was our inside connection to the facility."

Raina fell quiet with her questions as she tried to take it all in. I was grateful Patrick hadn't told her exactly what my connection was. I didn't think I could handle hearing Jacob portrayed as the bad guy. I prayed that wasn't the case, but I had seen them with my own eyes. Did my rapists even deserve such treatment? I wanted to say yes, but I had been so horrified by the conditions I had found, that I hadn't hit the yellow button that would have only opened the cages for those deemed safe. I had hit the green button that unlocked every cage in the room at once.

The hours spent driving home, were largely in comfortable silence as each of us internalized the events in our own way.

When we arrived back at the house I went straight to my room to see Liam. I needed him and I knew he would need me, too. He wasn't there.

I knocked on Kyle's office next, and he answered.

"Have you seen Liam?" I asked without even a hello, still feeling distraught and upset at what I had done.

"Hey, I didn't know you guys were back already. Did everything go okay?" he asked.

I nodded. "Raina's in the living room with Mary, doting over Zander. They just called Kelsey to come over, but didn't tell her why. You may want to be there when she arrives."

He released a huge breath and hugged me. "Thank God! I'll never be able to repay you for this, MC."

I just looked at him sadly. Where was my mate?

"Why do I get the feeling something more is going on?" he asked.

"I may have done something terrible," I confessed.

"Come on in," he said, opening the door wider and closing it after I had entered. "You know you can talk freely in here. What happened?"

I told him about my and Patrick's plans and how I couldn't leave any of them behind, but I didn't realize until too late that even included some very bad and dangerous ones. I told him about seeing the tigers.

"Shit! So it's true then? Oscar really could be half tiger?"

I nodded with tears streaming down my face. "It's been a really long and hard day, Kyle. Please just tell me where my mate is."

He grinned. "You know, today's the first time I've heard you call him that." Then his face fell. "He's not well, Maddie. I won't even try to sugarcoat it. He asked me to chain him up, knowing his wolf would overpower him and come after you."

"What?! How could you? He's your brother, not some animal!" I yelled, very near hysterics at that point.

"Don't you think I know that? And you haven't seen what this has done to him. He's barely hanging on. You two should have completed the bond first. It would have made things so much easier."

"Don't you think I know that? Don't you think I would, if I could?" He was making me angry and pointing out my biggest failure on what was already an enormously emotional day.

"What do you mean, 'if you could'?" Kyle asked.

"I'm not a shifter, Kyle. They- they killed my wolf the night they tried to kill me. I physically can't seal the bond. My human canines aren't enough." I sobbed.

He consoled me as he would one of his sisters. I was family already. I was pack and he was my Alpha.

"Shit. Why didn't you tell me sooner?"

"It's not exactly something I'm proud of and want to talk about, Kyle. Please, just take me to him. It'll still calm his wolf. I've told him since the beginning it would never work. If he's as bad as you're making him out to be, maybe I should just walk away. It would be best for everyone."

He snorted. "MC, that wouldn't be best for anyone. It's been a long day. Just promise me you won't make any decisions right now. I don't know if a wolf spirit can be killed without killing the human host. I've never heard of such a thing, but let me do some research and see what I can find out about that, okay?"

I nodded sadly.

"Come on. Let's go calm your mate, and you."

We walked out of the back of the house after stopping long enough for him to welcome Raina back. I didn't know where he was leading me. We headed into the thick of the forest behind the Alpha house. He peppered me with questions about my wolf. He didn't seem convinced about what I had told him. How I wished I was wrong!

As we came to a rocky section filled with caves, he headed into one. It was dark and moist inside, smelling earthy, and a lot like Liam. My stomach twisted as we headed deeper in and I saw signs of manmade things inside. Some looked like torture devices. There were chains attached to the walls.

"What is this place?" I whispered.

"It was once something of a jail for our kind. It hasn't been used in close to a hundred years, but when our pack first settled in this area there were humans everywhere. It took several decades to run the humans out. Our ancestors had traveled across the country, mostly in wolf form as it was a young, wild territory at the time. Readjusting to civilization for some of the shifters had been a struggle. This place was used to contain those that needed, um, a little more time to adjust. It's not a part of our heritage we're exactly proud of. Liam and I stumbled across this place when we were just pups. Scared the shit out of us."

"So, what are we doing here?" I asked.

He gave me an apologetic look just as an aggressive growl echoed through the chamber. Kyle picked up the pace, heading towards the noise. We came to an iron gate that was locked. He took out a key and unlocked it and we stepped inside.

"No!" I screamed as I saw Liam chained to other end of the room. He was human, but there was something feral about him. His eyes darted around the room and he growled and snarled at Kyle, showing all his canines despite being in human form. "Kyle, unlock him now!" I demanded.

"I'm sorry, MC. He's not right. His wolf is in control. He knew this would happen and begged me to do it. He'll change and tear me to bits the second he's free as man and beast fight for dominance. I'm going to give you the key and then I'm going to back out and shut the gate. He could never hurt you, not as man or wolf. You're safe, but I'm not. You need to calm him down and help Liam regain control."

I took the keys with shaky hands. He was little more than a feral animal before me. Kyle backed out of the room quickly and I waited until I heard the chains on the gate lock and Kyle gave the go-ahead.

Suddenly, I wasn't afraid anymore. My mate was hurting and he needed me more than ever. I ran to Liam and quickly unlocked the shackles holding him down. Strong arms wrapped around me, far stronger than Liam's human arms. He was generating all the power of his wolf but still in human form. I knew it was possible, but I had never actually seen it.

Crushed to him I breathed in his scent and kissed his exposed neck right in the place I desperately wished to mark him. I felt his sharp teeth press into my own flesh in the exact same place on me. Tears streamed down my face as I was unable to follow his lead. He pulled back and softened. I was crying and it drew Liam out quickly. He kissed the mark he had left on my skin, tracing light, feathery kisses up my neck and across my cheek till he found my mouth.

His body trembled in my arms as I returned his kiss and I could feel him coming back to me. Finally pulling back and leaving me breathless, he spoke in a hoarse voice.

"Just tell me you're okay."

"I'm okay," I said honestly. I knew it wasn't the time to tell him what I had done. He needed to get control of himself more before we had that conversation, but I was going to be okay, and I knew he would too.

"I'm sorry I bit you. My wolf doesn't understand and is angry you haven't completed the bond."

"Are you okay?" I asked.

"I'm going to be now that you're back. Just promise me the mission is over and you'll never do anything like that again," he begged.

"I can't promise that, but for now, it's over." I hoped beyond all hopes that what I was telling him was the truth.

Liam
Chapter 27

The calm that came over me just from Maddie's presence scared me almost as much as my wolf as he battled for dominance. To think one person had that much control over me was overwhelming, but if it had to be someone, I was glad it was her.

I hadn't meant to bite her, to mark her in that way. It wasn't right. My wolf had surged, insisting she was ours and calling out to her wolf. I couldn't help but think that if her wolf were truly gone, mine wouldn't continue calling her out. I imagined he'd be in mourning, not so insistent and impatient. Still, to mark her when she couldn't return it was wrong. Anyone who saw it on her now would know that I had marked her, but she hadn't marked me back. It was a sign of the ultimate rejection to our kind. Though I tried not to take it personally, it hurt on a deep level.

I wanted to kiss her again and a whole lot more, but not there. The place had always given me the creeps and before then I had only spent enough time in that place to satisfy a dare, since the first time Kyle and I had stumbled across it and asked Dad what it was. I knew it had been the right thing to do, but I was ready to take her home, shower, and claim my mate over and over again until my wolf was again at peace. So I did.

For the first week or two afterward, I could barely let Maddie out of my sight. I still didn't know all the details of what had happened, and wasn't sure I ever would, or wanted to, but something had scared her. I could tell, because she clung to me, too.

She asked if she could enroll in some online classes, saying that with Oscar she had never had the opportunity. Annie had insisted on her graduating high school, but college had never really been an option. Of course I encouraged her, and set up a second desk in my office for her to work and stay nearby. With the construction of the house wrapping up, I didn't expect her to work side by side with me much longer, but for the time I was grateful. It was exactly what my wolf and I needed.

With the tension of her mission behind us, we started to grow closer again. It was insane how much I had missed her in those weeks of distance where she kept her silence, as I had stubbornly asked, but causing a wedge between us in the process.

Somehow the mission had helped us in the bedroom, too. She was no longer freaking out or pulling away if I got a little aggressive. It was a good thing too, because my wolf was exceedingly aggressive these days and it was rubbing off on me, too. It wasn't all bad though. I felt stronger, more secure in myself than I ever had before. Kyle had even recognized me as an Alpha to the pack council. I had been a little surprised. I had never shown Alpha signs before, but they watched for them throughout the pack. Channeling Alphas in healthy ways that allowed them to be active members of the pack without causing problems was an important process within the pack. It helped guide and direct them into positions of power. My job as CEO already gave me that, so little was changing in my life in that regard.

Standing before the mirror, looking over my tux, on what was supposed to be the greatest day of my life—at least that's what the humans said—I thought life was pretty good. Lily and Maddie had spent countless hours making this day the greatest wedding in the history of weddings. I smiled to myself thinking about it. If this was what she wanted, what did it really hurt?

Oscar was still beyond excited. I had insisted on incorporating his adoption into the ceremony, despite my sister's protests. He was as much a part of this as Maddie and I, perhaps even more, because we both knew the only reason I had agreed to any of it was for him.

Dad knocked on my bedroom door and then walked in, looking like a slightly bigger, grayer version of me.

"How are you holding up, son?" he asked.

I shrugged. "It's all just a formality, really. They're already mine." My grin widened. We hadn't been able to seal our bond, but we would be legally tied to each other after today, a "real" family as Oscar liked to say.

Mom peeked into the room, and immediately started to tear up. “It's time.”

Dad went to his mate and consoled her, as he escorted her from the room before she could begin fussing over me. I said a quick prayer that my groomsmen had sobered up some. Since we were going all out, they had insisted on a kickass bachelor party the night before, and less than twelve hours ago had all been completely shitfaced—well, with exception of my best man, Oscar. Of course I didn't drink, so it wasn't an issue for me.

“Hey, look at you!” I said, seeing Oscar in his tux for the first time. He looked so grown-up and proud, with little Z toddling after him carrying the ring bearer pillow. No, we were not allowing a one-year-old to carry the actual rings. He had fake ones tied to it and they would only be for show.

Lily and Elise had truly gone all out. There was frou-frou girly stuff everywhere. My new backyard was covered in a kind of netting they called tulle and there were flowers brought in everywhere, even though we had asked to keep it small, it looked like half of San Marco had shown up anyway.

Maddie's family hadn't been able to make it, except for her sister Shelby, who was one of the bridesmaids. Collier Pack had three newly mated pairs and challenges had been scheduled requiring their Alpha. I knew the reunion of Maddie and Shelby must have been an emotional one, and I truly hoped my mate was okay. They had held their own bachelorette party and my sisters forbade me to come anywhere near her until the wedding.

We didn't get settled into the house yet as we had hoped, but I did have a surprise of my own for our honeymoon night. Our new king sized bed had arrived the day before and was set up in the master bedroom. It was the only piece of furniture in the house, but as far as I was concerned, it was the only one that mattered. The rest would be delivered within the week.

I didn't realize I was nervous in the least, until I saw Kyle, Patrick, Chase, and Cole Anderson dressed and at least sober, hopefully enough not to screw up anything. Relief washed over me. Chase hadn't yet met Madelyn, at least not since her return. He had driven in from college late the night before to stand up for me in the wedding. I knew he would love her and welcome her to the family.

“We're all ready, Liam. You have five minutes then we need

to start walking out. Cole will lead the way," Oscar informed me, checking his watch every few minutes to ensure we weren't late.

"Kid, you've been hanging out with Aunt Lily entirely too much." They all laughed, knowing it was true.

Walking to stand in front of so many family and friends was kind of surreal and a little nerve-wracking. Cole took his place in the center and I stood off to his left with Oscar, Kyle, Chase, and Patrick lined up beside me. Music started playing and Jessica Moore walked down the aisle first, looking lovely in a light-purple dress. She was ready to explode at any second, but being Maddie's first true friend, of course aside from Lily, in San Marco, she had insisted she could make it. Elise came next in pale-blue that made her teary eyes shine brightly, followed by Shelby in some light-peach colored dress. Finally, Lily made her appearance. I rolled my eyes and grinned at her pink dress with matching pink highlights. It was just so Lily!

At last the piano and harp strummed along with "Here Comes the Bride" as Maddie began walking towards me. I heard the oohs and aahs as she was getting closer, but obscured from my view by all the standing guests. Finally, she reached the aisle and I could now see clearly the most gorgeous woman I'd ever seen. My mouth dropped open and I gawked at the vision in white that was gliding towards me. She looked strong, and confident, and to me she was still my sweet and innocent Maddie in every way.

"Isn't she beautiful?" Oscar whispered, and all I could do was nod.

"Dude, close your mouth. You're embarrassing yourself," Chase chided in good humor.

Suddenly I got it. I understood why human men would go through all the wedding planning shit just to have this one moment. As Maddie finally reached my side, I grabbed her and kissed her as the guests around us hooted and hollered.

Cole cleared his throat, pretending to look annoyed. "Liam, that part comes at the end."

The crowd chuckled, but I didn't care. In that moment it was just me and Maddie . . . and Oscar, who had wedged himself between us, giving me a stern look that said I better pull it together. Maddie bit her bottom lip, trying to hide a smile, and blushed.

"Dearly beloved, you all know I have no clue what I'm doing here, so please bear with me," Cole started, inciting more laughter.

"And you all know why we're here today, to join this family in adoption and holy matrimony. Oscar," he started, sounding very official, "it has been petitioned and signed by the court for the legal adoption of you by none other than Liam Michael Westin. Technically it's already a done deal, but in light of the festivities, Oscar Jacob Winthrop, do you hereby take Liam Michael Westin to be your dad?"

"I do," Oscar said excitedly.

"You agree to listen and obey, respect, and love this guy?"

"Yes, I do," he said, more seriously this time.

"And Liam, do you take Oscar to be your son, to love and cherish and raise as your own for the rest of your life?"

"I do," I said, picking him up as his arms wrapped tightly around me.

"Well, then, by no power vested in me, 'cause like I said, it's already been filed with the courts and a done deal, I present Mr. Oscar Jacob Winthrop Westin."

Those present rose and clapped. Oscar glowed in the cheers. It was official. I was a father. My heart expanded just a little more at the thought.

"Now, now, calm down. Everyone take a seat so we can get this show over with. I hear there's a buffet with a carving station that's calling my name," Cole announced.

I looked back at Maddie, whose nose was pink, and her perfectly done makeup was starting to streak just a little. I didn't think she'd ever looked more beautiful, so I kissed her again. Cheers went up all around. This time Kyle chimed in.

"Might as well simmer down. This could take awhile at this rate." To me he added, "There's a thing called a honeymoon for a reason, so keep your lips to yourself until Cole tells you otherwise."

I grinned sheepishly. Nothing and no one was going to ruin this day for me.

Cole cleared his throat. "Are we ready to proceed?"

I shrugged and kissed her one more time. It was a quick, playful kiss and she was thoroughly embarrassed by the end of it, when I announced he could proceed . . . but to make it quick.

"Man, I rehearsed this part and everything," he said in exaggeration as he threw his notes into the air behind him. "I'll just wing it to speed things along. Maddie, do you take Liam to be your lawfully wedded husband, to love and cherish, and keep in line as best you can, yadda yada yada, as long as you both shall live?"

She giggled. "Yes, I mean, I do."

"Right answer," Cole praised. "Now Liam, you gonna love this girl with all your heart for the rest of your life? Protect and respect her, and even try not to complain too much when Lily tries to get her involved in one of her no-good plans?"

I laughed, glancing past my mate to my twin who was easily three shades pinker than her dress. Cole winked at her and I saw her stumble—swoon, I think Maddie would call it. I tried not to laugh as I said, "I do."

He called for the rings next. Maddie raised a shaky hand that calmed instantly as I took it and placed the ring she had chosen on her finger. I lifted it to my mouth and kissed her hand, hearing her heart rate increase.

"Dude, keep those lips to yourself, we're almost in the end zone," Chase announced, loudly enough for everyone to hear. I just grinned back at him.

Maddie placed the ring she had picked out for me on my left ring finger and the possessive feeling that washed over me had my canines elongating.

"Mine," I growled, pulling her toward me as I captured her mouth in mine and really kissed her this time.

"Close enough!" Cole announced. "Keep on kissing your bride. I now present Mr. and Mrs. Liam Westin." To Kyle he added, "I really hope this doesn't start a trend. I think he's a prime example of why shifters never caught on to the wedding trend."

Maddie finally broke our kiss, blushing and laughing along with our friends and family.

"We did it!" I announced, picking up my kid with my left arm, and wrapping my right around my bride as the band played more music and we headed back down the aisle with our wedding party in tow.

I headed into the house and kissed my bride again, as Oscar hugged us both together, before thanking the others, especially Lily, for making it such a wonderful day. I truly meant it, too.

The reception passed by in a blur of dances, hugs, and well wishes. I even took it well when Maddie smashed cake into my face at Lily's insistence. I never understood that tradition, and still didn't after experiencing it.

Life wasn't perfect. The Verndari were still out there. Jacob had been concerned enough that he and Annie had decided against coming to the wedding, for Maddie's safety. There was still evil in the world, but looking at Oscar it was hard to reconcile the nightmare Madelyn had faced with the amazing outcome of my son. *Mine*, I thought. From that day forward he would always be my son.

We said good night to each of our guests and looked around at the massive cleanup job we had before us.

"No," Lily said, doing that weird, awkward twin thing she sometimes did that felt like she was reading my mind. "We'll be over in the morning and all of this will be taken care of and cleaned up before you get back."

"Get back? From where?" Maddie asked.

"No clue," Lily said. "Liam insisted on handling that part all by himself, and he won't tell anyone a thing. Not even a teeny, tiny little clue."

"Go home, Lily," I said, hugging her tightly and picking her up and twirling her around as she giggled. "And thank you. Really. It was perfect."

She had tears in her eyes and for once was speechless as she left after hugging Maddie goodbye, too.

"So?" Maddie said awkwardly. "What's the plan?"

I scooped her up in my arms and carried her down the hall and up the stairs. "Well, Lily's going to inevitably put a major kink in them," I said, kicking our bedroom door open and hearing her gasp at the sight of the bed she had all but begged for and I had told her was too big for the room. "I hadn't really planned on going anywhere."

She looked back at me, smiling. "It's perfect. I really was dreading the idea of a car ride somewhere tonight. I'm exhausted."

"I hope not too exhausted," I growled, nipping her earlobe.

I carefully undressed her like the precious gift she was, and laid her on our bed. Making quick work of the penguin suit, I quickly joined her. I wanted to give her a sweet, beautiful moment to remember, but I had been hard since the first moment I'd laid eyes on her hours earlier. I wanted her too much to take it slow.

"Mine," I growled aggressively, encouraged by the smell of her arousal. She was mine, for always. We were married. It may have only been a silly human tradition, but it felt like more than before somehow, even if only in my own mind.

I feared I might be too rough in my need for her, but she met me with equal force. I was on the cusp of what I sought most when she gasped and jumped back. I looked at her, panting in the midst of our lovemaking, but there were tears in her eyes, happy tears. Grinning, she smiled brightly, showing me a full set of canines. Nothing could have shocked me more and I didn't even fully register it until I felt her teeth sink into the base of my neck. I followed her lead and a sort of frenzy started that sent us both into blissful oblivion.

When I finally came to my senses, she lay in my arms, sobbing tears of joy. I could feel that joy more clearly than I ever had before. Our bond.

“Mine,” I growled, stroking and kissing her. “Forever and always. Forever mine.”

Maddie

Epilogue

I sat on the back deck watching Liam push Oscar on the swing. *My guys*, I smiled to myself. Life might not always be exactly the way we want it, but mine was a pretty good one. I had a wonderful man who loved me unconditionally. Lord knew he'd proven that time and time again. I had a smart, funny, courageous son who filled my heart.

I was proud of how well Oscar had settled into San Marco. He might have even fit in better than me. The mystery of what he might or might not be only added to his popularity among the other children.

There certainly were few kept secrets in Westin Pack. Kyle and Kelsey believed in open honesty with their pack, for the most part. The truth about the Verndari was still kept to only a select few, and I understood their reasoning behind that decision.

I was worried about Annie and Jacob. They hadn't come to the wedding, and though we'd spoken a few times, not much was ever really said since the day I rescued Raina and the shifters being held as prisoners there. I wondered if Jacob even suspected it was me.

My parents and sisters were coming for a visit in just a week. I was a nervous wreck and had been obsessively cleaning the house for days in preparation. I guessed those extra bedrooms Liam insisted on adding to the house were going to get used after all. It had been wonderful to see Shelby again and she had stayed and been back to visit a few times, but I hadn't seen the rest of my family in over eight years. They hadn't met Oscar yet. It was going to be a tough reunion, but I spoke to at least one of them every day. Thomas still wasn't talking to me, but I hoped he'd come around eventually.

Lily was coming over tomorrow to help me prep some meals for their visit so I wouldn't have to spend all my time in the kitchen, though I already knew Mary was planning to have us all over at least one night. She loved cooking for a crowd. Me? Not so much, but I could learn. My kitchen skills would never be gourmet, but my cooking was getting better and my guys had no complaints, at least not that they'd admit to me. Who knew running a house was so much work?

As I sat there, I smiled to myself while contentedly sipping a steaming cup of coffee, and I thought back to all we'd come through, and all we have to look forward to. I was secretly hoping to make Oscar a big brother soon. I had finally made an appointment with Micah, the local physician, who had seen no physical reasons I couldn’t get pregnant again. I hadn’t told Liam yet, but I knew he would be over the moon about it. He was so good with kids.

I moved in my seat and my back began to itch. I scratched it, not giving it much thought. A few minutes later it started to kick in. I tried to think back through everything I had eaten that day. Nothing seemed off, but I knew I was about to have another allergic reaction. I was already rubbing my back against the chair, trying to find some relief.

I had battled these hives for as long as I could remember. Jacob had run every allergy test he could think of on me, and came up with nothing. They always came back fine. I wasn’t allergic to anything as far as the tests showed, yet I would still get these awful hives requiring massive doses of Benadryl to stop the itching. It always knocked me out and I hated that groggy feeling I'd always wake up to.

"Oh no," Oscar said sadly, walking towards me hand in hand with my handsome husband. "Looks like we won't be going to the movies after all?"

"What are you talking about? Of course we are," Liam assured him.

"No. Look. Mommy's having the allergies again," he informed him. "Mommy, want me to get your medicine?" Then he turned to Liam to fill him in. "The medicine makes the itchies go away, but it always puts her to sleep for a really long time.

Liam watched me curiously "Sweetheart, how often do you

get these, uh, itchies?"

I sighed. "At least once a month, sometimes more. They've been happening a lot ever since we got here to San Marco."

He closed his eyes and looked like he was biting back a smile. "And do you know what triggers them?"

"No. It's suspected to be a food allergy, but we've never been able to determine exactly what. All the tests come back clear." It was the truth.

"And how long has this been happening?"

"Nearly as long as I can remember. It worsened after Oscar was born. Annie says that's normal, that pregnancy can trigger heightened allergies."

"Uh-huh, okay, well for today, let's pretend that's not the case and try something new. Oscar, no meds for Mommy."

"But Daddy, you don't understand. It gets really bad and she's miserable without them. The faster she gets them, the easier it is."

"Sometimes life isn't meant to be easy, kid. Can you just trust me on this?"

"Liam, this really isn't the time. It's getting bad." He was starting to irritate me. I knew he hated human medicine, and I understood he wanted me off everything Annie had ever prescribed, but this was different.

I got up and headed to the door, intent on getting the pills myself. I had to stop in the doorway and use it to scratch my back again. It wasn't helping at all. This time it was coming on fast and felt worse than usual.

Liam laughed. He actually stood there laughing at me, grinning from ear to ear, like it was the greatest moment of his life watching me suffer.

"Sweetie, I just need you to trust me. It's going to be okay, I promise. Here," he said, walking over and picking me up. "Just try not to scratch. It doesn't help anything at all."

"That's easy for you to say, you aren't the one broken out in hives from head to toe, feeling like you're being eaten alive by a swarm of mosquitoes or something."

He carried me out into the yard and set me down in the grass.

"Great," I said, starting to get pissed. "Grass is one of the biggest allergy triggers for most people. Even those without the actual allergy are often highly sensitive to it. Are you trying to make things worse?"

I couldn't help it, as I was sitting on the grass, so I lay out flat and wiggled around on my back, just praying for some relief from all the itching. To make matters even worse, all it did was make Oscar join in on the laughing.

"Just laugh it up. I'm so happy to entertain the both of you."

"No meds, bud, no matter how much she begs. Just trust me, this is perfectly normal."

"There's nothing normal about this, you jackass. Oscar. . ."

"No!" Liam cut me off with a command while using some of that Alpha crap he'd started channeling when we met. It had helped a lot during several panic attacks, but right now it was just making me angry. How dare he?

He stood there looking at me, then kneeled down and gave me a quick kiss with an evil glint in his eye. "Trust me, Maddie. I love you. It's going to be okay. Better than okay, even."

He rose and began stripping his clothes off.

"Liam!" I scolded. Oscar was right there, and I definitely wasn't in the mood. What was he thinking? I swore he'd lost his freaking mind. It didn't even dawn on me what he was really doing until his beautiful white wolf stood before me.

"Oscar, I don't know what he's up to, but do Mommy a favor and go get the Benadryl."

The wolf growled and snarled at Oscar. My son wasn't intimidated in the least, but I jumped to my feet, towering over him. "Have you lost your mind? You did not just growl at our son!"

"Mommy," Oscar whispered in awe. "Look. You're doing it."

I glanced down to where he pointed to my hand, which was now sprouting fur—beautiful grey fur. I felt it and it was so soft then I started to cry.

Liam barked to get my attention and nodded his big wolf head up and down. I could tell he was grinning. It was really creepy looking at his wolf, if I were being honest. He lay down, then jumped up and did it again.

"I think he wants you to lie down, too." Oscar helped clue me in.

I did as my son recommended and Liam nodded, rising to do a little happy trot before he lay back down with me.

"Are you telling me that all that itching was my wolf trying to come out?"

He nodded up and down again. Next, he shifted back to human form.

"Madelyn, this is the most natural thing in the world. Your wolf, she's not dead. She's been there all along. That itchy feeling isn't hives, it never was; it's her signal to you that she wants out. Anytime we spend too much time in our skin that happens. We know the signs and address it quickly before it gets to the point of being so miserable."

"I don't know what to do," I whispered, both excited and scared half to death. I had never shifted before. They said it didn't really hurt, but I didn't see how that was physically possible. "What do I do, Liam?"

"Don't fight it. Give her the control she's searching for. I'll be right here the whole time."

"I'm scared," I whispered.

"You have nothing to be afraid of." He kissed me one more time before shifting back to his wolf form. He made it look so effortless. I wondered if I'd ever be able to do it with such ease.

His rear end was in the air, but his head was down. He barked at me. He howled. The sound was so beautiful it relaxed me. The second I relaxed, my body started to transform. It was so surreal. I didn't really feel a thing. I could feel some pulls and tugs here and there, but it was more like an ethereal experience. I knew what was happening now, but it felt more like I was watching it happen than actually experiencing it.

Soon, I was covered all in fur. I looked at Oscar, who was grinning.

"You did it, Mommy! You're a beautiful grey wolf."

I was grateful I hadn't just traumatized my son for life. Fortunately, he'd been around shifters just long enough to not be frightened and still be in awe at the same time. I glanced down at the ground below me and sighed. My clothes were ripped to shreds surrounding me. I loved those jeans.

Wait, did he say grey? I was a grey wolf? I shouldn't be surprised. I was a Collier, after all, but there was never a certainty on wolf coloring. A lot of shifters had wolves with similar coloring to their own hair, but not all. Liam's wolf was white, lighter than his sandy-blonde hair, but similar enough. No one knew for certain how wolf colorings were chosen. Some seemed to be more consistent within geographical areas, others appeared completely at random. Collier Pack looked as diverse as Westin in human form, but the majority of wolves turned out grey. *Like me,* I thought happily.

Liam barked at me and then nudged me with his nose to encourage me to stand. I did, then wobbled and fell back to the ground. Wow, it was such a strange feeling, nothing like crawling on all fours as we did as kids pretending we could shift. My legs, all four of them, felt unsteady beneath me. It took me a minute to find my coordination. I imagined I look much like a new calf struggling to stand and move.

I tested my stability and started to walk, then trot. I looked around. Everything was sharper, crisper somehow. I closed my eyes and listened. I could make out so many new noises. I could actually hear a squirrel gnawing on a nut high up in a tree and somehow I knew exactly where he was, too. I sniffed the air. Kyle and Kelsey were two miles out and I could smell the food they were cooking on the grill. I knew it was them because it was combined with the sweet baby smell of little Zander after a fresh bath. All of my senses were heightened. It was unreal.

Liam barked at me. It was loud because he was so close and startled me. I toppled over again on my not-quite-steady new legs. He chuffed as he laughed at me, but I forgave him quickly. Who could stay mad at his ridiculous wolf grin face?

I got up and shook it off before giving chase. Liam turned and ran towards the woods, but stayed in the clearing running in circles. Oscar jumped up and down clapping, cheering us on. It got easier with each step and once I got the hang of maneuvering four feet instead of two, I was good to go and almost fast enough to catch Liam.

I watched as he cut another corner and I changed paths to intersect, plowing into him and sending us both tumbling across the ground. Oscar shielded his eyes and shook his head at us. Liam looked at me with that stupid wolf grin still plastered to his face and gave my wolf a big lick right across my face. It totally disgusted me, but I laughed and pushed away to stand again.

I was a wolf. I couldn't believe it. She wasn't dead and she'd been there all along. I just didn't have anyone to help me see her signs. Joining with my wolf gave me much peace.

Liam changed back into his skin and stood gloriously naked without the slightest hesitation.

“Hey, kid,” he told Oscar. “Go pack your PJs and a toothbrush. I'm taking you to Grandma's. Mommy's going to be in this form for a while and I need to stay with her. Okay?”

He nodded happily on his way into the house, stopping when he reached me. He knelt down and wrapped his arms around my neck, burying his sweet face in my fur.

“I knew you could do it. I'm so proud of you, Mommy!”

He disappeared into the house, returning quickly with a backpack stuffed full. I could tell it was much more than his PJs and toothbrush, but I was unable to question him. Liam pulled on his own clothes, having been smart enough to remove them first, unlike me, and they got into the car.

For a moment, I started to panic. They were leaving me? I needed to change back, but I didn't know how. The irrational fear that I'd be stuck in my wolf form forever started to set in.

Liam jumped from the car and came to me. He must have felt my anxiety rising.

“Hey, it's okay. You'll change back, but it could be a few hours to a day. It gets easier, but she's been suppressed for a very long time. Best thing you can do is run.” I nodded my head to show him I understood, and started to calm. He took my big, fluffy head in his hands and stared at me in awe. “Most beautiful wolf I've ever seen.” He planted a kiss on my elongated nose before getting back into the car.

“Try to keep up,” he yelled from the window as the car lurched forward, leaving a trail of dust in my face. I shook it off and ran, feeling the weight of a lifetime lift from my chest, letting go of all the pain of the past and giving in to the uncertainty of the future as I ran faster and harder than I'd ever dreamed possible.

I couldn't have predicted how this year would turn out, or how much Liam would turn my life upside down in the best ways possible. I didn't know what the future would hold, but with Liam and Oscar by my side, I knew I was going to be okay.

Dear Reader,

I hope you enjoyed Forever More. Westin Pack has been such fun to write and share with you all. I love all the characters in this series, but may be a little partial to Maddie and Liam!

KEEP READING for a special SNEAK PEEK into Confusing Hearts. Poor Chase Westin doesn't know what to think! He feels the mating call one minute and then nothing the next. He doesn't realize his one true mate has an identical twin, AND she isn't even a wolf. He knows what his heart tells him, but will he listen?

For further information on my books, events, and life in general, I can be found online here:

Website: www.julietrettel.com

Facebook: http://www.facebook.com/authorjulietrettel

Instagram: http://www.instagram.com/julie.trettel

Twitter: http://www.twitter.com/julietrettel

Goodreads:
http://www.goodreads.com/author/show/14703924.Julie_Trettel

BookBub: https://www.bookbub.com/authors/julie-trettel

Amazon: http://www.amazon.com/Julie_Trettel/e/B018HS9GXS

With love and thanks,
Julie Trettel

SNEAK PEEK

CONFUSING HEARTS
A Westin Pack Novel

By

Julie Trettel

Coming Spring 2018

Chase

Chapter 1

I dropped my bag on the floor and collapsed onto my bed. Three weeks at home had been enough. I loved my family, but they had tried to cram so much into my Christmas break that I was exhausted. I knew they loved me and didn't want to waste a second of it, but I was ready for the break.

I had an easy semester of classes planned. My roommate was studying abroad, so even though I lived in the frat house with 36 other shifters, mostly wolves, I was looking forward to the space and the quiet. Okay, as quiet as a popular frat house could be.

Archibald Reynolds College, jokingly called the ARC, was a college specifically for shifters, all kinds of shifters. Archibald Reynolds had been a big proponent of shifter integration at the turn of the century. He had worked closely with our Grand Council that governed the wolf shifters to bring peace among all shifters, yet only in the last five years had there ever been a place to truly encourage that philosophy.

My brother, Liam, had been one of the first graduates of the ARC. I was in my second year now, and loved everything about it. I had been raised in a wolf pack, like most wolf shifters. Going to the ARC had opened my eyes to so much I had never been aware of or even thought about if I were being honest.

The pack gave us securities that other species simply didn't have. And I had known Westin Pack, my pack, was better off than most. I just didn't realize how much so, until I went to college and got to know people with very different backgrounds than my own.

I groaned at the knock on my door. "What?"

"Hey man, heard you were back," Matt Williams, one of my

frat brothers said walking in and plopping down on my roommate's bed.

Matt was a jaguar shifter, and while it was rare for felines and canines to mix, he had insisted on rushing Delta Omega Gamma his freshman year. We were in the same class and despite our differences, we'd hit it off immediately. He's put up with so much more as a pledge than I ever had to endure. They had even nicknamed him Kitty, and yet it never seemed to faze him. I asked him once why he was so determined to be a Dog and he said that he had always admired the sense of group, of family, that was instilled in the wolf packs. Felines tended to be loaners, and he craved that bond with other people like the canines had.

"What do you want, dude?" I asked him.

"There's a new sorority that opened up two houses down. They're having an open party tonight. You're going, right?"

"I just got back. I don't know if I'm up for a party tonight."

"Chase Westin is not up for a party? What happened to you man? You're the ultimate party animal. I've never seen you turn one down. Never."

"My nephews kicked my ass. You try keeping up with an eighteen month old and a seven year old hell bent on spending every waking moment with you. I love them, but I don't know how my brothers do it. I'm exhausted. Need a vacation from vacation."

"You can sleep when you're dead. Now get dressed and let's go." Matt told me, throwing my own phrase back at me. I had told my pledge class that every single day freshman year. It was what got us through to become full brothers of Delta Omega Gamma.

I kicked him out, grumbling in protest as I got dressed for the evening. Meeting up with Matt and two of our other brothers, we headed out walking down the short distance to the new sorority.

"DOGs in the house!" Matt announced as we entered. Our friends scattered to check out the new place.

A tall, thin girl with long straight black hair approached us with her arms crossed and a scowl on her face. She was sleek and sexy as hell. Despite the off-limits vibes she was sending, my interest in the night immediately piqued. I was up for a little challenge.

"Dogs are not welcome here," she said with complete arrogance.

I grinned enough that I knew my dimples were showing. Most girls found them irresistible, but this one seemed completely unaffected.

"You must be new here, 'cause I'm sure I would have noticed you otherwise."

She rolled her eyes. "My sisters and I just transferred. To encourage more of this nonsense and fraternization between species, our entire sorority was transferred. But just because we were forced to come here, does not mean your kind is welcome."

"Oh, now, come on darling," Brett, another of my brothers approached putting on his best southern charm. "This is the ARC where we encourage inter-species relations." He wagged his eyebrows and for a brief moment the ice queen thawed.

Game on, I thought. "Ignore the coyote. What's your name, gorgeous?"

She frowned at me. "You are clearly nothing but trouble." She turned to Brett with a look of disgust. "Coyote?" She whipped her long shiny hair as she turned and stalked away.

"Come on Chase, What was that all about?" Brett demanded.

"Dude, you totally cut in on my game."

"What game?" Matt laughed. "Hey, Ayanna," the ice queen turned and cocked her head in interested. "Don't be such a bitch."

She hissed as she turned and stomped off.

"Dude, you know her?"

"Chase, my man, you are aware that jaguars and black panthers are basically the same species, right?"

"Why would I know that?"

Matt laughed, "Well we are. Ayanna and her *sisters,*" he emphasized with air quotes, "are all black panthers. A bunch of elitist snobs. They even frown at fraternizing with my kind, even though the only difference is the color of our coats. Trust me, I did you a favor. Let's go grab a drink and find something better to distract you with tonight."

Much of the remainder of the night passed in a blur and my next fully coherent memory was waking up naked in bed and thankful I was alone. It wasn't like me to get that wasted, and I didn't like it. It made my wolf uncomfortable when I drank and I could feel my skin crawling with the sensation I knew as the sign I needed to shift.

I threw on an old pair of shorts and used the bathroom before grabbing a cold bottle of water from the fridge and heading for the woods. One of the things I loved about the ARC was the massive one hundred and eighty-seven acre forest surrounding the college. It was the perfect getaway, and since everyone on campus was a shifter, I didn't even have to hide when I needed time in my fur.

Once inside the cover of the trees, I started to discard my shorts.

"Chase Westin," a sexy voice purred behind me and I nearly tripped in surprise.

Turning I saw a girl that I didn't recognize at all.

"Um, hi. Have we met?"

"Chase, you rocked my world last night. I'm Anita, remember?"

Shit! I wracked my brain for any memory of the previous evening.

She started laughing, "I'm just messing with you. You were pretty wasted last night though. I really am Anita. You and some of your friends partied at my house last night?"

"Oh, you're a panther?"

"You say that with disgust. I suppose my sisters' reputations have preceded us. I suppose I shouldn't be surprised."

There was something different about the girl and I liked her immensely.

"And, you're not like your sisters?" I asked.

"Oh God no! I'm not a sex goddess, or think I'm the greatest thing ever to walk this earth. I actually love the inter species policy here at Archibald Reynolds. My sisters are just a bunch of snobs and our chief strongly encourages keeping our line pure, if you know what I mean."

"And you don't? By the way we call it the ARC—Archibald Reynolds College abbreviated it's A-R-C, kind of a pun from the...well, 'ya know the Ark, as in Noah's." I shook my head. It sounded stupid trying to explain it, but she just laughed.

"I like that. And no, I don't, though I'm not against finding my true mate of course. I just think it's okay to friend other shifters. I don't see the issue there. How about you?"

I shrugged. "Never much thought of it. I assumed I'd find my one true mate someday and settle down. In the meantime, I wasn't going to stress it. My brother went to school here, so I was exposed to all sorts of shifters before coming here. My nephew is half tiger. I guess I just didn't think it was really that big of a deal anymore."

"You have a half-breed nephew?"

"It's a long story, and not really mine to tell."

"I didn't even know that was truly possible."

"Why not?"

"Well, what is he going to be when he grows up?"

"Not real sure. We have a theory that God only gives us one animal spirit, so I guess he has a fifty-fifty chance of getting either a tiger or a wolf."

"Wolf?" she shrieked. "I thought you were a jaguar. You were hanging out with Matt Williams last night.

"Yeah, he's my brother. My fraternity brother."

"Matt's in a fraternity with a-a dog?" She must have seen the look of surprise on my face because she immediately began back stepping and talking really fast. "I didn't mean that like it sounded. I'm just surprised. Until yesterday I had never even met a shifter that wasn't a black panther or the occasional jaguar. And we were discouraged from even talking to the jags. So yeah, other species are kind of new to me. I guess I just assumed Matt hung out with other cats."

I snorted. "Nah, Matt was insistent he was going to be a Dog. Trust me he took a lot of shit when we were pledges, but now, he's just one of the brothers. They do call him Kitty, but don't tell him I told you that." I smiled enough to flash my dimples and unlike the ice queen Ayanna, Anita actually reacted to it.

"Wow, this is well, kind of cool. I've been excited to meet other kinds of shifters, just wasn't sure my sister was going to let me out of her sight long enough to actually make any friends here. Ayanna can be a little well... I'm not really sure how to describe her without it sounding horrible."

I laughed. "Ayanna is your sister? Like real sibling sister or sorority sister?"

She sighed, "My real sister."

"Wow, it must really suck to be you."

She grinned, "You have no idea. So, what are you doing out here anyway? I was just getting ready to go for a run."

"Same here, wanna join me?"

"A wolf? You want to run with a panther?"

"I promise not to eat you, and I'll go slow enough for you to keep up."

"In your dreams dog-boy!"

I wasn't sure why, but I turned away from her when I stripped out of my shorts and shifted. She was still in human form staring at me in shock. She put her hand out like one would when meeting a stray dog. I cocked my head to the side.

"What? I've never seen a wolf this close before. Okay, I've never seen a wolf in real life before. You're all black, just like me." I nodded and finally gave in and walked towards her outstretched hand. "Wow, your fur is so soft, too. Okay, so turn away or go over there or something while I change. I can't believe you just stripped right in front of me like that. Clearly dogs have no sense of civility."

I laughed and she jumped. I had no doubt it sounded creepy coming through my wolf. I ran a short distance away, and kept my back to her as I waited for her to shift. My heightened animal ears let me easily track her, even without seeing her.

I was surprised to find that she was as large as my wolf. I nodded my head towards the woods and took off. She easily kept pace with me. When we heard movement approaching she disappeared into the treetops. *That was definitely not something a wolf could do,* I thought.

Recognizing a small pack of my brother wolves running with Matt in his jaguar form, I nodded and barked, then joined them on their run. Anita would find her way back, of that I was certain.

Chapter 2

Half my closest, was strewn across my bedroom. It was my first day of classes and I had no idea what to wear. I had never been allowed to meet anyone or anything outside the family. My parents had kcpt both my sister and I close to them.

I was just a kitten when the panthers organized. Felines were already at a disadvantage because of our loaner personalities. We didn't run in packs or even prides, like the lions, but as our numbers dwindled, particularly the black panthers, we banded together and formed our own family unit. My father is the chief and my sister and I were considered the princesses.

It wasn't easy growing up as part of the royal family. We had been sheltered and protected our entire lives. While Tessa had rebelled starting in our early teen years, I had never even considered it. I was the epitome of the good girl. It was exhausting at times. I just wanted to be me.

When I had applied to Archibald Reynolds College, it was the only act of rebellion I had ever displayed. I hadn't considered Daddy would send Tessa and relocate our entire sorority to the other side of the United States just because I wanted to attend a different school. I tried not to resent them all. It wasn't their fault. When the chief issued a command, everyone followed. That's just the way it was.

I finally settled on a pair of jeans and a dark green shirt. I grabbed my backpack, shoving my new books inside and stepped out into the hallway. Tessa was there. I stared at her noticing she had on nearly the exact same thing, like my own reflection in the mirror staring back at me.

"Dammit, Tess. Now I have to change."

"You don't have time, we're going to be late for our first class," she scolded.

"Wait, we're in the same class?"

She shrugged. "Daddy's really worried about you, Jenna. He wants me to keep an eye on you, and you know if he's asking me, of all people, then he's really worried."

I sighed knowing it was pointless to argue. We headed across campus to our first class. I was excited despite the bomb my sister had dropped on me.

"Wait, I have calculus this morning, Tessa. How did you even get in the class?" I loved my sister, but Tessa wasn't exactly known for her brains. I had always been a nerd. I loved learning and got good grades. Tessa, well, she liked to cook, and dance, and was a phenomenal artist. Basically she hated all core classes, and only excelled in the electives in high school.

She grinned back at me. "I'm pretty much banking on you doing all the work for us in this class."

"Tess, I can't take two tests at the same time."

"Why not? It's not like we haven't done it before."

I looked at her like she had two heads. "That was high school. This is college. It's not that simple. Plus, we weren't in the actual same class. Remember?"

There were definitely benefits to being an identical twin, at least for Tessa. Okay, that wasn't entirely true. The only class I almost flunked was PE in the ninth grade. I wasn't really the athletic type, but that was Tessa's department. She was great at all sports, but especially volleyball. I didn't really envy her. I had my art, and loved seeing the world through a camera lens, but unfortunately physical education is still mandatory in high school.

You'd think that a panther, sleek in movements with great agility would excel in sports, but not me. I could dance. That was about the closest thing to an actual sport as I got, and that wasn't offered as a high school course alternative to gym class. The funny part was, while Tessa was extremely athletic, she had no rhythm and couldn't dance to save her life.

At that time, Tess had been failing algebra, and fortunately for us, the classes where on the same block. So she would pose as me and downplay her athletic skills just enough to get me a passing grade, and I attended her algebra class to do the same for her. It had been beneficial to the both of us.

It wasn't the only time we had changed places over the years either. Even our own parents had a hard time telling us apart, so it had always worked in our favor.

"Okay, you're right. Why didn't I think of this before? We can't both be in the class. I'm going to go over and see about transferring. Same classes, different schedules and no one ever has to know, especially Daddy. He'll just see that we had the same classes and assume we were in them together. Right?"

"I guess so," I said doubtfully. We were twenty-year-old juniors in college, and hundreds of miles away from our dad the chief. Why did we still care so much?

"Okay, have fun, take good notes for us," she said giving me a quick hug as she headed off to student resources in hopes of changing her class schedule.

I looked around me. Alone. I was alone, or as alone as a person could possibly be on a campus of eight hundred students. I couldn't stop the smile spreading across my face as I walked to class.

"Tessa, over here," I saw our friend Anita.

"It's Jenna," I told her.

"Oh, sorry. I thought Tessa said she was going to be in this class."

I tried not to laugh. "Tessa? In physics?" Anita laughed along with me.

"Yeah, it sounded like a long shot to me, too. I should have known."

"She actually did sign up, and then realized I couldn't do her work for her if she was in the same class, so she's working on getting her schedule changed now."

"Okay that sounds much more like Tessa," Anita said.

I followed her to empty seats at the front of the room as she chatted on. Anita was a true friend. I had always liked her, unlike her sister who came across as condescending. I was a princess. She was not. I had the right to be condescending, if I wanted to be, not her.

Who was I kidding? I just wanted to be left alone. I didn't have it in me to be as mean and calculating as Ayanna. She would definitely make a far better princess, and if I could give her the job, I would in a heartbeat.

As the teacher entered and called the class to order, I took in a deep breath. It was something I always did to calm myself before class, but as I inhaled, I was assaulted by an unfamiliar woodsy scent. No, I had smelled it before at the party we hosted over the weekend. It had caused such a tingling sensation across my skin that I had retreated to my room and locked myself in for the night.

I had heard of such a feeling. It was very much like my mother had described as the call of true mates. No no no no no, that couldn't happen here, I knew for a fact there were no male black panthers attending Archibald Reynolds. It was one of the things that had attracted me most. There were some male jaguars though. I said a quick prayer under my breath that my true mate was not a jaguar.

Daddy was very insistent on the purity of the family line. Black panthers were rare enough without polluting the gene pool. I had always assumed my one true mate would be a black panther, just like me, but technically there were several species of compatible cats to the panthers. I sunk down in my seat hoping the sensations I was feeling were nothing more than first day jitters.

As we were settling into class, Anita turned and waved to someone at the back of the room. I wasn't surprised to find she was already making friends. Most panther shifters were loaners. We didn't naturally run in groups like other shifters. Anita was somewhat of an exception. She loved people and was a quirky sort of extrovert.

"Did you know Matt Williams is in Delta Omega Gamma? The Dog frat. Seriously, I'm not even kidding. I met one of his brothers yesterday and I couldn't believe it. I mean he's cute and all, but I just assumed he was a jag. Imagine my shock when I went running with a wolf."

"A wolf? Anita, they're dangerous, you can't be hanging out with their kind," I reminded her.

She just rolled her eyes at me. "Jenna, we're at the ARC. Why else are we here if not to mingle with all sorts of shifters?"

Because they have the best photography program of any college Daddy would approve, I thought honestly. I wouldn't dare confess it though.

The teacher started class before I could answer, and I got out of there quickly the moment class ended. The smell had continued to haunt me throughout class until it became uncomfortable just sitting there. It had taken everything in my power not to turn around and search out the source of that delicious smell that caused goosebumps to rise on my skin. I just couldn't do it though. If my true mate was nearby, and he wasn't a black panther, it would be best if we just never met at all, because Daddy would never approve. Keeping our family line pure was more important to him than the bond of true mates. I had always known it, but until that moment, I had never given any thought to how that could affect me. For a brief moment I even considered switching classes. One thing was certain. I needed to stay as far away from that smell as possible.

Check out more great books by Julie Trettel!
The Compounders:
Book One

In the wake of terrorist attacks, economic collapse, and martial law, America has become a nation at war and a country at odds. Mike Jenkins was well prepared, and moved his family and friends to his totally secure compound on a remote mountain in western Virginia.

After several years, Holly Jenkins couldn't wait for the elders to open the bunker doors, allowing her to roam at will, and feel free once again. Escaping to the sanctuary of her hidden cave would set in motion changes in her life heretofore unknown.

The AMAN presented a threat to the compound and the nearby towns; a threat that could not be ignored. They were prepared for war, but nothing could prepare Holly for her own battle between the two men she had grown to love… and the third she might be forced to marry.

Chaos will reign! Will love survive?

Visit
http://www.amazon.com/dp/B018HKIU7O/?tag=kp-jtret-20

The Compounders: DISSENSION
Book Two

Holly Jenkins spent most of her life sheltered by the Compounders in a secure bunker on a remote mountain in western Virginia. After a battle with the AMAN, the oppressive group that reigns over the area, her life is set on a new course. Leaving behind the comfort and safety of the Compound isn't a choice for her. It's something she has to do.

When Griffon Maynor is captured by the AMAN, Holly's squad springs into action on a rescue mission without question, even when it becomes obvious to them that her feelings for him have changed. But can they rescue him in time?

New love ignites. New friends are made. New enemies are encountered. The lines between good and evil are blurred. Not everyone will survive. And when they finally make it home, everything has changed once again.

Visit
http://www.amazon.com/dp/B01N6FSGLE/?tag=kp-jtret-20

DISCONTENT
A Compounders Novella

Charlie Jenkins has big shoes to fill in the wake of his father's death. He hasn't always done the right things in the past, but he's trying his best for his family, the Compounders, and all the residents of nearby Wythel, Virginia, the small town just down the mountain from the Compounder's bunker. When his sister, Holly, goes missing, Charlie is fueled by anger, hatred, and resentment. Can he get past his emotions to be the man he was raised to be?

They aren't safe. People are scared. The stakes are high. The enemy now knows exactly where they live. Change is inevitable. With the Compound once compromised, and Wythel more vulnerable than ever, it's clear that both need a leader who can step up and give them hope. Can Charlie be that leader … or will his anger drive him to destroy them all?

Visit
http://www.amazon.com/dp/B07215QYL1/?tag=kp-jtret-20

One True Mate
A Westin Pack Novel

Kelsey Adams is alone, and has been since childhood. Running away is all she knows and necessary to preserve her deepest, darkest secret. She cannot afford for anyone to get close, or know about the monster within. But when she lands a lucrative job as an administrative assistant to Kyle Westin, CEO of the Westin Foundation, her life changes and everything's at stake. Can she conceal her growing feelings and her true self from this enigmatic, strong willed man, or will her world fall apart?

Kyle Westin, an alpha male who always gets what he wants, has watched and waited for the little she-wolf he knows is his perfect mate to show any signs of recognition. For two years he endures her unnecessary formality and daily rejections with a patience he did not know he possessed. But even Kyle has his limits.... Can he make Kelsey notice him as someone other than her boss and break down the walls she built around her heart? Or will Kelsey do what she has always done --- run?

Visit
https://www.amazon.com/dp/B071HXL3R2

What happens when you choose not to accept fate?

Elise Westin is obsessed with one thing. Avoid Patrick O'Connell at all costs. She knows the handsome foreigner is her one true mate. She knows they are destined to be together. Knowing it doesn't stop her from fighting it the only way she knows how.... run and hide. But hiding from him can only last so long. Fate, with the help of her family, forces her to come face to face with him. Will she be able to confront her own fears and accept love? Or will she lose it all by fighting her own destiny?

Patrick O'Connell has given up everything. Banished from his own pack and living in a foreign territory. He's chasing a dream that he was raised to believe doesn't exist. But he knows he's found his one true mate. She's real. One whiff of the dark-haired beauty changes the path of his life forever. With nothing else to lose, he won't stop until he finds her again. But Elise doesn't want to be found. Can he win the heart of his elusive mate? Can Patrick break down Elise's barrier of fears to find their happily ever after?

Visit
https://www.amazon.com/Fighting-Destiny-Westin-Pack-Book-ebook/dp/B07575HC9T

About the Author

Julie Trettel is author of the Compounders and Westin Pack Series, a full time Systems Administrator, wife, and mother of 4 awesome kids. She resides in Richmond, VA and can often be found writing on the sidelines of a football field or swimming pool. She comes from a long line of story tellers. Writing has always been a stress reliever and escape for her to manage the crazy demands of juggling time and schedules between work and an active family of six. In her "free time," she enjoys traveling, reading, outdoor activities, and spending time with family and friends.

Visit
www.JulieTrettel.com

Made in the USA
Monee, IL
20 October 2020

45614470R00154